Out of the Storm

By the same author

Rough Heritage
Maid of the Sea
A Song on the Wind

Out of the Storm

Janet Thomas

ROBERT HALE · LONDON

First published in Great Britain 2009

ISBN 978-0-7090-8902-5

Robert Hale Limited
Clerkenwell House
Clerkenwell Green
London EC1R 0HT

www.halebooks.com

2 4 6 8 10 9 7 5 3 1

Typeset in 10½/14pt Plantin
by Derek Doyle & Associates, Shaw Heath
Printed in Great Britain by the
MPG Books Group, Bodmin and King's Lynn

CHAPTER ONE

LOVEDAY 1901

I was gazing out of the cottage window at the angry water surging in the harbour and thinking of Joel of course, as I always did when the weather was rough. This was only a summer storm, though, and anyway the fishing fleet was many miles away from Cornwall.

Then I noticed a familiar figure carefully picking her way along the quay holding on tightly to her wide-brimmed hat with one hand. With the other, my sister was lifting her skirts clear of the cobblestones.

'*Kate*! What are you doing out in this weather?' As I opened the door, Kate was almost blown over the threshold by the force of the wind. Another gust brought with it a scatter of raindrops the size of silver threepenny bits.

'Phew!' She shook the dampness from her smart costume. That's new, I thought – another one! This was a navy-blue glazed cotton outfit, trimmed with white piping. It was expensive and the height of fashion; Kate was always dressed like a duchess. 'I didn't realize it was going to rain.'

Unpinning her elaborate hat, she hung it on the hallstand and tweaked her piled hair back into place. 'I've brought these, Loveday.' She looked back at me and held out a paper bag. 'You left them in the carriage when Arthur and I dropped you off yesterday.'

'Oh, my gloves! I was wondering where they were. I thought I'd left them up at the farm. Thanks, Kate.' She tossed them on to the shelf below the mirror. 'But you needn't have come down specially, not in this gale.'

She turned on a heel. 'Oh, I needed some fresh air, but I didn't realize it was quite so windy. It's even worse up on the cliffs. It's so exposed where we live. I've had more air than I wanted!'

I led the way into the parlour and Kate looked around the little room as she always did, not missing anything. It felt cosy today with its red chenille curtains keeping out the draughts. The red matched the bobble-edged runner on the mantel shelf where my pair of Staffordshire china dogs stood, along with a photograph of our family.

'Oh, you've finished your rag rugs then,' Kate crossed the room and glanced down as she went. 'They look good.'

'Yes, at long last.' I was pleased with them too. They really brightened up the polished boards. 'After spending most of last winter hooking until my fingers were sore, I'm not sorry to see them in use at last.'

Kate had paused to glance at the photograph of us all. She and I were standing solemnly beneath a potted palm, wearing smart skirts and pin-tucked white blouses. Behind us stood Papa in his Sunday best suit of black worsted. Mama was seated in a cane chair at his side.

I remembered when it had been taken, just before Kate's marriage. Ma had wanted a proper photograph of us all while we were still together at the farm, and we went into Mr Opie's studio in Helston for the occasion.

Kate sank into an armchair on one side of the grate. I lifted our little tabby cat from the other and sat down with it on my lap.

'That was a nice afternoon yesterday, wasn't it?' I glanced into the empty hearth, which I'd brightened up with a jug of foxgloves and ox-eye daisies. I'd picked them when I went out for a walk that morning. Smoothing the cat's soft fur, I reached for my knitting, but I couldn't manage both. 'Sorry, Smokey.' I put the purring animal down on the rug and picked up my needles.

'Mm, it's not often we all get together these days. It's a good thing we have birthdays!' Kate was fingering the cameo at her throat and her gaze was far away. The four steel needles clicked as I started another row.

'It's just amazing how quickly the time goes.' Kate glanced up at my childish sampler in coloured wools that hung on the wall beside her. 'I can remember you working that.' She pointed. 'It doesn't seem all that long ago. You always were good at stitching and making things, even then.'

'Loveday Anne Trevarthen, aged ten years.' I read it and smiled. 'I know how I wished I had a shorter name! My fingers were pricked so many times. But you remember how fussy Miss Bryant was about neatness. And then I had to do all the letters of the alphabet as well. It took me weeks of needlework lessons.'

'I was your age when Arthur and I were wed. Twenty.' Her eyes were far away.

'I know. Of course, I married Joel when I was only seventeen. Quite young.' I looked up at her and smiled. 'And you and Arthur first met at our wedding. People thought that was really romantic.'

Kate's gaze was fixed on the flowers as she bent to stroke the cat. 'Do you remember how Mama was nagging at me to find a husband and settle down before I was too old?'

I nodded. I did remember how the pert and pretty Miss Trevarthen had flirted wildly with all her suitors and ditched them one by one.

'You were always so pretty. You could have had any man you wanted with your big green eyes and blonde curls. Not a bit like my "broom-handle brown" as Ma used to call it!' I laughed and tucked a loose strand back into the low chignon on my neck.

I suppose I should have been jealous of my sister in the early days, she'd always been the favoured child, but actually we'd always got along really well. Probably because when we were small I'd been content to follow her lead. And far from resenting it, I'd been only too delighted to have all her cast-off finery handed down to me.

'I'd never met any man I could really love, you see. I'd only been having fun up to then, playing them along. Until Arthur. . . .' Her voice tailed off and she gazed vaguely into the middle distance. 'I *really* fell for him, Loveday – head over heels.' She turned back to me. 'He was so different from the local lads: such a gentleman. So charming, so handsome. I'd never met anyone like him before.'

She paused and twisted her fingers in her lap. 'The fact that he was rich beyond our imagining had nothing to do with it. Whatever the gossips said,' she added fiercely. 'Then when he asked me to marry him I thought, what did it matter if he was twice my age?' Half-talking to herself, she muttered, 'I didn't even stop to wonder why he wasn't married already. Or to think about Maud at all.'

I nodded. I'd heard enough tales about her martinet of a mother-in-law to understand. A silence fell as I concentrated on my knitting, counted the stitches and turned the heel.

'That reminds me,' Kate bit her lip. 'That brooch I gave you for your birthday, Loveday ... it wasn't my choice, you know? He – Arthur – chooses all my gowns, my hats, even my jewellery. I don't have any money of my own. I told him the brooch was too ostentatious and you'd never wear it, but he insisted.'

I wondered not for the first time, what lay beneath the surface of the Rosewarne household. Certainly Kate dwelt in the lap of luxury, but it sounded as if Arthur was very controlling. And living with her mother-in-law of course wasn't easy.

But then I gave a sudden start and cried out in surprise. 'What's the matter?' Kate's eyes widened and she looked at me with concern. 'Are you all right?' she asked.

I took a deep breath and nodded. A huge smile spread across my face. 'Kate, I felt the baby kick!'

I put my knitting down and laid a gentle hand on my swollen stomach. Each time it happened was a small miracle. Please God it would be all right this time. Third time lucky was the old saying, wasn't it?'

I glanced at the thick stocking of oiled wool that was taking shape on the needles. I loved Joel so much. As a fisherman's wife I had had to get used to his long absences, but he was always in my thoughts. He too, so desperately wanted to start a family. And after the agony and disappointment of two miscarriages, it seemed that our dream was coming true at last.

I tried to smooth my old brown skirt over the bump, but that only made it ride up under my bosom even more. My smile widened. Oh no, I wouldn't change places with my sister for all their wealth and the grand villa on the cliffs. With a handsome, loving husband like Joel, and a baby on the way! I'd not done so badly even though I was never a beauty and we would never be rich. What we *did* have together, though was priceless.

'When did you say you're expecting Joel back, Loveday? I can't remember how long the herring season lasts. July to – when?' Kate glanced towards me.

I folded my hands over my stomach. The baby was on the move again. 'Sometime in October. The fleet's in Whitby now, working their way down from Scotland. You remember that lovely Paisley shawl he sent me? He bought that up there.'

'Well, it's still only August,' Kate glanced out of the window, 'Although you wouldn't think so. He'll be back before the baby's born, won't he?'

'Oh, I *do* hope so.' I was picturing my husband's blond, bearded figure. Hearing his hearty laugh, feeling his burly arms enfolding me and seeing the smile in his sea-blue eyes.

'That's new, isn't it?' Kate had caught sight of a small painting I'd hung on the wall opposite the sampler. It was a picture of our home, here on the harbour at Porthleven. Red-sailed luggers were drawn up in the shelter of the granite wall, and gulls wheeled overhead.

'Oh, yes.' I laid down my knitting in my lap and glanced up at it. 'You know Joel's sister Meg, don't you?'

Kate nodded. 'She lives on the other side of the harbour, doesn't she? And has a big family.'

'That's right. Well, her eldest daughter, Jessie, is very artistic. She gave me that for my birthday.'

It was amateurish, of course. The perspective was a trifle out and the houses on the far side were climbing with the hill instead of being level, but it was a charming scene. 'She's quite talented.'

I dropped the knitting into the basket at my side. 'Let's have a cup of tea, shall we?' I started to drag myself out of the chair.

Kate raised a hand. 'You stay where you are, Loveday,' she said. 'I'll make it.' I gave her a grateful smile. 'Oh, right. We can have the rest of the birthday cake too. It's in a tin on the dresser.'

Kate rose to her feet and moved, a little awkwardly I thought, towards the door. I looked curiously after her. 'Have you hurt yourself, Kate?' She was walking stiffly, as if she'd been sitting still for too long.

I was surprised at the changing expressions that crossed her face in the fleeting moment as she turned back to me. She was in pain certainly, as she bit her lip and winced, but there was something secretive too, in the way she lowered her lids and bent her head. It was gone too quickly for me to be sure.

She put on a smile and raised a dismissive hand. 'Oh, I'm all right. I just twisted my ankle a bit when I was coming downstairs this morning. I missed a step, you know? And my back took the strain.'

Kate left the room before I could question her any further. Her explanation sounded plausible. I had to believe her, but I could not dismiss the nagging little doubt in my mind.

We had our tea and chatted of mundane matters for a while: of our parents; of the farm up at Sithney where we spent our childhood; of the new age that was upon us now that the queen had died. A companionable silence gradually fell, broken only by the click of my needles and the cry of seagulls out over the harbour.

'I suppose I'd better go soon.' Kate roused herself and glanced up at the wall clock, but she made no move to leave.

'You can stay as long as you like as far as I'm concerned. I'm enjoying your company. It gets very quiet here when I'm on my own.' I smiled up at her.

'Are you sure? I will stay a bit longer, in that case. It's so cosy and warm in this little place.' I caught a wistful expression on her face and my brows rose. After all the comforts of Kate's own sumptuous house, that remark was surprising. 'Yes, I suppose you must miss Joel a lot when he's away on these long trips,' she said.

I nodded. It was impossible to describe how *much* I missed him. 'Oh, Kate, I do. You can't imagine it, but all fishermen's wives have to put up with months alone. It goes with the job.'

And soon, soon I would have my little one. I smiled to myself and turned back to my knitting. 'But I get by. Ma comes down on the omnibus at least once a week. She says that old horse of Joe's is so slow, she has time for a cup of tea and a chat with me and still manage to catch him on the return journey!'

Kate chuckled. I turned another row. 'Then I go up to Pengarth to see her and Pa as well, whenever I like. There's Susan next door, of course, and Meg not far away. Apart from you in your perch up on the cliffs.' I smiled. 'So I'm not short of company.'

'You're not. You see more people than I do.' The smile slid from Kate's face.

She rose, putting a hand to her back as she did so, and picked up the tray of tea-things. 'I'll take this back to the kitchen.' She pushed the door wider with her foot. 'I think your cat's hungry, Loveday. I can hear her crying from here.'

'Oh, she's *always* hungry!' I laughed. 'I'll come and give her a drop of milk.'

I rolled up my untouched knitting and thrust it aside again. Levering my bulk out of the chair, I followed Kate down the passage. My kitchen was only big enough for the essentials. There was a rocker standing on one side of the Cornish range, Joel's well used and sagging armchair on the other. On the hearth lay his pipe and a jar of paper spills, awaiting his return.

Two bentwood chairs stood at the table which was covered in sprigged oilcloth. Against one wall was a dresser laden with china, and various jars and tins of commodities and leading off was my tiny walk-in larder, not much bigger than a cupboard. In here the zinc meat-safe hung on the coldest wall. On the slatted shelf beneath it stood a large stoneware bussa holding preserved eggs, my flour bin and various left-overs waiting to be used up.

Kate, swathed in a large apron, was already rattling dishes in the stone sink beneath the window. This room overlooked the backyard and a scrap of rough grass where the clothesline swung from a corner of the wash-house; on one side of this was the privy, discreetly screened by a large laurel bush and at the far end stood the shed where Joel kept his tackle and tools.

'There was just enough hot water left in the kettle, but I've used the last of the cold.' Kate looked over her shoulder, an empty earthenware pitcher in her hand. 'I'll take this out and refill it when I've finished.'

'Oh, right.' I joined her and removed some clean pots and pans from the wooden draining-board. 'I don't suppose you've washed many dishes since you got married, have you?' I smiled.

'Of course I haven't.' Kate's voice was scornful. 'Not with all the servants we keep. I wouldn't dare set foot in the kitchen – Cook's a proper old dragon! Apart from what Maud and Arthur would say.' Her smile didn't reach her eyes.

I'd been wondering for some time about the, well, defeated tone in my sister's voice today, but this was something new and I was concerned.

'Kate, is that really all that's the matter? You're sure there's nothing else? Only you seem . . . a bit . . . unhappy.'

She seemed to jerk out of her reverie then and gave another smile that didn't reach her eyes. In fact, the corners of her mouth began to tremble and she seemed on the verge of tears. Impulsively I held out a hand and caught hold of hers to give it a squeeze. 'Oh, Kate dear, *tell* me about it.'

I half-turned, startled, as the cat brushed against me, mewing pitifully, then twined itself around my ankles. Irritated, I gave it a push with my foot and began to fill a saucer with milk, still looking at Kate over my shoulder.

She reached up her sleeve for a hanky and dabbed her eyes. 'It's Arthur, you see.'

My brows rose. 'Arthur? What about him?' I paused and frowned.

I could feel the tension in her, and as she gripped the edge of the sink I noticed how white Kate's knuckles were. 'He's not the person I took him for, Loveday.' She gulped. 'He puts on one face for his public image. And another, quite different one for when we're alone.' She twisted the scrap of lace. 'He's a . . . bully . . . you see,' she whispered, her eyes huge in her pale face.

Startled, I gasped. '*What?* You mean . . . he knocks you *around*?' I found that hard to believe. I tried to imagine the suave Arthur Rosewarne as anything other than the soul of courtesy and consideration: Controlling, certainly, but a bully? By the misery on my sister's face, however, I knew she was telling me the truth. Absently I bent to place the cat's milk on the floor.

Kate nodded. 'And that's not all. . . .' Then she drew in a quick breath and cried, 'Oh, Loveday – watch *out!*' just as I staggered and was caught off-balance as the cat tripped me up.

No! Bent double, I gasped as I felt myself swaying. I – must – not – fall. I gritted my teeth. I – *would* – not – fall. I reached out a flailing hand to grab Kate's arm, and missed.

The nightmare went on. I caught a heel in the hem of my skirt and stepped on the saucer with the other foot. It tipped and slid out from under me. I was floundering in a stream of spilled milk. I heard a piercing scream – my own. Then finally losing my balance, I plunged to the stone-flagged floor.

CHAPTER TWO

LOVEDAY

'Loveday! What on *earth*. . . ?' Kate's scream echoed my own as she reached out to grab me, but she was too late.

All the breath left my body as I landed in an awkward heap, gasping for air. Close to panic I thrashed from side to side. Choking, gulping, retching. Kate bending over me, loosened my collar and tried to raise my head. At last I raked in enough blessed air to breathe again. Instinctively clutching my stomach to protect the delicate life there, I gritted my teeth and tried to think.

Lie still. I must lie still. It would be all right then, wouldn't it? Please God, please. I took another deep breath. I wasn't hurt that much, was I? A bruise on my bottom maybe, where I'd landed. I'd bruised my knee too. That was aching. I suppose I'd been lucky not to hit my head. But inside? I held the breath.

Something snapped. I felt a stabbing pain low in my back. Then a sudden rush of dampness. It was seeping through my underclothes. . . .

'Kate!' I cried. 'The baby! I think it's coming!' A searing pain turned my cry into a scream. I lay there on the cold stone floor, helpless. Writhing and groaning. While the pain stabbed again. And again.

'Lie still!' Kate's anxious face hovered over me. She reached for my hand and squeezed it. 'Loveday, try not to move. I'm going to make you comfortable. Back in a minute.' Kate was running for cushions, for blankets, calling over her shoulder. 'You'll be all right. Don't worry.'

Trying to convince herself as well as me. I clenched my teeth against the next onslaught.

'Now, raise your head a bit. Here's a pillow. Tuck this blanket under you. That's right. Where are you hurt most?' On her knees now, Kate's face loomed over me, taut with worry.

'Kate – I'm wet! The baby . . . oh what have you *done*?' I wailed. Another pain lanced through me, leaving me gasping with shock. No! This nightmare could not be happening. It *must* not be. It was too early. I bit down hard on my bottom lip as another searing pain convinced me that what I most feared was happening.

I'd been through all this before, hadn't I? Twice. Which left me in no doubt as to what to expect now. But maybe . . . a flicker of hope stirred between the pains . . . I was seven months gone after all. Maybe it *would* be all right. Premature babies had been known to survive. . . .

'What are we going to *do*?' Kate clapped a hand over her mouth. 'I . . . I'd better go and fetch somebody. Susan next door. I'll fetch Susan. She can send her boy for the doctor.' She scrambled to her feet.

'No!' I screamed, my fingers digging into Kate's hand, 'don't leave me! You can't . . . it's coming! It's coming!' My body contorted with a spasm that had me twisting in agony.

Kate, white with terror, was rooted to the spot. She loosened my clothing. She tried to make comforting noises. 'Hush – it'll be all right, don't worry.' She bent over me and smoothed back my damp hair. Her hands were trembling. 'It's just coming a little bit early, that's all.'

'. . . Your fault,' I muttered through gritted teeth, '. . . you distracted me.'

Kate gasped. '*My* fault? You can't say that! It was an accident!' I bit my lip. Now was not the time to argue.

The rest of what she did say was lost. I heard myself giving a series of primitive grunts as the urge to push began. My stomach heaved with a life of its own. An hour passed in hideous nightmare. Then another. So much for it coming quickly.

I was terrified of being left. Something dreadful would happen if I was alone. I held Kate's hand in a grip of iron. My sister made sympathetic noises and wiped my perspiring face. Between contractions I lay panting like an animal, gathering strength for the next onslaught.

Suddenly my body contorted again and I knew the end was near. I heard my scream of agony echo through the house. 'Ah . . . oh . . . it's tearing me apart!' Then with one almighty heave, my body at last released its burden. My child slithered into the world.

'Oh, Loveday! Oh, my dear Lord! What should I do?' Kate cried. She jumped to her feet and snatched down some clean cloths hanging above the range. Hesitated for a second, as if afraid to touch the tiny creature, but she managed to wrap it, cord, afterbirth and all, in a soft towel. She handed another one to me and I wiped my sweat-drenched face. 'It's a little boy!' she said with wonder.

'A boy!' I whispered. 'Joel wanted a boy so much. He'll be so thrilled!' Tears of rapture were running down my cheeks now. I held out my arms. 'Give him to me, Kate. Give me my son.'

I raised myself on one elbow. But as I watched Kate cradle the little body lying still, oh, so still, in her arms, my heart turned over. It couldn't be! Could it? I'd never been present at a birth. But I'd lived on a farm and was familiar with the sight of baby animals. This couldn't be so much different.

Surely it should be moving? Crying? This white little creature was lying motionless in her arms, its skin like wax. Kate gave it a gentle shake. Its head lolled to one side and stayed there. My stomach lurched. Was this my worst nightmare come true?

I dragged myself into a half sitting position, holding out my arms. 'Kate, give me my baby,' I demanded. 'Let me *see* him.'

Kate remained standing. 'Er . . . in a minute, Loveday. . . . There's something I have to tell you.' She must have seen my fear, for she swallowed hard. Her eyes were huge and dark in a face gone even whiter.

'There's something wrong with him, isn't there? Is he . . . not quite perfect . . . deformed in some way?' Even now I clung to a faint shred of hope. 'Kate, *tell* me!' My voice rose to a shriek.

Kate cleared her throat. 'No, it's not that, dear, it's . . . I'm afraid . . . oh Loveday, darling, I'm so *sorry*.' Her eyes brimming with tears, she held out her arms.

I grabbed the tiny bundle from her. It took only one glance and the flickering shred of hope died. I clutched the infant to me, howling to high heaven like one demented. Tears were pouring down my face as I rocked it to and fro.

Kate tried in vain to hush me. Standing over me, wringing her hands, not knowing what to do in the face of my appalling grief.

At last my shrieks and floods of tears subsided into a low keening, Kate put both arms round me. 'Loveday, darling, you should be in bed. Come on. Give him to me and we must get you up off this hard floor. We need to send for the doctor. He'll know what to do. He'll take care of you and . . . everything.'

'No! Not the doctor!' I heard my voice rise. 'He'll take my baby away. No one's going to take my son away from me.' I tightened my grip on the infant and glared at her.

'All right, darling, all right.' Kate was trying to pacify me. I suppose she thought I was too deep in shock to know what I was saying. But I knew exactly what I was about. 'Now you can't stay here. Let's get you on to the settee in the parlour. You'll be comfortable there. You're in no fit state to climb the stairs. Come on.' She put an arm around my shoulders and cajoled until slowly and stiffly I did as she said.

Once I was settled, Kate held out her arms for the baby. 'Just let me take him for a minute dear. To clean him up – and tie off the cord.' She looked warily at me as if afraid I was going to shout at her again. 'I'll bring him back straight away, I promise.' I nodded, for that made sense, and handed him over.

Much later, I fell into a deep sleep. Too deep for dreams or nightmares, born of sheer mental and physical exhaustion. When I woke at last, for a moment I could not remember where I was or how I came to be there.

I rubbed my eyes and looked around the room. I was on the settee in the parlour? And had been sleeping in broad daylight? But I *never* slept in the daytime. Then I looked down at the little bundle in my arms. Everything came flooding back with dreadful clarity. Tears began to pour down my cheeks again, silent, bitter tears. Dear God! This could not have happened to me again. It *could* not.

I stroked the little head. What a lot of hair he had! Thick, straight and the same shade of brown as my own, broom-handle brown! I gave a hysterical giggle that turned into a sob. He was sleeping so peacefully. In a moment, in just a short moment, he would wake up, my little son. And how hungry he would be then! I loosened my clothing and put the infant's tiny mouth to my breast.

Then a flash of sanity returned and with it came guilt. It poured in, consuming me, shrouding me in a heavy dark blanket of despair. For although my first reaction had been to blame Kate, of course it hadn't been her fault. I had got in her way in the tiny kitchen.

After I'd been so careful, for so long, for days, weeks, months. It had all been for nothing. *Again!* I closed my eyes and turned my face to the wall. I wanted to die too.

But I could get no rest from the workings of my over-stimulated brain. I would have to face what was done. Live with it for the rest of my life. I had no choice. The utter finality of death hit me like a physical blow and I clutched the child to me with a groan of agony.

However was I going to tell Joel? Terror seized me at the very thought. What could I say? How could I possibly put it into words? In fact, how could I even bear to look him in the eye, let alone confess what had happened? Joel's face had lit up like a beacon when I'd first told him the news – I could see it still. I pressed my cheek against the damp pillow, remembering. . . .

'. . . My dear maid, sit down and put your feet up!' Joel had said, springing from his chair and sending his newspaper flying. 'We're going to make sure everything goes all right this time, do you hear me?'

I had been laughing and crying all at once. 'Oh, I hear you, Joel. Of course we are. And pray God it will be!'

'Amen to that.' His face was solemn. I'm only sorry I shall be away for so many months and not here to take care of you.' His broad forehead creased in a frown and he ran a hand through his mane of thick hair.

I laid a hand on his arm and squeezed it. Don't worry so, Joel. Fishermen's wives have to get used to being on their own for months on end. I shall have Susan next door. Kate and Arthur not far away. It's no distance to Sithney either if I want to go up to Pengarth Farm for a chat with Ma and Pa. And of course, Meg's just across the way, too. I'll be all right.'

He nodded. That's right, my bird. Tis funny Kate settled in the village too, isn't it?' I smiled. 'Hardly in the village, Joel! That great villa on the cliffs?' He chuckled. 'Yes, well, you know what I mean.'

He'd been preparing for the longest trip of the year. Up through the Irish Sea, and then across Scotland. The luggers would be towed by horses through the Caledonian Canal, and into the North Sea, following the herring. 'What would you like me to bring you home for a present, my handsome,' his deep voice boomed. 'A bit of souvenir china, or maybe a piece of jet jewellery from Whitby?'

'You can just bring me back a bit of "nicey",' I said, as he took me in his arms to say goodbye. I could still remember how we laughed at the old Cornish word for a sweetmeat, neither of us with a care in the world. 'Because the only present I want is for you to come home safely.'

Now I began to imagine my husband's homecoming. I tortured myself with the thought, prodding and poking it like an aching tooth. His blond and bearded figure would be standing in the boat like some Viking warrior returning to his native land. His piercing blue eyes would be searching the quay for me. Then his mouth would widen in a welcoming grin as the boat came alongside. He would run up the steps towards me. His arms would be opening wide, ready to clasp me to him.

Then as his gaze raked me up and down and took in my slim figure, the smile would begin to slip. His eyes would widen in bewilderment and he would shake his head slowly in disbelief. Oh, dear God, it was bad enough to have lost another precious child. But to have to admit that I had lost it through what he would see as carelessness? *Never!*

I gulped back another flood of tears. Joel had only to raise his little finger to have girls throwing themselves at his feet, I knew that. And a fisherman away for such long periods could have a woman in every port and still keep a wife at home to bring up his children. His children! And if there were no children? My tortured mind saw the end of our marriage looming before me. And I was afraid.

At that moment, Kate's anxious face appeared round the door. Seeing that I was awake, she came all the way in. She was carrying a tray with two cups of tea on it. 'Here, give him to me and drink this, dear,' she said briefly, holding out her arms for the baby.

'No!' My vehemence must have startled her, as some of the tea slopped into the tray. 'I can manage.'

She touched my hand. 'All right, dear. Of course you're overwrought after all you've been through. Who wouldn't be? But you'll have to give him up sooner or later, you know. Anyway, we'll talk about it another time, when you're feeling stronger. I'll stay here tonight and look after you and send a message to Arthur saying you've been taken ill and need me.'

'Won't he mind?' Even sunk in my own misery I remembered how possessive Arthur could be.

'Oh, he'll mind all right.' Kate gave a mirthless laugh. 'But don't worry about it. I shan't. I will go down though, and see if I can find a boy to take a note to him.'

It sounded as if a group of youths were playing 'chicken' on the quay, trying to dodge the tremendous waves. I could hear their shouts and squeals from where I was.

'Hey, you!' I heard Kate shout against the wind. 'Who wants to earn a threepenny bit?'

'I do, missus!' . . . No, me! . . . 'Get off, I was here first!' Then came the sound of boys' hobnailed boots clattering on the cobbles. Sometimes they struck sparks from the stones. I heard Kate send him on his way, then close the door as she came back inside.

I couldn't sleep that night. I was haunted by nightmares, tormented by my own chaotic mind, I rose to my feet and slipped out of bed. Straightening my stiff and aching body, I paced the floor to ease it. Then I lifted up my baby and cradling him in my arms I crossed the room to look out of the window.

The storm was still raging. At its height now, it was lashing the water in the harbour into furious waves that came hurtling high over the quay, their white plumes flying. The wind was screaming in from the sea, tearing the dark clouds into black rags that scudded far inland, like ghosts fleeing an enchanter.

I pulled down the sash and stuck my head out. I lifted my face to the wildness, to the driving rain that soaked my hair in seconds and laughed. Now I knew what I had to do. I settled the baby comfortably in the crook of my arm, threw a shawl around us both and let myself out of the house.

*

I laughed aloud as I lifted my burden higher. Turning my face into the wind, my hair streaming out behind me, I made for the beach. Huge breakers were rolling shore-wards, black as the night itself. Their crests were tipped with silver by the fitful light of a pale moon which swam between the torn and racing clouds.

As the waves reared up, their ragged claws reached out for me. Ready to drag me down into hell itself. I took a few steps towards the water and raised both arms in greeting, holding my baby out like a sacrifice.

Soon all my problems would be solved. We would be together for all eternity, I and my infant son. Melting into this howling wilderness of sea and sky and becoming part of it forever.

Joel would be free to choose another wife. I would no longer have to worry about my failure to become a mother. Simple. It was all so simple.

I began walking around the point. Far away to my left I could see in the breaks between the clouds, a great ship. It was being tossed about on the enormous swell, bucking and diving like a huge sea-bird. Like the broken wings of a bird too, scraps of ragged sail clung to the splintered masts. A ghost ship, driven from hell.

I turned the point. Here beside a stretch of cliffs it was more sheltered, but thunder rumbled ominously all around. Suddenly the sky was lit up by burst after burst of sheet lightning. By this display of heavenly fireworks I could see some curious dark shapes nearby lying about on the wet, black rocks, as if they had been flung there by the sea. I stepped up on to a natural shelf to peer closer.

Bodies – they were dead bodies. Shock rooted me to the spot. But of course, this was hell, wasn't it? So they would be dead, I nodded. There was a man spread-eagled below me, half in and half out of the water. A plump middle-aged woman lay nearby, grey hair covering her face. Further away, a younger woman, about my own age. Her head was grotesquely twisted and her staring eyes looked straight at me – hypnotic and mesmerizing. This is how I'll be soon, I shuddered. My stomach heaved and I tore my gaze away.

Then I saw a flicker of movement below me. For an instant the outline of a big, burly man reared up in silhouette against the half-light. He had been bending to hoist a barrel or maybe it was a sack, on to his shoulder. His sudden appearance was so unexpected that I froze to the spot.

Could I be seen? There was no way to tell. He appeared to be looking straight at me. There was another man behind him, smaller and thinner. I shrank back into the shadows behind a spur of rock and tried to melt into the night.

Nothing was going to deflect me from my purpose, nothing come between me and oblivion. Soon I would be joining the ranks of these dead souls around me. Just another drowned body washed up by the sea. The nightmare went on.

Suddenly my baby began to cry. I could hear him quite distinctly, but when I unwrapped his shawl, my little son was as still and quiet as before. What a good child he was, he didn't howl like that. He didn't make that piteous mewing wail that filled my head until my nerves were ready to snap.

I could stand it no longer. I took a step towards the ocean. For this was why I had come to this place, wasn't it? To join these people in their eternal sleep.

But as the moon rocked free of its veil of cloud for a moment I saw, tossed up on the rocky shelf, the battered remains of a small boat. Curious, I peered inside. And in a fitful gleam of light, I could see a small bundle tucked under a broken seat. The pitiful wailing became louder.

Then I gasped and peered more closely. A tiny, furious baby lay there, tightly swaddled in a piece of yellow oilskin. Only its little face was visible, a pale and ghostly circle. A baby! My half-crazed mind did a flip. So this was where he had got to, the little son I had thought lost forever.

I laid down the bundle in my arms; it was very heavy. Why had I been carrying such a heavy burden all the way from home? I couldn't remember. I shook my head impatiently, trying to clear it. Then, kneeling down, I reached out for my baby.

I awoke to the sound of Kate's voice calling down to some women out in the street, presumably from her bedroom window. I sat up and glanced towards the light streaming into my own room. I must have slept very late if other people were up and about. I carefully crept out of bed, so as not to disturb the sleeping baby, and went to the window.

The storm had eventually blown itself out. The rain had stopped, the wind subsided and the sea smoothed itself out to its normal level. A sun of sorts had appeared – a weak, pale thing, it was gradually strengthening and smiling benignly down on a newly-scoured and gleaming world.

'So what happened last night? I heard the lifeboat go out.' Kate asked, her voice coming from above. I could see Susan Trembath, my next-door neighbour, shopping basket over her arm, standing in a group around another older woman called Jane Polglase. Jane was telling a long tale and pointing seawards.

Several of the women were knitting as they leaned against the harbour wall, their fingers flying as fast as their tongues, balls of wool stuffed into the pockets of their long white aprons. I well knew that seamen could never have too many thick stockings, or the traditional guernseys and jerseys of oiled wool – warm and weatherproof against the lacerating gales. These women's time was too precious to be wasted in idle chatter.

Kate had said several times how she felt very out of place with these local women. Although they were friendly enough to her on the surface, as my sister, she knew herself to be a 'stranger' in the eyes of the small and close-knit community. She had wealth and position and was not of the village in the way that these women were. They had all been born and raised here, like their forefathers, for generations past.

'Oh, 'tis terrible, terrible,' Jane called back, looking up. 'I just been saying – that there ship was lost with all hands!'

'*All?*' Kate's face must have registered her shock. I heard her voice rise up the scale.

'Ess like I said, 'twas some awful night. Bill said he've never seen nothing like it this time of year. Seas was higher than what they do get in the winter. Some upset he were – they couldn't pick up no survivors, see.'

The women's faces became even more drawn as details of the tragedy emerged. Jane Polglase had tears in her eyes. 'They could see the men on deck, hanging on for all they was worth as the ship was rolling and shifting. Six or eight men, Bill reckoned, and they just couldn't get no line over to them.

'Imagine it can you? They poor souls was only yards away, screaming and waving, but Bill and they couldn't do nothing.' She dabbed at her eyes with the corner of her apron.

'It was *that* rough was it?' Kate sounded horror struck.

''Twas some rough, yes, but really it were because of the ship being grounded on the bar, see.' I nodded to myself. Loe Bar was a notorious hazard to shipping.

'Lifeboat couldn't get near them because of the great seas tossing it all about like a toy, Bill said. Hours they was out there, firing line after line across, but they always snagged or fell short and was carried away. And the ship listing more and more all the time.' Jane sighed and shook her head.

'Then a huge great sea crashed right over the deck and washed all they men into the water. They was swept away so fast they couldn't even pick them up! The rip took them under in a second and out of sight.' Jane paused on a sob.

Susan was slowly shaking her head at the enormity of the tragedy. 'Some job, some job,' she whispered. 'I suppose the bodies'll start coming in soon, when the tide do turn.'

'What was the ship – where was she from?' someone asked.

'German cargo vessel,' Jane replied. 'Carrying timber. She had casks of ale and spirits on board too. Making for Hayle to deliver wood, then meant to go on to Falmouth. The gale swept her way off course and round Land's End.' She paused.

'Bill was in some state when he come in, I tell you. He'd think of all they wives what are widows now, and little children left without their fathers. They say the captain had his family aboard, too. It'll prey on his mind for days, because he do take it all personal like, Bill do.'

'But he did all he could – risking his own life – and so did the lifeboat crew,' Kate put in. 'No one could have done more.'

'Ess, but that's what it's like when the sea's in your blood.' The woman stared up at Kate. 'You aren't from round here, my handsome, see. Wouldn't expect you to understand.' And the circle closed in as the women put their heads together and changed the subject.

I heard Kate close the window and come downstairs. I slipped back into my makeshift bed before she looked in on me. Actually the settee was remarkably comfortable.

I was sitting up when she came in carrying a tea-tray. The baby was clasped to my breast. She kicked the door shut after her and tried to clear a space on the small table beside me to place the tray. She was about to speak when a sudden, angry squall from the baby gave her such a shock that the tea-things dropped to the floor with a crash.

I shifted my position and put the baby to my other breast. The yell subsided as he began sucking heartily.

'Wh-what. . . ?' Kate gulped, rooted to the spot. 'What have you got there?' A hand flew to her throat. What an inane question that was. 'Where did it come from? Oh, Loveday, what have you *done*?' She turned frightened eyes to my face.

'Hello, Kate.' I couldn't meet her gaze. For, my head reeled, what *had* I done? In the cold light of day the nightmare of last night had receded and sanity returned. 'I'm feeding my son, of course.'

Kate took a step closer and collapsed on the end of the couch as if her shaking legs would no longer support her. Her eyes widened as they caught sight of the pile of sodden clothing I'd dropped in a corner when I came in. My night-gown and the baby clothes. The linen binder, the shawl, and the piece of tattered oilskin.

'You went *out* last night! In all that storm. Didn't you?' Kate pointed, accusing. I hung my head so that my hair fell over my face and said nothing. 'Loveday – you could have *died*!'

Kate sprang up, arms akimbo. Then her jaw dropped. 'Was that. . . ?' she pointed a shaking finger at the baby. 'What you. . . ? Oh, I can't believe this!' She buried her face in her hands.

Then she edged closer. Lifting the hair none too gently from my face she yanked it back and glared. 'Loveday, look at me!' I had to, I was unable to turn away. 'Right. Now, *talk*!'

I moved the now sleeping infant from my breast and cuddled him close. 'Yes,' I said simply, biting my lip and on the verge of tears. 'Kate, I was at my wits' end last night. I mean that literally. I think for a while I was actually mad.'

I raised my eyes, pleading silently for her to understand. 'I can't really remember much. It was a dreadful kind of waking nightmare. I went down to the beach – to the sea – in the storm. I *must* have been mad. I was going to – to drown myself you see.' Kate gasped and stared at me in horror, both hands pressed to her face.

'There were these dead bodies lying about on the rocks.' I gulped. 'I thought I'd already died and gone to hell.'

'Oh, dear God! Go on.' Kate raised her head. Her gaze was fixed on my face, boring through my skull.

'Kate, I heard a baby crying, and because of the state I was in, I thought it was mine. I found it in a small wrecked lifeboat, thrown right up on to the rocks. How it had survived I don't know. I picked it up. I must have left m-mine there.' My eyes filled with tears as I shook my head. 'I just don't remember.'

Kate's face was grim. She drew in a breath. 'But Loveday, dear,' she began in a pacifing tone, as if fearful of my reaction. 'You can't possibly keep him, of course. You do know that, don't you?'

My jaw clenched and I clutched the baby more tightly. 'Oh yes I can, Kate, he's *mine*,' I said fiecely. 'I found him and nobody's going to take him away from me. Ever.'

'But you can't just *keep* him!' Kate cried, appalled. 'Another woman's baby?' Put bluntly like that, a shiver feathered down my spine. My determination wavered.

But only for a second. I flinched, but held my head high. I took a deep breath and when I replied, my voice was firm and level. 'Just think about it, Kate. I heard what those women out in the street were saying to you. Everybody on that ship perished. Everybody.' I stared her down. A hidden steely resolve that I'd never known I possessed, had surfaced and taken control.

Kate shook her head as if to clear it. 'But – but he'll have family somewhere – relations. You'll be found out! It's illegal! Dishonest! You could be arrested for kidnapping – for stealing someone else's child!' She babbled away, staring at me in horror. 'Loveday – you could go to *prison*!'

'Oh no, I shan't.' I stiffened my spine. 'When the bodies are discovered, even if anyone *did* know there was a baby on board, they'll find' – my voice broke on a sob – 'find . . . my little one, and assume. . . .'

Kate fell silent and regarded the sleeping infant. 'But,' she said quietly as her brow furrowed.

I leaned forward. 'Yes? What?' I demanded. Could she be right after all? Had she thought of something I'd overlooked? My heart began to flutter.

'Surely this baby isn't new-born? He looks bigger than . . . than yours did.' Our eyes met and she held my gaze.

I gulped. 'N-not *much* bigger though.' I tilted my chin in defiance. 'He can't be many days old because he hasn't shed the stump of his birth-cord yet.'

Kate sighed and nibbled her lip. 'Oh, I suppose so.' She paused, looking down at the infant. 'Oh, Loveday!' She nibbled her thumbnail and her green eyes were huge in her pale face.

'Actually . . . do you know, I think it might just work?' She slowly shook her head. 'I expect there's a snag somewhere, but my brain's too tired to think clearly at the moment.' She sighed and passed a hand across her forehead.

'Think of the other side of this, Kate,' I heard the note of steel in my voice. 'I saved this infant's life. How long do you think he would have lasted if I hadn't come along? He'd already been there for most of the night. I'd say his chances were pretty slim – maybe only hours, wouldn't you?'

I pointed a finger and stared into her face. 'This was meant to be, Kate. I truly believe that. God sent him to me – to save me from . . . from . . . taking my own life.' I gulped. 'We saved each other. So, he's *mine*.'

I looked down at the sleeping baby and stroked the top of his head. 'Do you see how blond he is? Just like Joel. He has blue eyes too. Our own baby,' I whispered, holding the warm little body close. Our little miracle.

I tried to convince myself I wasn't dreaming. Only a few hours ago I had been in a bottomless pit of despair. But now here he was, my little gift from God. An immense surge of love and protectiveness welled up inside me and I clasped him close. 'Kate, nothing and nobody is going to take him away from me.'

For Joel would never leave me now. Not now that I'd given him a son. I felt a smile spreading across my face, lifting the strain from my eyes. Smoothing out the worry lines that had been etched across my forehead. And I felt once more like the young woman I was.

Kate was stroking the baby's cheek with a gentle finger. 'He'll have to have a name, Loveday. Did you ever think of any – um – before. . . ?'

'Oh, yes. Joel and I talked a lot about names. He wanted Davy for a boy. I liked it, too. And if it was a girl we were going to call her Hannah.' I looked down at the little scrap in my arms, then smiled. 'So, Kate, this is our little son, Davy Penrose.'

CHAPTER THREE

KATE

I left Loveday's house physically and emotionally drained. I felt as if the whole nightmare had been going on for weeks rather than two days. I was dishevelled and dirty, wearing the same clothes in which I had dealt with the birth and all that had come afterwards.

I was partway up the steep incline towards the cliffs and Rosewarne Villa, but I couldn't face going home for a while. My head was aching, I hadn't been able to sleep much last night for the buzzing of my over-stimulated mind. I needed to think.

I leaned on a fence-post and looked out to sea. Up here the air had lost the tang of fish which always enveloped the harbour, and blew crisp and salty straight off the ocean. The sky was a bright sapphire blue, the landscape so clear it could have been sculpted and polished by some mighty hand.

To the left, on the eastward side, the sun was gilding the white-painted lighthouse on Lizard head. To the right, before the headland curved away out of sight, it gleamed on the weathered masonry of the old, abandoned Trewavas mine.

I averted my eyes from the bits of flotsam and jetsam from the wrecked ship that were forlornly slapping about at the foot of the rocks below. Broken planks, lengths of rope and other sad reminders of the tragedy. Mercifully I could see no bodies. They must have been discovered at first light and removed.

I was haunted by the enormity of what Loveday had done. I just could not take it in. When I was with her, faced with her determination and her conviction that the plan was foolproof, she'd managed to convince me.

But I was looking ahead now, to the weeks, months, years that she would have to carry on the deception. How could she live with herself, with Joel, knowing what she'd done? And surely the secret was bound to slip out sooner or later. It would only take one indiscreet word – from either of us really.

For *I* was going to have to hold my tongue too. For the rest of my life. Appalled at the prospect, at the responsibility which had been thrust unwanted upon me. I drew in a shuddering breath.

I dragged my weary body over the rise and there it was on its vantage point – Rosewarne Villa, ugly, pretentious and totally out of keeping in this glorious natural setting.

'Oh, it's you. You've come home at last, have you?' My mother-in-law was on her way out of the house and we met in the hall.

'As you see.' I wearily regarded Maud Rosewarne. Short and rotund, she was in black as usual and looked as dreary, as the brown painted dado and the bottle-green wallpaper. Over the ornate hall-stand hung a painting of Highland cattle in a large and dingy frame.

The woman's small and spiteful eyes raked me up and down. 'And looking like something the cat dragged in.' I automatically put a hand to my windswept hair and glared at her.

'Arthur wasn't very pleased when I told him you were staying away for the night!' Maud smirked and rubbed her hands together with what looked like glee. 'He was looking for you.'

I raised an eyebrow. 'I hope you passed on my message.' I turned with one hand on the newel post at the bottom of the stairs. 'That my sister had been taken ill and needed me. Her baby was born early this morning.'

I paused to peel off my gloves and remove my hat. Placing them on the hall-stand I turned back to her.

'I see.' The woman's eyes were cold. 'A pity it wasn't *yours*.' She sniffed. 'You've been married for two years and no sign yet of a son for Arthur.'

I felt colour creeping up my neck and wondered if she was aware of the rumours that were rife in the village about him, or whether she even knew of Arthur's proclivities at all, bearing in mind that remark.

Maud turned on her heel and took a step across the patterned tiles towards the door. 'Oh yes, I told him. But he didn't like it. Because as a married woman, of course, your first duty is to your husband, and your place is here, at home. And he missed you.'

Maud's head bobbed up and down and she pursed her mouth. 'It's a good thing he has me to turn to. I saw to it that he had a good meal last night and a hearty breakfast before he went to work this morning.'

My jaw dropped. '*You* to turn to?' I snapped. 'With all the servants we keep to see to our every need, I'm sure he could manage without me for one night.'

I was halfway up the stairs when the insidious voice came drifting up behind me. 'Well, he wasn't very pleased, and I expect you'll hear about it later.'

I half-turned and glared at her again. Clad in a costume of black gaberdine, Maud was standing with her arms folded, watching me. Her narrow mouth seemed incongruous in such a round, fleshy face. It was a face that looked as if it had originally been designed to be plump and jolly, but had been worn away over a lifetime of petty-mindedness.

I knew she'd been a widow since George, her husband, had died when Arthur was eleven and away at boarding school. But even given that the woman had had a hard life and probably a lonely one, not enough to justify her attitude towards me.

Now faced with my glacial stare, she went on her way, the black feathers on her hat nodding their agreement.

'No, Arthur didn't like that at all,' came the parting shot as I reached the landing. Out of sight, I raised a hand to my aching head. Maud never missed an opportunity to set Arthur against me. In small ways, not outward lies, but she was adept at seizing on a grain of truth and distorting it into something contentious. Then she would sit back with satisfaction as a row erupted.

Thank goodness she was going out. Maud was a person of strict habits, most of which centred around the Methodist chapel. This should have given her a more Christian attitude towards other people, like me, for instance. She must be the biggest hypocrite around.

On Wednesdays Maud took lunch in the chapel meeting room, with the ladies of the Missionary Society. Today was obviously no exception. As I entered the bedroom I heard the click of her hard heels crossing the tiles of the hall, before the front door slammed and she was away.

I sat down on the bed and sank my chin in my hands. I'd learned much during almost three years of marriage. I'd naturally assumed of course, that Maud would take second place and make way for me as mistress of the house. So it was a huge shock to find that she had no intention of doing any such thing.

I had soon found myself feeling like an interloper, and Arthur did nothing to help. 'Why should you want to run the house?' His eyes had widened at the preposterous idea. 'When Mother does it so efficiently? It will give us more time to be together. You can wear the beautiful clothes that I shall buy you, and just enjoy being my wife.'

And I'd believed it all at first. It had taken a long time for me to discover that Arthur only wanted me as a possession. As a doll-wife. One whom he could put on a pedestal and show off. Gradually he began to sap my will-power. And attempted to break my spirit. Too late I realized I'd been chosen for the air of respectability my marriage would bring to the house of Rosewarne. For respectability was the god revered by both mother and son. 'What will people *think*?' was their constant mantra.

'I think I'll have an early night.' I yawned as I rose to my feet at the end of that day. I was exhausted and longed for the comfort and oblivion of a good night's sleep. I replaced the magazine I'd been reading in the wooden rack. Maud was busy with some crochet-work. Arthur in his velvet smoking jacket was deep in the newspaper. Apart from the relentless tick of the grandfather clock in the corner of the gloomy drawing-room, there was not a sound.

Any sound would have been stifled by the dull maroon curtains, by the clutter of small tables, ornaments, and pictures that filled the room. I side-stepped a particularly hideous arrangement of stuffed birds under a glass dome as I moved towards the door. I'd made the move as much from boredom as fatigue.

'Good night,' I said as I passed Maud's chair. Arthur glanced over the top of his paper and remarked, 'I shan't be late myself.' My heart sank. I opened the door, skirting the velvet curtain which hung from a brass rail over it against draughts, and closed it carefully behind me. Sometimes he would sleep in the dressing-room, but apparently not tonight.

Arthur came in just as I was about to turn out the oil lamp and climb into bed. 'Leave it,' he commanded, 'I want to look at you.'

I did as I was told, feeling like a rabbit trapped by a snake. Already clad in his habitual striped night-shirt, he took a couple of steps across the room. Laying a heavy hand upon my shoulder, he turned me round to face him.

'So.' His fingers bit into my flesh, 'you decided not to come home to your husband last night. What sort of behaviour is that for a respectable married woman, eh?' The voice was dangerously quiet.

I squirmed, but his grip was like iron. His hot eyes bored into mine. I lifted my chin. 'I left you a message. I only went to visit my sister, but while I was there her baby was born, so of *course* I stayed the night. I – that is – *we* have a new little nephew.'

His lip curled. His nose wrinkled. 'What sort of behaviour is *that* for my wife? Attending at a childbirth! I thought I raised you above the level of the farmyard and the fish cellars when I married you.'

His hot breath on my face was making me want to gag. He squeezed my shoulder again and I flinched. 'Your place, madam, is here with me. In this house. And when I come home I expect my wife to be around to greet me. At any time.'

I gritted my teeth against the pain and stood my ground. 'Yes, Arthur, I'm your wife. But surely I'm entitled to visit my relations. As often as I want to. And so I shall.' I knew that defiance would only enrage him even more, but I would not meekly submit to his bullying.

Arthur's expression had changed to one of sullen fury. He jerked me towards the bed. 'You, madam – will do – as you are *told*!' he hissed, pushing me backwards on to it.

I sat down with a jolt and my night-gown rode up past my knees. Hastily I tried to drag it down again. But Arthur was leaning over me, his hands pinning me to the pillows. He thrust his face down to mine.

'And how do I know that you're telling me the truth, anyway?' Snarling, he grasped my shoulders and shook me. 'You could have been spending the time anywhere. With anybody.' He was breathing more rapidly and his face had flushed to a dull brick-red.

'Of course I'm telling the truth!' I squirmed and tried in vain to free myself. 'For goodness sake – why would I lie? You've only got to ask the neighbours if you want *proof*.'

'But you weren't *here* – that's the main thing.' I noticed his moustache was flecked with little drops of spittle, and my nose wrinkled in distaste.

'And for that,' Arthur's voice dropped to a sinister whisper, 'you must be punished!' With a lunge he seized me round the waist and flung me face down on to the pillows. Seizing my nightgown at the hem, he ripped it over my head and tossed it to the floor.

'No! Arthur. Please. NO!' How I hated myself for pleading. But he was reaching under the bed for the leather belt. I knew it was useless to struggle. I'd married a devil with the charm of an angel. Now I was paying the price of his deception. But maybe there was a way I could dissuade him. Anything was worth a try.

'Please Arthur – I'm still hurting from last time. Isn't there another way that I could – er – *please* you. Help you to. . . .' I raised imploring eyes to his face.

'*What?*' As if thunderstruck, he stopped with the belt in his hand, glaring at me in horror. Then his anger erupted. My heart sank as I realized I'd only made matters worse.

'You trollop!' I flinched at the fury on his face. 'How dare you suggest. . . .' He was spluttering with rage. 'What lady would even begin to imagine the needs of a man? To – to presume that she. . . . What could a real lady *know* of such things? You madam, have the morals of the *farmyard*. Of the muck-heap you came from. You need teaching a real lesson!' He raised the belt above his head.

I cringed as I surrendered to the inevitable, clenching my hands into fists as the blows rained down. I stuffed the corner of the pillow into my mouth and bit down hard.

When he'd finished, Arthur took me. Brutally and briefly. Like an animal. He gave a shout of triumph as he climaxed, then collapsed sobbing on to the bed.

I rolled away. Forcing myself to raise my aching body to its feet and reaching for a robe, I hobbled into the dressing-room and rang for hot water. I could hardly sit comfortably in the hip-bath without easing myself up on my hands, but the warm water was a blissful relief. It was however pink-stained. I drew in a sharp breath as I realized with foreboding that I was bleeding internally as well as outwardly.

When at last I returned to the bedroom, stiff and pain-racked, thankfully Arthur had gone. I reached into the drawer where I discreetly kept my 'headache medicine' and took a swig from the little brown bottle. I quickly stifled the guilt I felt at doing this more and more frequently. For it was the only way I could find escape from my battered body and tortured soul.

When I managed to drag myself downstairs the following morning, I found Arthur sitting at the breakfast table, his own dapper self again, beaming at me as if nothing had happened.

Maud was at the head of the table, presiding over the teapot. She looked me up and down as I slipped into my seat. I wondered how much the woman had overheard the night before. Maud slept on the far side of the house however, and it was impossible to tell.

'Ah, Kate! Good morning my dear.' Arthur rose and pulled back my chair. I raised an eyebrow. There was a small velvet-covered box beside my plate. It was always the same. Whenever Arthur had had 'his way' the previous night, there would be an expensive present to follow. Flowers, or jewellery, or perfume. Conscience money? I sniffed. Blood money was more like it.

Both pairs of eyes were fixed on me as I picked up the box. 'Go on, open it,' Arthur urged. 'It's an early anniversary present, for my beautiful wife.' I gave him a scathing look. For an instant the smile wavered.

I lifted the velvet lid and peered inside. It was a gold watch, its dainty face encrusted with tiny jewels. I stroked it with a finger. In any other situation I would have been thrilled to own such a delicate thing. 'It's lovely.' My voice was toneless. 'Thank you, Arthur.'

Maud, spreading marmalade on her toast, was watching through half-lowered eyes. She *must* have some idea of her son's proclivities; her eyes met mine as she raised her head to take a bite, and I was sure.

'Kate, I've planned a little surprise for you.' Arthur made his announcement at the dinner table that evening. He reached for a napkin and carefully wiped his dark moustache.

'Oh?' I raised an eyebrow. 'Yes?' We were seated around a mahogany dining table big enough for ten people. I felt marooned on a sea of starched white damask. Arthur, as master of the house, was sitting at the head, Maud and I at either side. Awaiting orders, a uniformed maid hovered beside the matching sideboard. On this stood an array of covered silver dishes holding enough food, I knew, to keep Loveday and Joel for a week.

My husband smiled, showing sharp white teeth. 'Yes. As you know, it will be our wedding anniversary in the spring.' He leaned forward, held my gaze and paused for maximum effect. 'We'll be spending it in Paris.'

'*Paris?*' Jolted out of my lethargy, I couldn't suppress a gasp of amazement. And a surge of interest. I'd never been out of Cornwall, and even with Arthur as company it was bound to be exciting. New sights, new people, different food. 'Oh, how lovely!' For once my face lit up with a genuine smile for him.

Arthur gave a gratified smirk as Maud chipped in. 'Oh Arthur, how thoughtful of you. No-one could wish for a better husband – or son.' She looked fondly at his bent head. 'I hope you realize how lucky you are, Kate, and are suitably grateful.' She raised a soup-spoon to her mouth and fixed her beady eyes on me. 'There are not many men as considerate as Arthur, you know.'

I ignored her. 'How long will we be away, Arthur?' I broke a piece of bread and nibbled it.

He swallowed before replying. 'I thought about two weeks.' He laid down his spoon and pulled a notebook from the waistcoat of his dark, pin-striped suit. 'Yes, I can manage a couple of weeks.'

Maud raised an imperious hand and the maid came forward to remove the empty soup-plates. Arthur smoothed back his black hair, so slick with macassar oil that it could have been painted on his head. 'Yes, I shall have to arrange to take some leave from the office. It won't be all that convenient, but I shall tell them that my wife comes first.' He beamed patronizingly at me. I gritted my teeth and said nothing.

The maid placed a joint in front of him and he picked up the carvers. 'I think Richards is quite capable of dealing with things temporarily.' Plates loaded with slices of beef appeared before us. 'I've trained him thoroughly enough, and if anything major crops up of course, he can always turn to John Stephens.'

Arthur was a partner in a small firm of solicitors, Stephens, Rosewarne and Vigus, in Helston. It had been the family business for several generations and brought in a steady, but modest income.

The wealth which enabled us to live in luxury, I gathered, came principally from his father's mining investments. Also in rents from the properties he had bought in and around Porthleven. These had naturally come down to Arthur. From listening at keyholes and peeping when they thought they were alone, I learned there was also an annuity left to Maud by her own father. Naturally, Arthur administered this for her. All of which meant that we wanted for nothing.

The roast was followed by cabinet pudding and custard, after which we rose to take coffee in the parlour.

'Of course, my dear,' Arthur's dapper figure was leading the way. He looked back over his shoulder. 'You'll need new clothes for the trip.'

I thought of my already brimming wardrobe and stared in amazement. 'But Arthur, I've so many gowns! You know I have. Surely I can't need any more?' I glanced down at the maroon shirt-waist I was wearing at that moment. Trimmed with expensive lace at neck and cuffs, the cost of which would have kept us for a week at Pengarth.

Maud, pouring coffee from the silver pot, raised an eyebrow. She is thinking what an ungrateful chit, I am, I assumed. I stared her down.

Arthur waved a dismissive hand. 'You've absolutely nothing suitable for travelling in.' He spoke to me like a child. 'We'll go into Truro and visit the emporiums there.' He replaced his empty cup and left the room, nodding in his mother's direction and giving her an oily smile. 'If you'll excuse me, Mama.'

I glared at him with irritation. Why did he always have to rap out orders as if I was a servant? Surely we could have a civilized conversation just once in a while. But, Paris! In the spring! As I hugged the idea to me like a comfort blanket, the corners of my mouth lifted. I could put up with anything to see Paris.

'What a generous man he is!' Maud rang the bell for the maid to clear away. I glowered and kept my mouth shut. At least I would be getting away from my mother-in-law for a while and that would be a holiday in itself.

CHAPTER FOUR

LOVEDAY

The fleet was coming home! The luggers had been sighted off Land's End. I had joined the other women on the quay, all in our sober dark dresses, or skirts and high-necked blouses, and long white aprons stiff with starch. Waiting for the return of our men.

I was clasping little Davy in my arms. It was now three weeks since the great storm, and the memory of that momentous night seemed more and more like a dream. For the sake of appearances I had spent the usual amount of time 'lying in'. Ma had come down regularly to help, and with Meg – Joel's sister – and Susan my neighbour dropping in, I had no lack of company.

And the company kept my mind occupied. While I was chatting to others I could forget the reality. When they had gone however, I had time to think, alone in the silent house. Then there were moments when I quailed at the enormity of what I had done. And I dreaded my husband's return.

'Some fine little boy you got there.' Jane Polglase chucked the baby under his chin and cooed to it. 'Your man'll be some proud of he. Know you've had un, do he?'

'I hope so,' I stroked the tiny cheek. 'I sent him a telegram care of the post office in Scarborough. He was expecting a letter from me, so I hope he called in. But I haven't had any reply.' I bit my lip as my stomach tightened.

'Big boy for his age, isn't he?' Susan Trembath joined in. 'Who do he take after, do you reckon?'

I swallowed hard. To hide my reddening cheeks, I bent over the baby and fussed with his shawl. 'It's a bit early yet to tell, but of course he has Joel's colouring.'

'Dear of him.' With feeling, the woman added. 'You won't never have so much time to give to a cheeld again like you do with your first.' She hefted her own youngest into her arms and restrained a toddler who was heading towards the edge of the quay.

'Some lucky weren't you, that your sister was with you when you started?' Susan turned back. 'I didn't know nothing about it till it was all over, else I would have come in. You could have called me even so, you know.' A flicker of something, hurt maybe, or disappointment, crossed her face and was gone in a second.

'It all happened very quickly.' I smiled. 'And it was such an easy birth that we managed it well between us.'

How easily the lies slipped off my tongue. Me, who had never told a lie in my life. Now I was living one. I tightened my grip on the sleeping infant. Davy was worth any amount of lie-telling. I would have sold my soul for this precious scrap of flotsam that had drifted into my life when I had been at my most desperate.

'That's right – you *was* some lucky to have your sister there,' chimed in another voice. I turned to look at the speaker – what was her name? Ah, Ruth, that was it. She nodded as the woman held her gaze. 'Funny you should both have come to live so near to each other when you was married.'

She gave me a level stare. 'Um,' she paused, 'happy is she, your sister, up there with Mr Rosewarne and his mother?'

Surprised, I stared back. What a strange thing to ask. 'I – er – as far as I know, Ruth.' I hardly knew what to say.

Ruth must have seen my reaction for she took a step back. 'Sorry, that sounded awful nosy.' She clapped a hand over her mouth. 'Dick my husband do always say I ought to learn to mind my own business.' She giggled.

'But I only asked because I used to work up to Rosewarne Villa myself, see. And there was stories going round then about Mr Arthur.'

I frowned and changed arms with Davy. He was getting quite heavy these days. 'Really? What sort of stories?'

Ruth lowered her voice. She raised a hand to shield her mouth, and her round blue eyes met mine. 'Well, the other servants used to say how he couldn't keep his hands to himself, like.'

She looked over her shoulder, and satisfied she wasn't being overheard, went on. 'Now, that's only hearsay mind, he never laid a finger on me, but some said his tastes weren't quite ... *normal*, you know?'

I felt my eyes widen at this.

'Lots of the maids didn't mind a bit of slap and tickle, no harm in that. But the Rosewarnes couldn't never get girls to stay there long, and rumours went round that 'twas because of him.'

She stepped away and shook her head, 'But there I go again – Dick do always say I let my tongue run away with me. I'm some sorry, Loveday, I was forgetting how you're related.'

'That's all right.' I nodded and changed the subject. This was something to think about in private. 'Yes, it's quite a coincidence we live so near each other. Of course, I met Joel when we came down from Sithney to the Gala Day.' I cast my mind back, remembering.

'I was down on the quay not far from here. I'd become separated from the family by all the crowds and I was on my own. I was looking for Kate and the others when this group of drunken louts jostled me. They were shouting and leering and I was getting quite frightened.

'Anyway, Joel came up and saw what was happening. He went for one of them, and whether he meant to or not, I don't know, but he gave him a push and the man fell off the edge, right into the harbour.' I bit my lip. 'I didn't know whether to laugh or cry.'

Then I'd looked up to thank my rescuer and met the full force of those sea-blue eyes. And the tanned and bearded face was full of concern. I was lost. I fell in love with Joel Penrose from that moment, when I was not quite eighteen. And had loved him ever since.

'Joel must have seen how shaken I was,' I went on. 'He made me sit down, and then we started talking. It all went from there. He told me he was entering the rowing competition later that afternoon, so of course I made all my family watch it – and he won!'

'Aw, that's really romantic,' Ruth replied, her head on one side and a beaming smile across her face.

I nodded and smiled too. 'Then of course, Kate met Arthur at our wedding. He was some kind of official at the Methodist chapel.' I paused to change arms with Davy again. Then both Ruth and I were distracted by the shout that went up.

'There they are!' several voices called at once. I raised my head and looked out to sea. Sure enough there were sails on the horizon.

'That's the *Mary Anne*, my Jim's boat. I can see her white foresail. She'll be first one in at this rate.'

'Some handsome sight, aren't they?' Jane Polglase beamed with pride as the boats made rapid headway. They were scudding over the water in the stiff on-shore breeze. She stood on tiptoe and craned her neck over the other heads. 'No sign of the *April Joy* yet. Harry, my son's on that.'

My heart had started madly thumping. Soon Joel would be here. For an instant I felt a surge of pure panic. As if Joel, knowing me so well, would be able to see right through to my soul. Would discover my secret. Don't be so foolish, I chided. You'll give yourself away just by looking guilty.

But even at this last minute my mind was running over the details of the baby's rescue. Had I overlooked anything vital? The bodies I'd seen had been re-discovered by a man walking his dog. They had been buried along with the other recovered victims when the sea had released them. I tried to empty my mind of the whole incident. Davy was mine, mine and Joel's and would remain so.

'Here they are!' cried a voice as one vessel entered the outer harbour and an excited cheer went up. ' 'Tis the *Mary Anne*, with *Seamew* close behind her. . . .' My stomach lurched. Joel was on the *Seamew*.

Soon they were tying up in the inner harbour, closely followed by the remainder of the fleet who were crowding in behind. I was oblivious to the bustle and noise. All my attention was focused on the steps up which Joel must come.

There he was, his eyes scanning the crowd, searching for me. My legs felt like jelly. I raised my free hand in a welcoming wave. He took the steps two at a time. 'Oh Joel, I'm so *glad* you're back!'

Wrapped in his embrace I heard his shout of joy as he gazed down avidly at the tiny child in my arms.

'Aw, my handsome, fancy you having to go through all that on your own.' His voice was tender. 'Ever since I had your telegram I've been that on edge, you wouldn't believe. Couldn't get here fast enough. Skip was on my side and we piled on the sail. Only the *Mary Anne* managed to beat us to it at the last minute.' He grinned and bent to kiss me tenderly.

At that moment Davy, disturbed from his sleep by all the noise, screwed up his face and began to wail. 'He's hungry,' I smiled. 'It's past his feeding time.'

Joel put out a finger and stroked the furious baby's cheek. 'Come us on then, let's get home out of this here crush. I'll have to come back later and help unload, but I had to see my family first.' And I heaved a sigh of pure relief at the note of pride in my husband's voice.

It was going to be all right. Wasn't it?

I was sitting in the open doorway, enjoying the late summer sunshine, my eyes on the sea. With Davy clasped in my arms, I was thinking how thankful I was for the way my life was turning out.

For the last couple of months the three of us had been living as a normal family. I'd stopped holding my breath and looking over my shoulder. Stopped thinking about every word before I uttered it, in case it was incriminating. I'd convinced myself that I had overcome my fear of being found out and that everything was all right.

I glanced around the busy harbour and listened to the cacophony of various noises that filled the air. The clang of metal on metal, that would be from the blacksmith's forge. Hammer blows and sawing from Kitto's ship-building business. The shouts of men's voices on the fishing boats, and overall the endless screeching of the gulls. Smells of tar, paint, smoke and fish mingled with the salty breeze from the sea. I took a deep breath of it and smiled.

For Porthleven was a far cry from the peaceful farm where I had grown up. It had taken me a long time to adjust to life in the bustling port. But this was home now and I revelled in our little family and watched my baby thrive. He was my pride and joy and the apple of his 'father's' eye.

A few months passed. Autumn turned uneventfully into winter. Soon it would be Christmas, but of course, Davy was too small to know anything about that. Next year though, oh the fun we would have! He would be old enough to enjoy his presents, to marvel at the flickering candles, the shining tree.

I went singing about the house. My dreams had come true. The nightmare past was buried. And almost forgotten.

'Well, Loveday my handsome, before I go to sea again we must have our boy baptised, mustn't we?' Joel and I were sitting at the kitchen table over dinner, while little Davy was asleep upstairs.

I pushed back my plate and steepled my fingers. 'I know – it should have been done before now, of course.' I smiled across the table. 'But we just haven't got around to it. At first I was waiting for you to come home. Davy couldn't very well have a christening without his father, could he?'

It couldn't happen soon enough for me. For the occasion would be more than a conventional ceremony; it was a formal and public acceptance of Davy as our own child.

Joel chuckled. 'It would have been a bit unusual.' He tapped his fingers on the tablecloth and his brow furrowed. 'He'll need two godfathers and one godmother, being a boy. How about having my brother David for one, seeing they share the same name – and Arthur and Kate for the others?' He filled his mouth and wiped his plate with a crust of bread.

'Yes, of course.' To me it was not that important, as long as it actually became official. 'I'll leave the arrangements to you, shall I?' I reached across the table for Joel's empty plate and moved away to the sink.

The christening was held in the parish church after morning service on a soft November day of pale sunlight and occasional drizzly showers. Davy was now three months old, and as we left home Joel remarked with pride, 'What a fine family we look, all decked out in our Sunday best!'

I glanced up at him, smart in his one good suit. He was indeed a handsome man: tall, broad-shouldered, a smile never far from his face. The black of his clothing set off his fairness to perfection. How I loved him! I slipped my free hand under his elbow and squeezed it.

Cradled in my other arm slept the star of the show wearing a cream-coloured frilled and tucked gown and bonnet. The outfit was borrowed from Joel's sister Meg, each of her large brood having worn it in turn.

Joel covered my hand in his big one and beamed down at me. 'Soon got your figure back, didn't you, maid? After the birth, I mean. You're looking so slim now as what you did before.'

I smiled up into his eyes. 'Oh, you know me, I never had much of a figure in the first place. Always flat as a board, I was. Not like Kate,' I added as the Rosewarne carriage drew up outside the church and my sister stepped out.

Tightly corseted into the fashionable 'hourglass' shape, Kate was wearing a costume of claret jersey trimmed with white fur, and an enormous matching hat crowned with flowers and feathers.

I looked down at myself, comparing her outfit with my own bell-shaped skirt of lilac wool. I also wore a cream blouse and a long jacket with braiding down the front. My own hat was simple, trimmed only with velvet pansies, but I felt neat and comfortable. And happy.

Kate raised a gloved hand in a wave. 'Ah, your sister's a fine-looking woman. Can't deny that.' Joel was gazing at the dainty ankle in its kid boot that was revealed as Kate stepped down.

A sudden churning of the old insecurity clenched my stomach. Lightly I said, 'You know Joel, I used to think that you and Kate – well, that you were attracted to her at one time – more than you were to me.'

I knew I was being ridiculous, we'd both been married women for years now. But with Kate seeming none too happy, and Joel's open admiration for her, what guarantee was there that she wouldn't turn to him? And maybe by a casual remark betray my secret?

My heart began to pound. Oh, not intentionally. I knew my sister better than that, but by accident, a slip of the tongue. It could so easily happen.

I needed reassurance from Joel. To hear him say that it was me whom he had always loved. To have him put that into words – something he seldom did.

Joel was following Kate's progress to the church door with a thoughtful look on his face. 'Oh, I don't deny she used to be a pretty girl, but she seems to have aged recently, don't you think so?' Then his eyes, as blue as flecks of the sea where he spent so much time, twinkled down at me. 'Anyway, 'twas you I wed, maid, weren't it?'

It wasn't enough, but I hadn't really expected anything different. I swallowed on a lump in my throat and proceeded towards the church.

Davy Penrose behaved impeccably by sleeping throughout the service, only flinching when the touch of water on his head woke him up. By the time he had opened his mouth to protest, it was all over and he was back in my arms.

'Oh, the dear little soul, wasn't he good? Let me hold him for a minute, will you?' Meg came out of the church with her own brood clustering around her. I was reminded as I always was, of a bustling mother hen.

Meg had been a mother for most of her life. Joel had told me that soon after we met and how his eldest sister had brought him and his siblings up as both their parents had died in an outbreak of typhoid fever that had swept through the village. Yes, Meg had had a hard life.

As Joel was the youngest of the family, I could understand the close bond there was between him and his sister. 'I'm the only one left at home now,' he'd said. 'I think Meg and Matt are quite looking forward to having my room when I leave, now that the children are getting bigger. Not that they've ever even hinted at it, mind.'

And sometimes in my lowest moments, I wondered whether this had been another reason why he'd married me after so short an engagement. I gave myself a little shake, now was not the time to dwell on things like that.

'Oh how I do love babies,' Meg crooned, cuddling Davy close. 'And all mine are growing up so fast. So's this little one, isn't he? He's such a big boy for his age.'

It was an innocent remark, but in spite of it my heart lurched and my answering smile was automatic. Of course, I told myself firmly, Davy had been as good as newly-born when I'd found him – he just was a large baby. It was only my guilty conscience pricking. I moved away before my sister-in-law could say anything else,

I withdrew from the huddle around my son. Mama was fussing over Davy now. Pa, uncomfortable in his Sunday best, was fingering his tie and talking to Matt about the weather.

I wandered down a grassy path where I noticed a huge, newly-erected granite cross. Tall and stepped, it had an inscription picked out in lead lettering. When I reached it, the name 'Meervogel' leapt out at me as if the letters were ten feet high. Then I wished I'd stifled my curiosity and stayed with the family. For this was the memorial to the mariners of the wreck. I leaned forward to read the inscription. 31 August 1901.

And gasped in fright as a figure stepped out from behind it. I had to clutch the stone to steady myself. I hadn't heard a sound. Not a footstep to warn me I was not alone.

'Abe Russell! What do you think you're doing, jumping out at me like that?' One hand to my throat, I tried to still my thumping heart. For I recognized him of old.

Abraham Russell was the fellow whom Joel had pushed into the harbour, the day we first met. My stomach churned. I knew he'd never forgotten the humiliation of it. For as he had dragged himself out spluttering and gasping, his friends had laughed at him, and that to him was unforgivable. He had been a deadly enemy of us both ever since.

The sprawling Russell family, countless numbers of them, were a feckless lot who never did an honest day's work if they could avoid it. Petty criminals, public nuisances, a drain on society, they lived up on the moor behind the village in a couple of ramshackle cottages.

When minor offences occurred in the district – drunken brawling in the street, dogs chasing cattle, petty thefts – their reputation preceded them and the police always knew where to call first. Not over-blessed with brains, the Russells were shrewd enough however to evade the law. With the backing of their numerous relations they could usually produce a plausible alibi.

He leered down at me, a great dark hulk with bushy black beard and whiskers, and I quailed. He had been in my class at the village school and was well-known then as a brute and a bully. Younger children were terrified of Abe, both of his size and his unstable temper. And he never forgot a slight, no matter how long ago it had been.

'I seen you down on the beach at midnight when that there ship went down,' he said casually, jerking a thumb towards the stone.

My heart lurched. Of course! The silhouette of a big, swarthy man, outlined against the night sky. I'd never forgotten the fright I'd had.

So it had been *him*! And his brother and side-kick, Billy. My mouth dried up and I was speechless.

'Creeping about. Hiding away. Didn't think I'd spotted you, did you?' He gave a cackle and stuck his hands in his pockets. Rocking back on his heels he went on. 'What was you doing so secret-like, eh?' He took a step closer and I cringed. All my childhood terror of this brute came flooding back. I felt ten years old again.

Licking dry lips I tried to stare him down. 'It w-wasn't . . . I wasn't. . . .' I realized I was stammering. Just as if I had a guilty secret to hide. 'That is,' I forced myself to appear calm, 'you've made a mistake, Abe. It must have been someone else you saw. That was the night my baby was born. I'd hardly have been walking on the beach at midnight, in a storm, would I?' I shrugged and pasted a smile on my face.

'Yeah?' his stony eyes bored into mine. I knew how a rabbit felt, hypnotized by a snake. 'Well, *there's* a coincidence.' He grinned, showing brown stumps of rotting teeth. 'Because, this here woman what I saw – either you or somebody not known – she was carrying a bundle in her arms. And it just happened to look exactly like a baby.'

He was idly stroking his beard with thick, hairy fingers. Much as one would stroke a small animal. Or a woman. . . .

I shuddered, went rigid and felt icy-cold. Fighting against shock. He knew! He couldn't. How could he? He suspected something! He was bluffing. But why? Just to scare me?

Of course it was my imagination. And guilty conscience. My attempt at a reply came out as a mouse-like squeak. I cleared my throat, took a deep breath and tried again. Oh dear Lord, help me. I sent up a silent prayer.

How I managed it I'll never know but when I spoke, my voice was as calm and serene as if I hadn't a care in the world. 'I'm sure it was only a trick of the light, Abe. At the height of a storm over the sea there would be moving shadows everywhere.'

I forced myself to keep breathing deeply. Then tilted my chin in defiance. Holding myself ramrod straight I stared him down. Attack is the best form of defence. I'd heard that somewhere. So, I would counter-attack.

'Anyway, what were you doing down there yourself at midnight, when all *honest* people were in bed?' I stood my ground and held his stare.

Taken aback, my tormentor opened his mouth, but no sound came out. Gaining confidence, I pressed home my momentary advantage. 'My guess is you were out looting wreckage from that ship. *Weren't you?*'

I'd caught him off-guard with that one. He continued to goggle at me as he struggled for words. And I knew how slow-witted he was.

'I heard it was carrying drink,' I taunted him, 'casks of ale, crates of spirits. Just up your street I'd say.' I took a step forward and pointed a finger. 'I noticed too, how your Ma's cottage has been shored up recently. With planks of new wood. That ship was carrying timber, too. How's that for *coincidence*, eh?'

'P-prove it,' he growled and shuffled his great feet.

'I just have,' I said lightly and turned on a heel. 'Well, I must get back to the others. They'll be wondering where I am.' I swung my skirts aside and brushed past him. Steeling myself not to run all the way, I returned to the church.

We were sitting over a leisurely meal one Sunday a few weeks later. Fishermen never went to sea on the Sabbath, no matter how enticing the weather or how plentiful the shoals. Joel had been largely silent throughout the meal and I frowned as I thought how glum he was looking. 'Is something the matter, Joel? You don't seem very happy today.'

Joel heaved a sigh. 'I was miles away, maid. Thinking about the fishing.' He chewed on a piece of roast mutton. 'Tis in a bad way, see.'

'Oh, really? Why's that, then?' I'd overheard snatches of conversation around the harbour and seen a few solemn faces, but hadn't taken much notice.

'Trawlers, my handsome, trawlers coming down from up-country to fish round here. That's the problem,' Joel replied grimly. 'Scrape along the sea-bed they do, and scoop up everything as they go.' He waved a fork to demonstrate. 'Fish too young to be caught, as well as other creatures and their spawn, what do feed the fish, see.'

'But that's never right, Joel!' My voice rose in indignation. I laid aside my knife and fork and stared at him. 'Can't anything be done about it? Where are the authorities? Why don't they stop them?'

Joel shook his head and speared a crisp potato. 'No, 'tis gone too far for that now.' He sighed and pushed back his empty plate. 'Nice bit of mutton that was, maid. There's nothing to beat a Sunday roast to my mind.' He frowned. 'Although the way things are going we'll be eating less meat and more mackerel at this rate.'

He crossed his arms and leaned his elbows on the table-top. 'Ess, snatch our fish from under our noses, they do, and there isn't no way we can stop them.' He scowled. 'There was some trouble when they first started, I tell you. I've heard my uncle say there was tales of boats fouling and cutting the nets of the drift-men. Some swore they did it deliberately. Still do.'

'Oh, that's awful!' I frowned. 'What a mess. And it's so unfair, too. There's surely enough fish in the sea for drifters and seiners alike, if they weren't so greedy.'

Joel shrugged his broad shoulders. 'Like I said, bird, no-one do know for sure what goes on out at sea by night.' He flattened his hands on the table and levered himself to his feet. 'No, we shall just have to work longer hours for smaller catches. That's all there is to it.'

I leant my chin on an elbow as I gazed out of the window. 'I was just remembering something Meg said the other day, too. About Matt.'

'What about him? Not sick, is he?' Joel's bushy eyebrows rose.

'No, no, he's all right. But he was telling her that orders up at Kitto's are falling off too. It seems that more and more boats are being built of steel now instead of wood. They might have to lay men off, she said.' I looked up at him and our eyes met. 'She sounded quite worried. So it's not only the fishing.'

Joel nodded. 'I heard that too. And with these here engines on them, there aren't the number of men needed to crew them, neither. Sail-makers, net-makers, they're all going to be hit, way things are going.'

He stroked his beard as he always did when he was thinking. 'Lots of men are going overseas. Know that, do you? Like the miners. All over the world. America and Australia, South Africa. . . .' He shook his head. 'Don't know where 'twill all end, my handsome.'

'It isn't *fair* though Joel, is it?' He smiled down at me, and I knew my face must have shown how angry I was. 'Life's never been fair, maid, nor ever will be. Now, give us a kiss and I'll go out and chop that pile of wood for kindling. I can hear young Davy stirring upstairs. He's looking forward to his bit of "Sunday roast," too. Takes after his father, he do!'

Chuckling to himself, Joel reached for his cap and left the house. I watched him go down the path, my heart beating a little faster as it always did when he made remarks like that.

I lingered at the table for a moment before going upstairs, turning over what Joel had said. It seemed as if this so-called golden age of opportunity was a mixed blessing. Progress and change was not good news for everybody.

I spooned mashed vegetables and gravy into Davy's eager mouth. He was just about weaned now. As I marvelled at how fast he was growing, my head was still full of what Joel had been saying. How he was having to work so hard and keep such long hours. And I came up with an idea.

I put it to him when he came in a couple of hours later for a cup of tea. When we were sitting one on each side of the range, Davy on the rug between us, banging happily on the floor with a wooden spoon.

'Joel,' I said, as I laid aside my darning. I was mending a sock of Joel's, stretched over a wooden mushroom. 'I've been thinking about what you were saying at dinner-time. And I was wondering . . . I know most women and girls in the village work down in the fish-cellars, gutting and packing. And in the smoke-house too, to earn a bit extra for their families.' I spread my palms and leaned closer. 'And there's the basket-making. . . .

I could do something too, if it would help us out,' I said eagerly. 'I could leave Davy up at Pengarth for an hour or two. Ma would be delighted, she's always saying she never sees enough of him, so. . . .' But my voice trailed off at the sight of Joel's stormy expression and I ground to a halt.

Joel was frowning, his face set. His lips narrowed to a thin line of disapproval. '*What*? Me send my wife out to work! Because I can't support my own family?' He cast aside the newspaper he'd been reading. It fluttered to the floor and Davy seized it with glee.

'Oh no, Loveday, we'd have to be really on the breadline before we came to that.' Joel leaned closer and his eyes, cold as polar ice, glared into mine.

'Don't I bring home enough for you, eh?' He stabbed a finger. 'Surprise me, you do. I never thought you was one for frills and fripperies. Not like that sister of yours. But it seems I was wrong.' He thumped the arm of his chair with a huge fist, and the mug of tea in his other hand wobbled alarmingly.

'Joel!' I was almost in tears at this unwarranted attack. 'Calm down for goodness' sake. You must know I didn't mean it like that. Of course I can manage perfectly well on what we have. I was only trying to help.' I swallowed on the lump in my throat.

Joel's expression softened. 'Yes maid, I suppose you was. But even if I let you, you're too gently reared for standing in they open sheds all winds and weathers. You don't know what you'd be letting yourself in for. Your little hands would be chapped and raw with the salt in five minutes. You'd be in agonies, my handsome. And making they baskets idden so easy as what it looks either. You've got plenty 'nough to do here, looking after we.'

He drained his tea, bent to rescue the tattered paper and shook it out. 'So I'll hear no more about it.' He placed his empty mug on the fender and pretended to read. I knew it was yesterday's, and he'd read every word of it then, but I recognized it as a barrier. It implied that the matter was settled and that was the end of it.

I kept quiet after that, and took up the darning again. I understood Joel's fierce pride in his independence. It was part of the Cornish character.

Our partnership seemed to be unique, in that Joel handed all his earnings over for our joint management. We trusted each other completely. But conversely, it meant that I never had any money I could call my own, that I could spend as I liked.

I'd mentioned something of this to Joel in the early days of our marriage. And had been met by a look of such astonishment and hurt that I wished I'd never opened my mouth. He had repeated my request, which had seemed eminently sensible at the time.

'An *allowance*? Oh, come us on, Loveday – you know that everything we've got is as much yours as mine! You can spend whatever you like. Buy what you want. You don't have to ask me for pocket-money like a child!' Then he'd shrugged and spread his arms wide as if meaning, 'What more can I say?'

This of course had the immediate effect of preventing me from spending anything at all on myself. Or being racked with guilt if I did. Especially as Joel spent very little. He seemed quite content with the occasional drink down at the 'Ship Inn' and a pipe of tobacco of an evening.

So I rarely indulged in any little extras for myself or for Davy. Since this latest outburst I decided to give up buying even the books I loved, and purchased second hand at the market. I joined the circulating library instead, but it wasn't quite the same. Of course I confided nothing of this to anyone, least of all Joel, and outwardly our life went on in a serene and uneventful way.

Until to my amazement a year slipped by and it was almost Davy's first 'birthday'. As we celebrated with an iced sponge I'd made, with one candle on the top, I convinced myself that my secret was buried for ever.

CHAPTER FIVE

KATE

The winter days were becoming shorter. Soon it would be Christmas. Nothing remotely festive, however, was happening in the mausoleum that was my home. Depressed, unable to settle to anything, I decided to walk down as far as Loveday's. It would be good to have a chat. See what she was doing and catch up on any news of the family.

My sister opened the door with a frown on her face, which turned into a smile of relief when she saw who it was.

'Oh, Kate, I'm so glad it's you! Come in. Come through.' She bustled down the passage towards the kitchen, talking over her shoulder. 'I'm stirring up the Christmas puddings while Davy's quiet and I've got a moment. They should have been done before now if they're to mature properly.'

We reached the kitchen and she gestured towards the mass of baking things spread across the central table. 'You won't mind if I don't stop, will you? You can see what a mess I'm in.' Gabbling away, she returned to the bowl of raisins she'd obviously been de-seeding and raised sticky hands to me.

'Of course not.' I went further into the room and peeled off my gloves. 'It smells wonderful in here, Loveday.' I sniffed in appreciation. The kitchen was fragrant with the smell of spices and fruit. 'What did you say you were making?'

'The Christmas puddings. And a tub of mincemeat to lay by for pies later on. I've got the cake in the oven as well.' I watched as she neatly swathed the tops of a couple of puddings in white muslin and tied them firmly, then set them aside for boiling.

'Well, you *are* a busy little bee.' I laughed, but felt a pang of envy too. I would have welcomed the chance to try my hand at baking, especially Christmas food, but I quailed at the mere thought of suggesting it to the formidable Harriet. And as to what Arthur would say if he found me mixing up puddings, with a smudge of flour on my nose, I could only imagine.

I crossed the room and began talking to Davy, who was fastened into his high chair. I picked up his ball from the floor and handed it to him. With a cheeky grin he immediately flung it down again.

'He'll have you doing that all day long if you let him.' Loveday smiled. 'You'll get tired of it before he will!' She tipped the raisins into the mincemeat mixture and set about blanching almonds.

My gaze lingered on the child's bright face and I stroked his silky hair. I would never have a little one of my own to love, either. I choked back the lump that had risen to my throat.

Loveday and I never talked about Davy's 'birth'. But what more was there to say? I behaved towards him exactly as if he were my natural nephew. And even sometimes actually forgot he wasn't. As to what went on in my sister's mind, I didn't ask.

'Are you getting a Christmas tree in for him, Loveday?' I ignored the ball and handed Davy his stuffed dog instead.

'Oh, yes, of course. He'll absolutely love it.' She started to clear away the baking utensils and wipe down the oilcloth table cover. 'Joel's making him a wooden train. I think he's getting as much pleasure out of it as Davy will!'

She ruffled the child's hair as she passed and paused for a moment, her eyes far away. 'Last year of course, he was too small to know anything about it. But now . . . Kate, isn't it incredible to think he's sixteen months old!' I nodded and a meaningful look passed between us.

Loveday snapped back to the present, took off her apron and wiped her hot face with it, then dropped into a wooden chair and rested her elbows on the table. 'What are you and Arthur doing at Christmas, Kate?' She looked expectantly at me.

I shrugged. 'Oh, the same as usual. We'll be going to chapel in the morning. Arthur's preaching. Then to lunch at the "Royal Standard". After that, when we get home Maud will fall asleep in her chair.' My brows arched and I spread my hands, indicating the boredom of it all.

'Then Arthur will expect me to take a sedate walk through the village with him, in order that we can meet the people who were at the morning service. So they can tell him what a wonderful sermon he gave. That's about it.'

It sounded a bleak prospect. I suppose it must have been reflected in my eyes, for Loveday was looking at me with sympathy in her warm brown ones.

'Couldn't you come up to the farm with us?' she said. 'At least to have tea with Ma and Pa. Surely that's reasonable, after spending the rest of the day with them, isn't it? We shan't be staying late because of Davy's bedtime.'

I met her eyes and tilted my chin. Of course it was reasonable. 'Yes, Loveday,' I nodded. 'It is.' I nibbled my bottom lip in thought. 'Naturally I'll have to invite Arthur as well, but I know he won't want to leave Maud on her own. And you know she wouldn't lower herself to come to Pengarth, even if we asked her. To a smelly, muddy *farm*?' I made a face.

Loveday nodded. She would understand perfectly. In the early days of our marriage she'd attempted to visit several times, as had Mama. But the formidable Maud had made it clear they weren't welcome. I tried to make a stand and insist, but I was no match for both her and Arthur.

She implied that Arthur had married beneath him. That I should think myself lucky I'd been rescued from the lowly condition into which I'd been born. It had been humiliating and highly embarrassing and they'd never called again. Instead, I always came here or to the farm.

'So yes, I will try and come, Loveday.' I didn't mean to blurt out what came next, but contrasting her cosy, fulfilling life with my own, I couldn't help it. My throat constricted as I added, 'Although I shall be made to pay for it. . . .'

Loveday looked up with an air of surprise and there was concern on her face. She must have noticed how pale I'd become. 'Kate, are you all right?' Her brow puckered.

'I do have a bit of a headache.' Which was true. I heard my voice waver and couldn't contain myself any longer. I gave a strangled sob, dropped my head in my hands and burst into tears.

'Kate, darling, what is it?' Loveday came across and put an arm around my shoulders.

I sniffed and tried to control myself, reaching in my bag for a handkerchief. Then I drew in a deep breath and mopped my eyes. 'It's Arthur.' I bent my head and stared at the hearth rug as if I'd never seen it before.

'Arthur?' Loveday's voice rose. 'What about him? Is he ill?'

I raised my head and twisted the sodden hanky between my fingers. 'No, nothing like that. But, Loveday, do you remember, ages ago, I started telling you about him? It was when you had that fall, and the baby started coming . . . and well, so much has happened since that we never got back to it.'

Loveday frowned, then her brow cleared. 'Oh, yes! You said he, um, bullied you.'

'Yes, but there's more to it than that. Loveday, Arthur has . . . certain *habits*.' I was whispering, ashamed to be uttering such things aloud, and she had to peer closely into my face to hear.

'In b-bed. And I can't stand it any more. It's been three years now and I've tried to put up with it. Because I made my marriage vows . . . "for better or for worse" . . . you know? But I just have to talk to somebody. I can't tell Ma. She could never imagine such things. Wouldn't understand. So – so I came here, to talk to you.'

I saw Loveday's jaw drop and her eyes widen. She didn't know how fortunate she and Joel were in their mutual love and respect for each other's feelings. I gathered from what she'd said over time, that my sister's experience of marital relations had always been blissful, but she must have known that not everyone was so lucky. Many of the fishermen drank, and beat their wives as a result of it.

'Tell me about it, Kate dear,' she said quietly. 'Does Arthur . . . he beats you, you say. Is that it?'

I bit my lip and nodded. 'Yes. Part of it. Because it's the only way he can – um – perform.' I ground out the words through gritted teeth, 'and then. . . .' I couldn't hold back the sobs.

'He's unnatural, Loveday. The way he does it, I mean. Like . . .

animals. . . . Do you understand?' I sniffed as she stared at me in horror.

'Of course I do.' Her fingers tightened on my shoulder. 'I was raised on a farm.'

I wiped my eyes. 'I was so thrilled when he proposed to me, Loveday. . . . I didn't stop to wonder why he wasn't already married . . . a man of his age. I j-just thought he had to look after his mother and wasn't free.'

I sank my chin in my hands. 'How was I to know he was – well, *warped*? I didn't know anything about men. When I think how naïve I was – we both were—'

'Oh you poor thing!' Loveday squeezed my shoulders again. 'Can't you leave him, Kate?' she whispered, her eyes huge and dark with pity. 'Go back home to Pengarth?'

I stared at her out of eyes made sore with weeping. 'Do you think I haven't thought of that? If only I could, Loveday. But you don't imagine he'd let me, do you?' I spread my hands at the hopelessness of it all.

'The scandal there'd be! You know what a pillar of righteousness he is around here. There isn't a position of office that he doesn't hold – or has done in the past.' I sniffed and ticked them off on my fingers. 'Justice of the Peace, Chairman of the Board of Magistrates, and he sits on goodness knows how many committees. Why, he's even a Methodist lay preacher!' I broke into hysterical laughter.

Shaking off Loveday's arm I stood up and began pacing the room, livid with indignation now. 'Oh no. Who would believe a word of mine against such an influential figure? They wouldn't dare.' I clenched my hands into fists.

'I should either be pitied for my foolishness or condemned for defying my saintly husband. A man can do what he likes to his wife in private, Loveday.' I rounded on her, my tears giving way now to bitter anger. 'The world will turn a blind eye and pretend that it doesn't happen.'

I snorted. 'You wouldn't think women had any rights, Loveday.' I jabbed a finger. 'Once married, our husbands seem to think of us as their *property*, you see to do what they like with.' As she watched and listened open-mouthed to this tirade, I threw up my hands in despair. 'Oh, you just don't know how lucky you are to be married to a normal man!'

Then a frown creased Loveday's brow. As if a shadow of doubt had crossed her mind. Maybe she thought I might be exaggerating. I had to admit it did sound a little far-fetched.

She bit her lip, hesitating, and I knew I was right. 'Well Kate, if you don't mind me saying so, you don't seem to – um – have any bruises, for all that you say Arthur does to you.'

I came closer and placed both hands on the table between us. I glared at her. 'You don't believe me, do you?' I snapped, feeling my colour rise. 'You think I'm exaggerating? Well, come away from the window and take a look at this.' I flung off my wrap. Then turning my back to her, I lifted my skirt and pulled down my drawers.

As Loveday gasped, horrified, I knew I'd proved my case. I took a quick glance over my shoulder. Both her hands had flown to her face.

I knew my buttocks were covered in red weals and that these were overlaid with purplish-yellow staining of old bruises – the abrasions reached from halfway up my back as far down as my stocking-tops. Seeing this had obviously convinced her.

'Oh, you poor *thing*!' Loveday sounded overcome with genuine pity. And with guilt that she'd doubted me. Suddenly she flung away, furious. 'But it's too dreadful for words!' she blazed. 'For a man to do this to anyone is bad enough, but to get away with it because his victim is his wife is . . . is . . . intolerable!'

I nodded and tidied myself. 'Arthur's cunning, you see. He never hits me where it'll show.'

'B-but,' Loveday was stuttering with indignation, 'can't you go to a doctor and explain? Get *him* to do something?'

'Pooh!' I gave her a scathing look. The very idea was ridiculous. 'Even if I could prove it, which I can't, they're all in the same clubs, these professional men. He'd tell me I'd fallen down the stairs and made up the tale to shame my husband. I'm sure half of them enjoy humiliating their wives. It gives them a sense of power, and bolsters their self-importance.' Loveday fell silent as this sank in. I must have convinced her at last.

'I must go,' I said shortly. I turned away, slipped a hand into my bag and took a quick sip of my 'medicine' for comfort. I needed it after all that.

But Loveday had noticed and my heart sank. She frowned and narrowed her eyes. 'What have you got there, Kate?' She was trying to read the label, her head on one side, but I was too far away.

I pushed it quickly back in the bag. 'Oh, um, it's only some medicine that Dr James gave me for headaches. I get these dreadful sick headaches, you see. . . .'

Loveday's mouth narrowed and she held out her hand for the bottle. 'Show me.' Cornered, I reluctantly handed it over.

'Laudanum!' Her eyes widened as she glanced at the label. 'Oh Kate dear, you shouldn't be taking this stuff – don't you know how addictive it is?'

I tossed my head and snatched the bottle back. 'I can manage, Loveday. Mind your own business.' I stuck my nose defiantly in the air. 'It brings me relief from all the horrors. And if mothers can give it to their babies to make them sleep, it won't do me any harm.'

I grabbed her arm and looked her in the face as a sudden thought occurred to me. 'But Loveday – don't tell anybody about all this, will you?' I pleaded. 'Especially not Joel, I mean. I couldn't stand his knowing – I'd feel so humiliated.'

'Of course I won't.' Loveday's voice was warm. 'But promise me you'll go easy on this stuff. All right.'

Dumbly I nodded and turned to go, fighting back feelings of guilt, anguish and despair. Nothing had changed, nor was likely to.

After I'd left Loveday's house I took my time walking round the harbour, before I tackled the steep path to the cliff top. I needed to think. Really think. Although my situation remained the same, I did feel better at having unburdened myself at last and shared my dreadful secret with her.

And strangely, talking about Arthur's behaviour had put it in perspective for me. For the first time since my marriage, it had jerked me out of my lethargy.

With my eyes on the sparkling sea, I felt my depression lifting. I actually began to toy with the idea of leaving him. It seemed impossible at that moment, for all the reasons I had given Loveday. But maybe . . . one day . . . if I could only think of a way.

I leaned on a bollard for a moment, watching the boats bobbing at their moorings. I was in no hurry to go home. I'd been reading in the newspapers these past weeks, of this new 'golden age' of opportunity that was apparently opening up with the coming of the twentieth century. Opportunity for women especially. It was becoming more respectable for single women to find employment outside the home.

I tried to imagine what this actually meant for women. Emancipated, liberated women who were taking responsibility for their own lives. Working in offices, as typewriters, as clerks. In hospitals now that nursing was becoming recognized as an acceptable occupation.

To be truly independent! How strange it must be. But how exhilarating too. My spirits sank. For what had I done with my life? I'd thought marriage was the only option and had welcomed it. Now I saw it only as a painful trap. I sighed and straightened up, suddenly feeling cold in spite of the warm rays of sunlight on my face.

Weeks passed. And months. Christmas came and went and winter came to an end at last. By March there were daffodils in the cottage gardens and creamy primroses dotting the hedgerows. Housewives were busy beating carpets and scouring away the grime left by smoky chimneys. Down on the quay, boats were being caulked and repainted ready for the new season. The days of mists and the soft, steady drizzle of a Cornish winter were giving way to a stiff breeze. It was crackling the washing on the many clothes-lines, and whipping up the water beyond the harbour wall into a tumble of foam.

Our wedding anniversary was in May. The intervening months soon passed, and as they passed, so my spirits rose in anticipation. To my amazement, I actually found myself singing about the house.

CHAPTER SIX

LOVEDAY

After Kate had told me her horrific story that day I couldn't get her and her problems out of my mind. At one point I recalled something one of the village women had told me when we were waiting for the boats to come home, just after Davy had been born. My thoughts wandered. It was incredible to think he was now nearly two. The time since that day had passed in a blur, and my baby was now fast growing into a little boy.

Ah, Ruth, that was what that woman was called. I could remember the hints she had let fall then, about Arthur's tastes being, 'not quite normal'. In the excitement and apprehension of Joel's homecoming I'd thought no more about it, dismissing the whole thing as village gossip, but now it all made sense. So it was common knowledge. Oh, poor Kate. No wonder she'd never felt she belonged in Porthleven.

I frequently took Davy up to Pengarth Farm to see Mama and Papa. They doted on their first 'grandchild' and the little boy dearly loved the animals and all the attention he received there.

I would have liked to confide in Ma, tell her what kind of life Kate actually had, but of course as my sister had already said, there was no point. Such behaviour was so far beyond her own experience, she would think I was making it up.

No, Kate would have to keep her secret as surely as I was keeping mine. Both of us weighed down with our own problems, hers physical, mine emotional. We just had to put up with them and get on with our lives the best we could.

'How he's *growing*, the dear of him!' Ma took Davy from me on one of these visits, and sat down with him on her lap.

She'd been baking and the room was full of the smell of new bread and saffron buns. As round and dumpy as one of the cottage loaves cooling on the window-sill, Ma's face was flushed from the oven's heat, and several wisps of greying hair had worked loose from the bun at her neck.

'I know. He's getting quite heavy to lift. At least, now he can crawl I don't have to carry him everywhere.' I ruffled the child's soft blond hair. 'He's beginning to pull himself up by the furniture too. I should think he'll be walking soon.'

We were in the big farm kitchen where nothing had changed since my childhood. The same picture on the wall, with a faded Jesus still commanding, 'Suffer the little children to come unto me'. Even the geraniums in pots on the windowsill looked identical.

I felt as well, if I opened the big wooden cupboard in the corner our toys would tumble out, mine and Kate's, just as they used to. As the years fell away, I could almost hear our childish voices playing 'mothers and fathers' with our dolls. It must be because I was now a mother myself that all these jumbled thoughts were filling my head. I was viewing the past from a new perspective.

Davy was now starting to struggle and kick in Ma's arms. 'You'd better put him down,' I laughed. 'He's been sitting still long enough!'

I couldn't believe it when she went to the cupboard and brought out a box of farm animals that had been mine when I was about two years old.

'Here you are my handsome,' she bent down and placed them on the hearthrug beside the little boy, 'these'll keep you quiet for a minute or two.'

'Ma! You've kept those all these *years*!' My jaw dropped in amazement. 'What else have you got stowed away in that cupboard?' I crossed the room to have a look. And there on the top shelf were our well-thumbed story-books; two or three stuffed toys; some board games, and the clockwork mouse which always terrified me because it moved so fast and erratically.

'I thought you'd have thrown all this stuff out long ago!' I turned to her in amazement.

'Oh, no.' Ma shook her head and there was a dampness about her eyes. 'Call me a silly old woman if you like, but I always hoped I'd have grandchildren one day, you see. And my dearest wish was to see them playing on the floor with these old things, just like you two used to do. And now watching that dear cheeld coming on, it'd make up for losing you when you grew up.'

She bent down and tenderly removed a stuffed toy rabbit from Davy's mouth. 'It's some quiet here after you and Kate got married. So I can't tell you how much that little fellow do mean to me.' She dabbed at the corners of her eyes. 'But listen to me going on – and I haven't even offered you a cup of tea!' She bustled away and started clattering kettle and crockery.

I was almost in tears myself by this time, and I bit down hard on my lip to stop its trembling. I felt lower than the most crawling creature on earth, to be deceiving her so badly. For if ever, *ever*, my dreadful secret did come out, it could easily be the death of her – from shock, disillusionment and grief – my own mother.

The ramifications of what I'd done reared up to haunt me again, just as I'd thought them buried for ever. Was I never to be free of this great burden of guilt and fear?

I glanced at the clock and rose to my feet. 'We'll have to leave soon to catch that bus back, but I must go and have a word with Pa first. Do you know where he's working?'

'He was ploughing the bottom field this morning, my handsome. He'll be down there somewhere. Don't be too long. I'll keep the tea hot until you come back.'

I was glad of a quiet moment to compose myself. It was a dry but cold day, with a hint of east wind in the air. There had been a frost earlier and white crystals still lay on the grass verges. The rutted path was dry and hard, with the glint of ice on the puddles. From the top meadow a peaceful vista of fields unfolded, rolling down towards the hidden sea. The muted colours of winter: ochre; sienna and deep purple in the shadows, made a perfect foil for the intense blue of the sky and the low, pale sun.

By the time we met Papa coming up the lane I had a smile on my face as I raised a hand. He was leading the two great plough horses, Gog and Magog, their breath rising in clouds of steam on the still air. Davy chortled and kicked at the sight of them and struggled to be put down. Pa waved a hand and when we were near enough to speak, lifted him up for a ride.

'It's amazing he's not afraid, isn't it?' Pa said, as Davy crowed with delight, looking like a little doll perched up so high. Pa held him securely as the great beasts lumbered on at their own steady pace, with no need for guidance.

He smiled with pride, his eyes twinkling in his craggy face. It was as lined as one of his own ploughed fields and as brown. 'Oh, our boy'll make a proper farmer one day, you wait. He's not afraid of any of the animals, you know. He was nearly in the pen with the pigs t'other day. I only grabbed him just in time!'

'Our boy'. There it was again. I suppose in time I would stop noticing these allusions. Stop feeling the stab of guilt that always lay just below the surface. I would have to for my own peace of mind, but it was hard.

By the time we got back to the farm Davy was tired and fractious. We trundled home on the omnibus and he was asleep in my arms long before we arrived.

Christmas came and went. Several months rolled uneventfully by, and one day in May as I was standing in the open doorway, enjoying the first warmth of the spring sunshine and watching over Davy, who was never still, I began thinking about the dreadful Arthur.

Poor Kate. If only there was some way out for her, but of course there was nothing anyone could do. She was tied by the laws of the land to her monster of a husband. She had vowed before God to stick by him, 'until death do us part'. I shuddered and turned my attention back to my son.

Today his toys were out on the small patch of rough grass at the front of the cottage. The stuffed dog with one eye missing, which was his constant companion. The wooden engine Joel had made him for Christmas. The little boy was in a world of his own, playing his imaginary games and talking in a language all his own as well.

'You'd need eyes in the back of your head when they're that age, don't you?' Susan Trembath was looking over the low dividing wall between the houses, her knitting in her hands.

I turned and laughed. 'I should say so. There's no holding him. Susan, he's never still unless he's asleep. He fair wears me out sometimes! Look at him now.'

Davy was trying to push the engine along and cram the dog inside it at the same time. The dog was twice the size of the engine and kept falling off again and again as it trundled down the path. But Davy would not be beaten and toddled after it every time.

The other woman nodded, counting stitches. She looked up and her nimble fingers paused for a moment. 'Been nice and quiet round here lately, haven't it? Since they Russells was put away. You heard 'bout that break-in upalong, I suppose, didn't you?'

'Break-in? No, I didn't. What break-in?' I gave her my full attention.

'Oh, I thought with your people living up to Sithney you would have.' She turned her needles at the end of a row. 'Yes, they was caught redhanded, they two brothers, stealing chickens. Just before Christmas 'twas. I suppose they was going to sell them, see, that time of year. But they took on more than they bargained for. The chickens made such a racket the farmer thought there was a fox, and came out with his gun. He took a few pot-shots before he realized it was them. Caught them red-handed he did, when they started shouting for help.'

I burst out laughing as I imagined the scene. 'That would be Abe and Billy, of course, wouldn't it?'

'Oh, yes. Always is, isn't it? Feckless lot, they Russells, and those two are the worst of them. Wouldn't trust them further than I could spit, I wouldn't.' Susan pursed her mouth and nodded as the needles clacked on.

I leaned a shoulder on the wall and folded my arms. 'How long did they get? In prison, I mean.'

Susan sniffed. 'Don't know. Couldn't never be long enough, I say, whatever they gave them.'

A silence fell while she concentrated on her knitting and I digested this bit of news. So that's why I'd heard no more from Abe. My heart lightened a little.

Susan had raised her head at a shout from Davy and her gaze was following his progress over the grass and down the path in pursuit of his engine. 'Big boy for his age, isn't he?' Her eyes met mine.

A familiar hint of anxiety prickled down my spine. 'Oh, yes,' I stared her down. 'But he was such a large baby if you remember. Joel's family are all big-boned, you know.'

' 'Course, he's going on for two now, isn't he? Twelve months younger than my Sammy.' She glanced down at her own youngest, who was chasing their kitten down the garden. The animal jumped on to the wall out of his reach and sat there smugly washing his whiskers. 'How they grow up. Where do the time go, know do you?' Susan's needles started clacking again.

'I know. Davy's bursting out of all his clothes. I've just made him a couple more little smocks. At the rate he's shooting up they could be the last before he's breeched. Then we shall lose our baby for good.' The smile slid from my face at the thought.

'That's the way it do go.' Susan chuckled. 'But he'll make some fine little boy, Loveday. And perhaps you'll have another one by then, my handsome!'

I started. Such a thing had never occurred to me. I'd had too much on my mind to even think about it. But to my neighbour it must be completely logical. I'd borne one child. There was no reason why I should not bear another.

It was a beautiful morning in early May. The strengthening sun was sending down fingers of brightness upon a world well rinsed and scoured by a night of rain. The last remnants of dampness were visible only in the light, pearly haze far out at sea. Along the quay the polished cobbles were glistening in the light.

'It's some lovely day, maid. Go out in the boat, shall we? Like we used to. Haven't done that since Davy was born, have we?' Joel had pulled aside the net curtain and was peering out of the window. 'I've got to take her out and pick up they crab pots I set last night. We could take a picnic. Like to, would you?'

He turned back into the kitchen. I was kneading bread and Davy on his hands and knees, was investigating the whole new and fascinating country he had discovered under the table.

I looked up and pushed back a stray lock of hair with the back of my hand. 'You've left a floury smudge on your nose.' Joel chuckled.

I laughed and wiped it off with a corner of my apron. How perfect everything seemed on this glorious day. I'd left my worries behind with the winter, and for long periods I found I could actually forget them.

'What a lovely idea, Joel! I've nearly finished here. I can put the dough at the back of the range to rise while we're gone. Give me a minute or two to get Davy ready and put some things together.' I undid the strings of my apron and reached for a clean one.

Down in the harbour the luggers of the fishing fleet, gleaming with fresh paint and moored in neat rows, were making the water almost invisible. They were packed so tightly together that anyone could have crossed from one side to the other dry-shod.

Joel's little dinghy was lying to at the bottom of the weed-fringed steps. 'Manage can you, Loveday?' He swung Davy up in one arm and the basket in the other. I nodded and bunched up my skirts. 'Careful now, 'tis some slippery.'

When we were settled he picked up the oars. Soon we were leaving the shelter of the harbour wall and heading for the open sea. The air was warm and balmy, herald of the summer to come. I trailed a hand in the translucent water and lifted my face to the soft breeze. With the other I clutched the tail of Davy's little smock as he knelt up on the thwart beside me and looked over.

The boat had begun to rock with the swell now, and as it dipped and rose over the waves, the child's face began to pucker. Then he burst into tears, turning towards me to bury his face in my lap. I picked him up and sat him on my lap, holding him close, trying to reassure him.

'There, it's only the sea, Davy, look. And see those big birds up there.' I tried to distract his attention to the seagulls squawking above our heads. 'Isn't this lovely – out in Papa's boat?'

But try as I might, even offering a few of his toys I had brought along, the little boy would not be comforted. Soon his wails had turned into full-throated roars. He held himself rigid in my arms and his little body stiffened alarmingly.

'What on earth's up with him?' Joel's brows drew together in a frown as we reached the mouth of a large cave. He shipped the oars. 'I got to pick up they pots here.' He went to the stern and leaned overboard, dragging in the ropes of the crab-pots with a grappling hook.

It was all I could do to restrain Davy now. The boat was rocking and lurching even more as Joel's weight shifted about and he was getting short-tempered. I could hear his grunts and see the angry look on his face.

He took his place again and pushed off. 'Was it a good catch?' I tried to appear interested, but it was hard to make myself heard above the clamour.

'Not bad.' Joel's face was like thunder. 'Can't you keep him quiet, Loveday? What is it – hungry is he?'

I shook my head. 'I think he's frightened.' A cold hand clenched my stomach into a knot of something like panic. My head began to pound. Suppose, just suppose, it was some hideous quirk of fate. Could Davy, having once almost drowned, retained a trace of ... not memory exactly, but an innate sense that the sea meant danger?

Could the seeds of terror have been planted subconsciously in his new-born brain? And would they grow into a fully-fledged fear of the water? Oh, no! I sent up a silent prayer, please no. For the consequences could well be disastrous as far as Joel was concerned. I knew it would damage his pride severely to have to admit to his mates that his only son was afraid of the water. He would lose face, and that was unthinkable.

He was muttering something into his beard as he turned the boat, and we headed back to the harbour. Davy's screams had subsided now into heartbreaking sobs. Worn out with crying, he was falling asleep in my arms.

Joel was ominously quiet until we reached home. Then he growled as he tossed his cap towards a peg and his temper exploded.

'Dammit all Loveday! I thought 'twould be a treat for him. Screaming like that – a son of mine! I ask you.' He spread his great beefy hands, seemingly at a loss for words, then spluttered, 'And it were flat calm too!'

'Oh Joel,' I felt myself shaking. I rocked the child on my shoulder. 'Davy's only little still – not quite two. You're expecting too much.' I did my utmost to pacify him. 'He'll grow into it, you'll see.'

Please God. I mentally crossed fingers. 'The sea must have seemed so enormous to a little chap his size. Don't you think so?' I went upstairs and laid the sleeping child in his cot. Then straightening my shoulders I swallowed down my fears for the moment.

Back in the kitchen I set about unpacking the abandoned picnic. After that, I tried to soothe my disgruntled husband with the panacea for all ills – a cup of tea.

I was humming away to myself one morning while I donned a large apron and swathed my hair in a kerchief. I was preparing to clean the fat, black Cornish range. Every housewife took great pride in having a gleaming 'slab' as it was locally called, in spite of all its brass knobs which needed constant attention from a tin of Brasso and a soft cloth. Joel had removed the oven lining for me before he had gone that morning, and had taken it outside to brush off the soot.

I'd been on my knees for some time with a brush and Zebo, blacking the monster, and had almost finished when a knock came at the front door. 'Drat! Who on earth's that?' Muttering to myself I glanced down at my filthy apron. 'And look at the state I'm in! Well, it can't be helped.' At another imperious rap I sprang to my feet and went to answer it.

'You!' My heart sank. 'I thought they had you locked up, out of harm's way.'

Abe Russell was standing there with a smirk on his face, the familiar basket of produce beside him. 'Ess, bin on my holidays, haven't I? Now I'm back, doing me rounds again.' He puffed out his chest and rocked back on his mud-covered heels.

'Pity. Shame they didn't throw away the key,' I retorted.

His face darkened and I felt a stab of fear. Why oh, why couldn't I keep my mouth shut? It would do no good to antagonize the lout, more likely it would have the opposite effect.

'Well, I don't want anything,' I said quickly, putting my hand to the latch. But he'd placed one booted foot inside the door and I couldn't close it.

'Get off my step!' I hissed under my breath, as a woman and child passing by glanced towards us.

'Not so fast, missis.' He glared. 'I haven't finished with you yet.

Better let me in and close the door, private-like. Unless you d'want all the neighbours listening.' He jerked his head towards the couple. Then he insinuated himself over the threshold and stood in the passage, smirking.

What could I do? What did he want? How could I get rid of him? Thank goodness Davy was asleep upstairs, out of the way.

'Well?' I stood with arms akimbo, keeping him in the passage. 'What's all this about?'

He leaned a brawny shoulder against the hall-stand and folded his arms. The rank stench of his unwashed body and dirty clothes filled the small space. My stomach began to churn.

'Ah,yes. Well, 'tis like this here, see.' He studied a grimy fingernail, put it between his teeth and nibbled on it. 'I bin thinking over what we was saying the other day. About you being out on the beach, that night of the storm, with yer baby.'

'But – I. . . !'

'Shut yer gob.' He raised a hand and cut me off before I could protest. 'I knaw 'twas you, so cut the cackle.' He jabbed a finger at my chest. 'I ain't fergot what your bleddy husband did to me, even if he have. Pushed me in the harbour, didn't he? I could have bleddy drowned.'

Pity you didn't, I thought. Aloud I said, 'But, Abe, that was years ago! You can't still bear a grudge for that, surely.'

'Oh, I don't forget nothing, maid. Said then I'd get me awn back, didn't I? And so I shall. Now listen to me. And listen good. Because this is what we're going to do. You,' he pointed, 'and me.'

He took a step nearer. The narrow passageway was full of him. I fought back the claustrophobia threatening to choke me. I was determined to keep him from coming any further in. I swallowed hard and tried to breathe deeply in spite of the reek.

The insidious voice went on as his black eyes bored into my head. 'Right. You're going to have to pay me a little . . . um . . . *consideration* . . . like, if you want me to keep quiet, see?' He rubbed a finger and thumb together expressively. 'Just a little bit each week when I call in on my round. Got the idea?'

'*P-pay* you! For what? Why on earth should I?' My jaw dropped in amazement.

He leered down into my face with a waft of foul breath that had me gagging. 'Because, if you don't I'll have to whisper a few words in your goody-goody husband's ear, won't I?' He drew back and shoved his hands in his pockets. 'Reckon he'd be really interested to knaw what his wife d'get up to when he's away.'

I gasped and a hand flew to my throat. 'B – but – that's ... *blackmail!*' My voice shook.

'Call it what you mind to, maid.' He propped himself against the wall, took a breath and puffed out his chest. 'Call it a little reward for what I suffered back along. Justice done.'

'He'll never believe you!' I said with defiance. 'It's only your word against mine. You can't prove a thing. Joel wouldn't take any notice. He trusts me.'

I stopped short and my heart missed a beat as I realized what I'd said. For he did. And I'd betrayed that trust, hadn't I?

'And he knows what a liar you are, Abe Russell.' I glared at him, but I was shaking in every limb now. My mind reeled. Oh, dear Lord, what had this evil creature stirred up? The ramifications would be endless. I knew it would only take one small poisonous whisper in Joel's ear. Down at the 'Ship' probably. Only a hint would do it. He wouldn't need proof.

Once the seed was planted he would dwell on it. Fill in the rest for himself. Churn it round and round in his head until his imagination would exceed anything this odious man could ever dream up. I quailed. Again I saw the end of our marriage looming. And in the cry of the seabirds overhead I heard the fisher-girls laughter.

'Of course, if he don't believe me,' went on the relentless drip of words, 'there's always the kid, see. Wouldn't like anything to happen to he, would us?' A sudden wolf-like grin crossed his face.

'No!' That shattered my outward composure at last, and I cried out. I couldn't help it. All my brave show of defiance had crumbled away. He'd goaded me too far this time. Not Davy! I silently pleaded. Please. Not Davy. I made one last desperate attempt at bravado, and raised my chin. 'I'll call the police, Abe Russell. You'll be taken in again, for threats ... and blackmail ... and stealing from the wreck.'

The villain must have seen the fear in my eyes, for he chuckled. 'I don't think so.' He swaggered his way to the door. 'Well, I'll be off now,' he announced. 'I'll leave you to think it over. See you next Thursday, Missis Penrose. Have some money put by ready. Half a crown should do it, I think.'

'Half a *crown*!' My eyes widened and my heart began to pound. 'Where do you think I'm going to find that sort of money?'

'That's up to you, maid, innit?' He smirked. 'See 'ee next week.' He looked back over his shoulder. 'And if you was thinking of going out fer the day – don't.' He shook his head. 'Because I can always come back, see? Maybe when Joel d'come home fer his dinner.'

I slammed the door behind him and leaned on it. My shaking legs would no longer support me. Slowly I sank to the floor and put my hands over my face.

What had I got myself into? My plan I had thought so foolproof had been shattered in seconds by this evil lout. And he didn't even have a shred of evidence. That was the most galling thing. Because of course, he didn't need any. This battle was to be played out in terms of my mental stress. And I was impotent to do anything about it. Oh yes, I knew I'd brought this on myself by my own deceit in the first place, but that was scant comfort.

I clenched my fists in fear and frustration until the nails drew blood. For there was no reason why he shouldn't increase his demands if I once gave in to this blackmail. I'd heard of bullies doing that. Squeezing their victims dry. Ruining them.

But what was the alternative? The *only* alternative was to confess everything to Joel. Tell him of my deceit. Tell him that Davy was not his child. Break his heart, break mine and break up our marriage.

And where was I going to get money from, anyway? Any money? I nibbled a thumbnail to the quick. I had no funds of my own. I had always been so proud that Joel trusted me to handle all his income. Now I wished he had been less generous in spirit. Had he only divided up the housekeeping money into compartments for the various expenses, given me a sum for myself and taken his own pocket money, like other husbands did.

Kate? I wondered. Would Kate help me out? Her husband would never miss a small sum from his vast wealth. But hadn't Kate said she had no money of her own either? And why should she take the risk in any case? It wasn't her problem. Added to which, hadn't she as good as said in the first place it was a crazy idea to keep Davy as my own? Now she'd be able to say, 'I told you so.' I decided against asking Kate, then.

If only Joel had let me take on a job when I'd asked him. If I could earn something it would be an easy matter to keep my tormentor quiet. Was there any thing I could do? Without Joel knowing? It would have to be from home, because of Davy. I racked my brains and started on another fingernail.

Joel's next long trip would be for the mackerel season. But that wasn't until January. He'd be away then for several months, though. Which would give me a chance, if I could only think of something. But it was only July now. How was I going to manage the payments until then?

As a temporary measure I could pilfer a few coins bit by bit, so Joel wouldn't notice, from the old toffee tin on the dresser. We each put our spare change in it and only rarely counted up what was there. It would make me feel like a thief, but I was already a liar, wasn't I? What was one more sin on top of everything else? But I couldn't keep on doing that for six months. He'd be bound to notice.

I felt I was sinking deeper and deeper into a sticky morass, which would eventually drag me under to oblivion. Just like the 'sinking sands' of our childhood when we'd been brought down for a day on the beach. We would play near the Bar. Squealing as our feet sank one after the other in the squelching mire. Pretending to be stuck. Pretending to be terrified, but safe in the knowledge we were in full view of the grown-ups and there was no real danger. We would drag ourselves out, each foot as heavy as lead, then collapse on our backs, weak with laughter. If only I could get out of this one as easily.

I was looking out for Abe Russell the following Thursday. With Davy in his perambulator I met him at the gate on my way out to the village shop. There was no way I was having him anywhere near my house again. Making sure no-one noticed, I slipped the money into his dirty hand, stuck my nose in the air and pushed past him without a word.

He gave a mock bow, grinned and touched his filthy cap. 'Thank you, milady. I'll see you next week, same time.'

The following Thursday however, he arrived a lot earlier and was on the doorstep before I saw him coming. Much against my will, I was forced to buy something for the sake of appearances. Susan Trembath was outside her house, cleaning windows, and she never missed anything.

I passed over the right money for the cabbage I'd chosen and pushed the blackmail money into his dirty hand at the same time. I was preparing to shut the door on him when he peered closer and grinned. 'Make it five bob next week,' he hissed.

'Five *sh-shillings*. . . !' I clutched at the doorframe as the sky tilted. I heard a roaring in my ears and my legs turned to jelly. 'But, I *can't*. Oh, *please*. I just haven't *got* money like that.' I heard my pleading voice and hated myself for it. 'You can't do this to me.' My stomach was churning and I felt sick.

He chuckled hugely. 'Oh, but I can. What's to stop me?' He picked up his basket and went whistling down the path.

Horror-struck, I was left staring after him, one hand at my throat, trying to take in what he'd said and what it would mean. How could I possibly cope. . . ? I chewed my bottom lip until it began to bleed. I just couldn't! There was no way. . . .

But I was suddenly jerked back to the present. Joel was striding towards me along the quay, a couple of mackerel swinging from one hand. He was looking after Abe Russell with a frown.

As soon as he was near enough to speak, I tried to summon up a smile. 'Joel! You're back early.' Desperate for a way to deflect his attention, I pointed to the silver-and-rainbow coloured fish. 'What lovely big mackerel. We'll have those for tea tonight.'

'What was Abe Russell doing here, talking to you?' Joel jerked a thumb at the retreating figure.

'Oh, you know he's doing a vegetable round now, don't you? I bought this cabbage just to get rid of him.' I held it up for Joel to see. 'Then, um,' I improvised, 'he said I hadn't given him enough money. But I had.' I nearly burst into hysterical laughter. For if this *double-entendre* hadn't been so grim, it would actually have been funny.

'You're sure he wasn't bothering you again?' Joel glowered. 'If I thought he was, I'd do more than knock him into the harbour this time. I'd break his damn neck.'

I laid a pacifying hand on his arm. His voice was rising and Susan had already glanced our way once. 'No, no, of course not. Come on in so I can close the door.' I forced my shaking legs into action and moved aside.

I knew Joel meant what he'd said. And he had a terrible temper when provoked. If he *did* happen to get wind of what Abe was up to, I knew he would snap. He might even *kill* him! And go to the gallows for it. I gulped and clutched the cabbage tightly to still my shaking body.

All the time as I went about the daily round, I couldn't get my tormentor out of my mind. Weeks and months of Thursdays stretched before me into infinity. Where *would* it end? In a moment of panic I could see myself being prey to his demands for the rest of my life.

CHAPTER SEVEN

KATE

We travelled up to Truro in the carriage for the shopping trip Arthur had arranged. To add to my brimming wardrobe the articles he deemed necessary for our trip. Of course, the quicker and more convenient journey by the Great Western Railway was not for us. The ostentatious carriage pandered to my husband's considerable vanity, allowing him to see and be seen.

'This way, Kate.' We were crossing the cobbled square in the centre of the city. Behind us the soaring spires of the cathedral pierced the sky of cloudless blue and a clock chimed the hour. 'You'd better take my arm again.' I obediently placed my gloved hand on his elbow.

I glanced up at my husband and for a moment my gaze stayed on him. In a light-weight, three-piece suit of grey, impeccably tailored, Arthur looked every inch the gentleman – suave and urbane. Passers-by would take him for a caring, loving husband. In fact, we must have looked the epitome of a prosperous, middle-class couple.

Here, away from his mother, I glimpsed a hint of the person Arthur might have been under different circumstances, and sighed as my throat constricted.

Catching my glance, Arthur beamed patronisingly down at me. 'Here we are.' He led me up the steps of a select dress-shop. 'We'll spare no expense today, eh?' He looked back with a roguish smile. My eyes widened and I stared at him in surprise. Arthur, being roguish? There must be something about the air of Truro. 'As part of my anniversary present to my beautiful wife.' He beamed again and squeezed my arm.

I cringed inwardly, not a bit taken in by this false air of bonhomie. I had suffered too much last night during another bout of Arthur's excesses. And far from celebrating this coming occasion, I was wishing it had never happened in the first place.

However, the roguishness soon vanished. Soon I was trying on gowns in an elegant showroom with thick carpet and an atmosphere of almost reverential hush. Black-clad assistants scurried about like so many worker ants under the eagle eye of their queen, a hatchet-faced woman also in black. Elegant gowns were displayed on life-sized models around the room. Day-gowns, tea-gowns, travelling gowns. Sumptuous gowns for evening wear. Each with its lavish accessories and not a price ticket to be seen.

Arthur had ensconced himself in one of the dainty gilt chairs. I could see his eyes getting hot and excited as I was paraded before him in one outfit after another, a living model. I began to feel quite faint. And stifled by the scented warmth of the place. My husband's gaze never left my figure as I was turned all ways like an automaton.

When we were shown drawer after drawer of delicate lingerie and nightwear, I saw him actually lick his lips like a predatory animal. My stomach churned.

And by the time Arthur had selected several elaborate gowns, hats and sets of underclothing, I was feeling physically sick. In fact, I felt like a whore. As sullied and cheap as if I'd been exposed near-naked on a street corner. But maybe it was all over now.

It wasn't. There was jewellery to come yet. We were ushered like royalty into an adjoining room. Each new outfit had to have an accompanying necklace, or ear-drops. Or rings, bracelets, a brooch. What appalling lavishness! I almost found myself envying the little black-clad 'ants' around me.

At least when they left work they could choose for themselves what clothes they wore. Having to save up to pay for them too, would make the outfits far more precious. Arthur's extravagant purchases were now being packed into gilded boxes and taken out to the waiting carriage. 'Madame' was bowing and scraping as she prepared to usher us out. Arthur acknowledged this as no more than his due and reached for his hat and cane.

I was getting to my feet, ready to leave, when suddenly the walls of the room began to tilt. Then to whirl around me as a dull roar filled my ears. I stumbled, reached out to grasp the chair-back and missed. I was aware of a warm trickle running down my legs beneath my skirts, then I blacked out. The carpeted floor came up to meet me and I knew no more.

I drifted in and out of consciousness, oblivious to the passage of time or to my surroundings. Sometimes icy-cold, I'd pluck feebly at my covers and clutch them round me as if they were never enough. Then stiflingly hot, I would cast them all restlessly aside as I sweated and gasped for air. I knew that kind hands came and went, water was dribbled into my dry mouth and cool cloths placed on my aching forehead, but my eyes remained closed. I didn't have the strength, or inclination, to open them.

A male voice was there once or twice too. I felt my face pressed into the pillow. Strong hands turning me over and touching me in intimate places. I stiffened then and tried to scream. Arthur! Was he here? He was! No! Oh, please, no! But no sound came from my mouth. I was helpless, powerless to resist him. And I could hear faintly whispering voices in a far corner of the room; other people were watching! For seemingly aeons of time I lived in own private hell; haunted by frightening dreams. Tears of weakness and despair trickling from the corners of my closed eyes.

One day I awoke from a period of calm, natural and refreshing sleep, realizing that I felt better. Not knowing whether it was night or day, or how long I'd been ill, I tried to raise my head with my eyes fully open at last. I tried to see if it was light or dark outside, but my whole body was weak as a baby's. I was forced to slump back on to the pillows with a sigh.

Then memory returned in a blinding flash. Arthur had been here, hadn't he? Or had I dreamed it? No. I'd felt his fingers on my body, probing . . . I put my hands over my face in despair and burst into tears of hopelessness.

I sniffed and helplessly wiped my nose on my sleeve like a child, then stared. This wasn't my nightgown. Mine had a frill of ruffled lace around the wrist, not plain stitching like this one. I was wearing someone else's clothes!

Slowly I turned my head and looked around me. White walls, curtains of an unfamiliar pattern. Stiffly starched sheets. Where was I? Then I became aware of a figure sitting by the bed. I rubbed my eyes as the person rose and came to my side.

'Mrs Rosewarne! Oh, at last. You're awake! We've been worried about you!' A uniformed nurse was bending over me. Oh, hospital. Of course. I feasted my eyes on the tall, slim figure. The first flesh and blood person I'd seen for . . . how long?

I moistened dry lips. 'How long . . . how long have I been ill?' My voice came out as a croak.

'Almost three weeks.' The nurse placed a thermometer in my mouth and cut off any further conversation. She reached for my wrist and timed my pulse against her fob-watch.

My memory was returning in snatches. I'd fainted, hadn't I? In the dress shop, when Arthur . . . we were going to Paris. . . .

The nurse whisked away the thermometer and shook it. 'Mm,' she murmured and made a note on her pad.

'Three *weeks*!' I started up in the bed and forgetting, winced as pain sliced through my head.

The nurse placed a hand on my shoulder and pressed me back on to the pillow. 'Don't try to move just yet. You've been in a coma. You'll be very weak for a long time. Dr Roberts said so.'

My mind had begun to turn things over. A doctor? A ray of hope stirred deep within me. 'Has, has anyone come . . . to see me?' I whispered.

The nurse had gone to the window to draw back the curtains and blissful sunshine was slanting into the room. 'Is that too bright for you?' She glanced over her shoulder.

'No, it's wonderful,' I managed, through lips that felt thick and swollen. 'W-water – please, I need a drink.' The woman raised my head and held a glass to my lips. I drank deeply and leaned back with a sigh. 'Apart from the doctor—'

'Your husband, of course.' Her mouth narrowed and a frown creased her forehead.

I gulped. Arthur. It had been him, then. But . . . in a hospital, surely he couldn't have . . . have. . . .

'Your sister visited, with your mother, but you didn't know anything about that, either.' She was turning to go but I clutched her arm.

'Where is this place, please? Am I still in Truro?'

'Yes, you are.' She smiled and patted my hand. 'This is the Royal Cornwall Infirmary.'

'Oh what a lot of worry I must have caused everybody.' I felt tears rising again. I seemed to be crying at the slightest thing.

She shook her head. 'They'll all be just so glad to have you back with us again.' She picked up her clip board. 'I must go and tell your doctor the good news. I'm sure you'd like a cup of tea too, wouldn't you?'

Tea – it sounded like heaven. I nodded and gave a weak smile as the nurse bustled off. Suddenly, I realized that in fact I was ravenously hungry.

'Light meals and frequently,' said the doctor after he'd examined me. 'And you know that it'll be several weeks before you'll feel anything like your old self, don't you?' I nodded. My head felt like a lead weight. The way I was now, I could believe it. 'Oh. . . .' I gave a sigh of disappointment. We would have to postpone our trip to Paris.

'What's actually been the matter with me?' I asked him when he called round again later. Fortified by a bowl of soup, I was feeling slightly stronger.

'Mrs Rosewarne.' His face was grave. 'You have had a complete mental and physical breakdown, preceded by a haemorrhage. At one point we feared for your life.'

My eyes widened. My life? It had been that bad? My jaw clenched. My husband had a lot to answer for.

After a few days I was feeling strong enough to be wheeled into the day-room where I could look out over the spires and rooftops of the city, for the Infirmary stood at the top of a steep hill. I passed the time in idle chat with the other patients, and in reading newspapers and magazines. In one of these I came across a long article about the suffragette movement. I'd heard of it of course, but had never realized how highly organized it all was. I read it through with interest. It was an account of a huge rally that had been held recently in Hyde Park.

I read it word for word, engrossed in the story. '. . . Hundreds of women in their colours of green, purple and white turned out to march to the call of the bugles with banners waving'.

Hundreds? I'd no idea there were so many involved. 'Unperturbed by the heckling and stone-throwing of the large crowd that had turned out to watch, they assembled in the park where Mrs Emmeline Pankhurst gave a rousing speech concerning "The Cause". The meeting concluded with their Great Shout, and then a petition was handed in to Mr Asquith at Number Ten'.

A photograph accompanied the article. Row upon row of women, their faces alight with the glow of fanaticism. I laid the paper aside. Could I, I wondered, ever feel as strongly as this about 'The Cause'?

In all honesty, I doubted it. I began to wonder whether the Vote, if they ever achieved that goal, was actually going to stop husbands ill-treating their wives – a subject dear to my heart.

And as I lay resting and slowly regaining my strength with plenty of time to think about it, I realized that what I would really like to do, was to offer practical aid in some way to women and girls who had had similar experiences to mine. I imagined a refuge, providing medical help and advice, and the company of others who understood what mental and physical abuse was like.

Oh, banners and rallies were all very well, but immediate help for these suffering women seemed to me more important than the suffragists faraway dream which might or might not one day become reality.

I had as much chance of achieving my own dream as of flying to the moon, though, and all this thinking had made my head throb. Forgetting where I was, I automatically reached into my bag for the comfort of my 'medicine', but I realized with a shock that the bottle was almost empty.

I wondered as I yawned hugely and settled back on to my cushioned chair, whether the doctor who was attending me here would give me another supply. I would ask him when he called next . . . for I wouldn't be able to go out myself for a while . . . I drifted off into a deep and wholesome slumber.

I was dreaming of Pengarth and home. Loveday and I were children again, helping with the hay harvest on the farm. It was June, I could feel the sun beating through my starched white bonnet. I could smell the sweetness of the mown grass. Bees were buzzing lazily in the clover at the edge of the field. The farm-hands were loading up the huge wagons, tossing the dried hay high with their pitchforks, their brawny arms bared and brown, sweat streaming down their faces.

Soon the sun would go down. We little girls would get a longed-for ride back to the farm on top of the swaying load. I came half-awake, lost in nostalgia, wishing I was back in that happy, carefree childhood. Then dozed off again.

I was awakened by a visit from a doctor I hadn't seen before. 'Mrs Rosewarne,' he extended a hand. 'Jonathan Roberts. I've been attending you since the onset of your illness. But I've been on leave until this morning. Dr Harrison's been filling in for me.'

I looked up into a face surely not much older than my own. Well, thirty-ish at most. A narrow, intelligent face. Warm brown eyes and a silky moustache of the same colour. In fact he was altogether a brown man. From his flop of straight, shiny hair which owed nothing to macassar oil, to the suit of fine tweed he was wearing, and his highly-polished brown boots.

'Dr Roberts,' I smiled as I took his hand. It was warm and firm. Here was a man I immediately liked. One who inspired in me a feeling of instant and total trust.

'It's good to see you sitting out at last.' He stood over me, smiling, a clipboard under his arm. 'But I need to check on a few things. I'll get someone to take you back to the ward.'

Once I was in bed again he sat down in the chair beside me and reached for my pulse. 'How are you feeling generally?'

'Much better, thank you, but still very weak. Or a bit "whisht" if you like,' I added with a flash of mischief. 'To use the local Cornish expression!'

'Oh yes, this land of the Celts is full of expressions like that. Since coming down here I've learned a lot!'

The twinkle in his eyes made me laugh out loud. The first time I'd laughed for a long time. He joined in, showing white, even teeth. I noticed his face and hands looked unusually tanned for an English summer. 'Where do you come from?' I asked.

'Surrey,' he said briefly, taking a stethoscope from his Gladstone bag. Which hardly explained the sun tan. 'Forgive me, but I need to listen to your breathing. To make sure there's no remaining trace of fever.'

The doctor hooked the instrument round his neck and bent over me. 'If you would just loosen your nightgown, please.' I felt myself flush. My fingers seemed to have become all thumbs. I blamed illness for my weakness as I struggled with the tiny pearl buttons.

He leaned closer with the instrument. Warm fingers brushed my bare neck and I recoiled as if stung. I caught the fresh aroma of his skin. It was lightly scented and smelled like soap and shaving cream. And something else. Well, just *maleness*.

There was something so ... I struggled for the right word ... so *wholesome*, that was it, about this man. He was fresh, clean and wholesome; the complete opposite to my husband.

A lock of his brown hair brushed my face and my heartbeat quickened. What on earth was the matter with me all of a sudden? I bit my bottom lip as a flush crept up my neck. Why should I feel so embarrassed? He was only a *doctor*, for goodness sake.

'Where were you when you were taken ill, Mrs Rosewarne?' He removed the stethoscope and straightened up, folding it away.

I bent to fasten my nightgown. 'I was shopping, with my husband, and I fainted.' I raised my face. 'And, Doctor Roberts, I'm just so grateful for the treatment I've had here.' I slowly shook my head. 'Until the nurse told me, I'd no idea I'd been ill for such a long time.'

The doctor's face was solemn. He cleared his throat and looked into the middle distance. 'Er, you're aware of course madam, I had to examine you internally while you were unconscious. In order to find out the cause of your bleeding?'

Heat flooded through me again as my fevered dream came back. Of course it hadn't been Arthur. How stupid I'd been. It had been this man. 'Oh? Um – yes.' I kept my eyes on my hands and plucked at the edge of the sheet.

'I discovered you had an infection there. I had to give you several injections. But I'm delighted to say the problem has cleared up now. You must be feeling much more comfortable.' He raised an eyebrow.

'Yes.' I nodded and smiled. 'Yes, I am. Thank you so much.'

He paused. 'I'd like to assure you that a nurse did stay in the room each time.' He cleared his throat again and this time his eyes met mine. 'And I gather from the nature of your injuries that they were inflicted by – your husband?' The voice was soft and gentle.

He knew! But of course he did. How else could I have come by them? And his face was full of sympathy. 'They were, yes.' My teeth clamped my bottom lip and I looked away.

The doctor rose abruptly to his feet. Angrily muttering something I couldn't catch, he took a turn around the room. 'And is he coming to visit you, this husband of yours? Let me know when he does. I'd like to speak to him.'

I looked at him in alarm. 'Oh, no, please don't do that. He'll think . . . think I've been . . . telling tales.' And I'll be punished, I could have added, if it hadn't sounded so childish. I hung my head.

'My dear lady,' the doctor patted my arm and his face was grim. 'Don't distress yourself. I shall make sure he never gets a chance to hurt you again.'

I looked up into the kindly eyes and felt my own expression brighten. I gave a sigh of relief. At last – an ally! Someone of standing who could face up to Arthur with authority. 'You will? You could? Oh, thank you – thank you so much—' I stammered. 'You've no idea what that means to me.'

'Oh, I do, believe me, Mrs Rosewarne.' He lowered his voice. 'I've seen many cases of brutality, but I have to say that most of them were in the slums. They occur among the poor, the ignorant and the hopeless, and owe more to drink than intention. In a professional man there's no possible excuse for such behaviour.'

He stood up and picked up his case-notes. 'I'll call again before you leave hospital, which you should be able to do soon.'

He was turning to go as I remembered. I swallowed hard and realized this was the moment. Now, or it would be too late. I took a deep breath and held out the brown bottle.

'One moment before you go, Dr Roberts. I wonder if you could possibly get some more of this for me, please.' I handed over the bottle. 'My doctor gives me a regular supply for my headaches. It helps me to sleep after . . . after . . .' I gulped. 'But I need some more. It's nearly run out. I'd be so grateful.'

He frowned as he read the label. Then looked at me in horror. 'Laudanum! Whatever possessed the man to give you this stuff?' He glared. 'It's pure poison. It's just opium under another name. Didn't you know that?' I quailed at the force of his stare and shook my head.

'Don't you know *anything*?' He glowered. 'Like how insidiously it creeps through your body? That in time you become totally dependent on it? Until the time comes when you can't live without it?' Mesmerized by his fury, I could only shake my head and cringe further back on to my pillows.

'My dear lady.' He was so worked up I could see his hands actually shaking. 'I've seen people ruin their lives and those of their entire families. All their money goes upon this evil, evil, stuff. *Medicine?* It's a travesty of the very word.'

He raised the bottle in his fist. 'No, I certainly won't supply you with any more. I totally refuse. This should only be given in small doses by a professional person – just as a temporary sedative. It's certainly not for long-term use.'

I felt my face fall. But the doctor must have noticed my alarm. 'Look,' his voice quietened. 'What I will do is prescribe you something else. Something less addictive. So don't despair. I know it's hard to come off this stuff, but the other will soften the transition.'

He twisted the bottle round and round in his hands. 'And really, you know, now that your husband is aware that his – inclinations – are no secret any more, you shouldn't have any call to use it. Your headaches I'm sure were caused by related stress. Now the cause has been removed they should disappear. All right?'

I looked dubiously into his face. 'I suppose so,' I said, wanting to believe him.

'Good.' He passed the bottle back to me. 'Now, you've enough left for a few more doses. See if you can manage not to take them. Of course, if you're absolutely desperate – for I don't know how dependent you've become – then you'll have to. I'll be round in the morning with the alternative.' He turned towards the door again. 'Good day to you, Mrs Rosewarne.'

I managed a wan smile. I felt totally exhausted. 'Good day, doctor. And thank you again. For everything.'

Mindful of what the doctor had advised, I resisted the urge to take another dose from the brown bottle. I found I was looking forward to his next visit, so I could tell him so. It was probably nothing to him. He must see similar cases every day, but I felt strangely anxious to gain his approval.

So I pushed the bottle to the back of a drawer where it was out of sight, took a deep breath and tried to stifle the cravings and the cold sweats by thinking of other things.

Then I had a pleasant surprise when visiting time came round and there was Loveday crossing the room towards me. We'd written to each other, short notes to keep in touch, but I knew how difficult it was for her, with Davy to think of, to make the long journey to Truro very often.

'How lovely to see you!' We hugged and she held me at arm's length as her eyes raked me up and down. I knew I was looking a mess, because of the withdrawal symptoms I was having.

'How are you feeling?' she asked with concern. She laid a posy of wild poppies and ox-eye daisies on my night-stand.

'Oh, how pretty! Thank you. They remind me of home. How am I? Um – not too bad really. Not as bad as I look!' I smiled and told her the reason.

'Oh,' Loveday's face brightened. 'That's wonderful. Kate, I'll be so relieved if they can wean you off that dreadful stuff'

I nodded. 'So shall I. Now tell me about you. What have you done with Davy today?'

'Meg's looking after him. She says she doesn't mind a bit, but I don't like to bother her too often. Joel's up in the Irish Sea off the Isle of Man, after herring.'

As she pulled up a chair and slipped her coat off, I noticed how pale she was looking. Not that she was ever exactly rosy-cheeked, her complexion was naturally sallow, but there were worry lines on her face as well, just above the bridge of her nose, two grooves I'd never seen there before.

'So, what does the doctor say about you? I suppose he' – she lowered her voice – '*knows*? About Arthur, I mean?'

I nodded and plucked at the bedcover. 'He's a really nice person, Dr Roberts. And he was horrified when he found out. He's promised to speak to Arthur when he comes. Loveday, he said he'll make sure Arthur never hurts me again.'

'Oh, that's *wonderful*. Kate, I'm so thrilled for you.'

'Mind you, I'll believe it when it happens. It sounds too good to be true.' I changed the subject. 'But are you all right yourself? You look a bit pale.'

Head bent, she gave a sigh and played with the gloves in her lap. 'Not really.' Then her head jerked up. There was an anguished expression on her face as she blurted, 'Oh, Kate, I wasn't going to bother you with this, being ill as you are, but I just *have* to tell somebody. I don't know what to do.' She was obviously on the verge of tears.

Full of alarm, I reached for her hand. 'My dear, of course you can tell me. What on earth's the matter?'

Then out poured the whole tale, of the sordid blackmail, her fear of Joel finding out, her struggle to find the money each week. My eyes grew more and more round as each incident unfolded. I was filled with pity for her suffering, and rage that she had been forced into such a situation.

'But Loveday, *listen* to me,' I urged as she came to a shuddering halt at last. I had to keep my voice low as we were not alone. If we were, I would have shouted and raged at her for letting herself be so intimidated by this lout.

'Listen, what did he *actually* see that night?' I held on to her hand and made her look at me.

'He says he s-saw me with a baby in my arms. He knows it was me, Kate . . . I tried to shrug it off and say it was a trick of the light, but. . . .'

'What proof does he have?' I demanded.

Loveday shrugged her narrow shoulders. 'N-nothing really. But his brother was there too, and he would say anything Abe tells him to.' She leaned closer. 'I tried to stand up to him, Kate, I told him I knew he was stealing stuff from the ship, but it didn't make any difference. . . .'

Sternly I said, 'So when he came to the house, you panicked, didn't you?'

She hung her head and nodded. 'I suppose I did, but Kate, he was so huge . . . and horrible . . . and he threatened to hurt *Davy*.' Her face crumpled. 'What else could I do?' She raised pleading eyes to me. I squeezed her hand.

'But I do feel better just for talking to you about it.' She sniffed.

I was thinking hard, although it wasn't easy. My head felt full of cotton wool and it was beginning to ache again.

'Well, you can't go on like this.' I frowned. 'How long will Joel be away?'

'About a month.' Her hand was still gripping mine like a lifeline.

'Right.' I patted it absently as I tried to come up with some comfort for her. 'So while he's out of the way Abe can't do anything. He's only bluffing about Davy – what harm can he do when the child's always with you?'

I shrugged. 'It's not as if he goes to school or anything. So forget that. Be out of the house on Thursdays. Go up to Pengarth, go anywhere.' I waved a finger at her. 'Abe will soon get fed up and find somebody else to torment. That's what bullies are like.'

Loveday gave me a dubious look and nibbled her lip. 'Oh, Kate, I only hope you're right.' She gave a huge sigh and relaxed a little.

'Of course I am.' I tried to sound as reassuring as I could. Anything to take that haunted look from my sister's face.

With a glance at the clock above us, Loveday began to pull on her gloves. 'Oh, dear, I have to go. I told Meg I'd be back on the next train. And we seem to have spent the whole time talking about *my* problems. I'm sorry, Kate, really I am. I was supposed to be coming to cheer you up!'

'Don't worry about it.' I shrugged. 'If I've cheered you up instead it's been well worthwhile!'

'I'll come again soon,' she promised, and hurried away.

I looked thoughtfully after the scurrying figure. For all her confession, I could tell there was something still worrying her. I knew my sister well and there was another, underlying, reason for that haunted look in her eyes.

CHAPTER EIGHT

LOVEDAY

It was all very well for Kate to be so dismissive of Abe Russell. I still had doubts. Once I'd left the Infirmary, all the hope she'd given me soon evaporated.

The whole situation was ridiculous. Also, there was no way I could raise the sum he was asking now. And the more I thought about it, the more clearly I realized there was only one course of action I could take, one thing I could do that would end his hold over me: I would have to tell Joel. But something so startling and unexpected happened that it drove everything else from my mind. I discovered I was to have another child.

I'd been aware of missing my monthly courses a couple of times, but had taken no notice of it. I was never *that* regular. And I'd had too much else to think about. After the third month had come and gone with no sign, though I had to accept the obvious. A visit to the doctor in Helston confirmed it. Susan's prediction was coming true. Torn between delight, and fear that this would end in another tragedy, I broke the news to Joel.

We were sitting at the kitchen table having dinner. I'd made pasties for us, and a miniature one for Davy. I laid down my knife and fork and pushed my plate to one side.

'Joel, I've got something to tell you.' I looked tenderly at his bent head. He was eating his pasty the traditional way, in his hand. Holding it upright by the crimped crust and biting downwards to the gravy-filled corner at the bottom.

He looked up with his mouth full. 'Mm? What's that then? Picked up a bit more gossip from she next door, have you?'

'No, nothing like that.' I smiled and patted my stomach. 'Joel, I'm – we're – going to have an addition to our family.'

'*What?* Oh, my handsome, that's wonderful!' Joel jumped up and his unused knife and fork fell to the floor with a clatter. Coming round to my side of the table, he put an arm around my shoulders and gave me a huge bear-hug. 'Feeling all right are you?' he asked with concern.

I raised my face for his kiss. I loved him so much. I looked into his honest, open face. Joel had never needed to keep a secret in his life. He had no idea of the stress, of the strain I'd been under for so long and still was. I was weary at having to think twice about every word before I spoke. Having to dissemble all the time, to pretend. 'So far, yes,' I returned his kiss.

'Well, we must make sure you take care of yourself.' Joel went back to his pasty. 'And it's just the right time, now our Davy's getting past the baby stage. Good thing he's getting about a bit by himself too. You don't want to have to lift him more than you've got to. He's some weight now.' The little boy was sitting in his high chair, pasty in hand. Joel ruffled his blond hair.

He resumed his dinner, looking up at me from under shaggy brows. 'You know how I always wanted a big family, don't you maid? Like I was used to.' Joel nodded with satisfaction. I smiled and turned to wipe a dribble of gravy from Davy's chin.

Joel pushed back his plate and brushed crumbs from his beard. 'We shall have to take out the old cradle again. I must mend that broken rocker. . . .' Eventually he went off whistling down the path. I leaned both elbows on the table amid the dirty dishes, lost in my own thoughts.

Why, oh why, I asked myself yet again, hadn't I told Joel the truth right from the start? Faced his wrath? Whatever the consequences. Wouldn't it have been worth it for my peace of mind? I nibbled a fingernail to the quick as my mind turned over and over, round and round and always came back to the same thing.

With the ever-present threat of Abe Russell hanging over me, and now this latest event, it was becoming more and more imperative that I should confess. Own up to everything, right from the beginning.

This would blow apart all my carefully plotted web of lies and deceit, and rock our cosy world to its foundations.

Could I bring myself to do it? As a muffled cry announced that Davy had woken from his nap, I pulled myself together. I must do it and it would have to be soon.

But when? And how? Under what circumstances could I ever find a right time to break such momentous news?

In bed maybe? 'Oh, before we go to sleep, Joel, I must just mention that Davy's not actually your son. I found him on the beach. Good night, dear.'

Perhaps over a meal? 'Oh, Joel, there's something I must tell you. Davy's not our son, you see. He's a foundling. More tea?'

Out walking? 'Oh, Joel, that's the place where I found Davy. I didn't tell you he's not our child, did I, dear?'

I couldn't do it! I had to. The more I watched Joel whistling about the house and garden, patiently playing the repetitive children's games that Davy loved and displaying his tender concern for me, the more depressed I became.

I began to hate myself for treating this kind and loving man as I'd done. How much worse though was it going to be when I did pluck up enough courage to confess?

I watched my knuckles whiten as I gripped the sill and leaned out of the bedroom window, gazing over the sea. Joel was kicking a ball about on the beach for Davy to toddle after. The little boy's shouts of excitement were an exquisite torture as they drifted up to me. What had I done to that innocent child?

True, I'd saved his life, but I'd deprived him of his birthright. For in spite of all I had said to Kate at the time, I knew that if I'd really wanted to, I could have traced Davy's family somehow. But I hadn't wanted to. I could see no further than my own needs. I'd used Davy as a prop for my own feelings of insecurity, hadn't I?

Because I'd been terrified of losing my husband. This bluff, kind-hearted man who had never given me any reason to doubt his shining love for me. I desperately needed someone to talk to. Kate? But what could Kate do, even if she were here? Ultimately the only person who could help me was myself. And surely anything would be better than this self-torture.

Then one day at last, came the perfect opportunity. 'You're some quiet lately maid, feeling all right are you?' Joel asked one evening. 'Or is that there baby kicking you around again?'

Davy was in bed and we were sitting in the little parlour for a change. Usually we lived and ate in the homely warmth of the kitchen. But I'd wanted a comfortable seat to ease my aching back, and had taken my sewing there. Joel had followed with his newspaper and we were sitting side by side on the couch.

As he spoke, Joel slipped an arm around my shoulders in a gentle hug. I could see the concern in his eyes. 'I thought you was looking a bit whisht at tea-time. Don't you go overdoing things now, my handsome. I love you too much to see you worn out by the evenings.'

I gulped and my mouth dried. Here was my chance. If I didn't grab it right away, there might never be another one. I kept my eyes on the little shirt I was sewing for Davy and jabbed the needle into it to occupy my shaking hands.

'Joel,' I whispered, 'would you love me the same whatever I did?'

' 'Course I would, you ninny. You're my wife aren't you?' Joel shook out the paper and turned a page. He scanned the headline and snorted. 'They suffragette women are at it again – demonstrating outside the Houses of Parliament. Votes for women! What claptrap! Pity they can't be content with their homes and families like you, my bird.'

'Even if I'd done something really dreadful and hadn't told you?' I persisted. I was sure Joel could hear the hammering of my heart, we were so close together. I laid my head on his shoulder and looked up into his face.

'Loveday, what is this all about?' Joel tossed the paper to the floor, looking exasperated. 'You're not making any sense. Surely after six years of marriage we don't have any secrets from each other. What on earth's bothering you?'

I gulped and clutched at his arm. This was it. 'Wh-what if I was to tell you that Davy. . . .' I choked, unable to finish the sentence.

'Davy? What about him?' Joel was frowning now. I removed my hand and sat up, twisting my fingers in the crumpled sewing on my lap. 'You love him dearly, like you do me, don't you Joel?' I took a ragged breath. 'As dearly as if he were your own son.'

In the stunned silence that followed I felt all the blood drain from my face. I waited not even breathing, for the storm to break. I fastened my gaze on a pink and white decorative jug on the mantelpiece 'A present from Scarborough' it proclaimed in letters of gilt. Joel had brought it back for me from his first long trip away after we were married. It had been our only ornament then and I'd treasured it ever since.

'My . . . own . . . *what*?' I steeled myself to raise my head and look at my husband. His eyes were round with shock and hard as ice-blue pebbles. They bored into my skull. His face had turned scarlet. His brows steepled into his hairline. Although his mouth was working, no sound came out.

Suddenly he jumped up, grabbed my wrist and hauled me to my feet. Gripping my shoulders so hard that I winced with pain, he stared intently into my face. 'Do you mean to tell me,' his voice was dangerously calm, 'that Davy is not *my child*?' I hung my head in misery. Joel seized my chin and jerked it up again.

'Did I hear you right? Look me in the eye, woman, and let me hear that again. I understood you to say that I'm not Davy's *father*?'

Silently I shook my head. This was as bad as all my worst imaginings. Joel jerked his hand away and pushed me back on to the couch. '*No! No-o*!' He was shaking his head and roaring like a wounded animal. Both hands covered his ears as if to blot out the terrible news.

Then he took a step towards me and raised his fist. I flinched and cowered away. But Joel managed to control himself and refrained from striking me.

'So help me, I've never hit a woman yet,' he hissed. 'Let alone one who's carrying a child.' He took a ragged breath. 'Well, *this* one mine is it, eh?' He stabbed a finger towards my stomach. His voice rose up the scale. 'Or are you going to tell me you're growing another bastard in there to pass off under my name?'

I tried to seize his hand. 'No!' I cried. 'Oh no, Joel, listen. . . .'

But he tossed it away and began pacing the room. 'To think that the wife I worshipped . . . *worshipped*.' His voice broke. 'Has been with another man, and. . . .'

'I haven't – I didn't – Joel, *listen*, please. . . .' I stifled my sobs, stumbled after him and clutched at his hand. My nails drew blood as

I shouted into his face, 'He's not *mine either*!'

Shock momentarily stopped Joel in his tracks. His mouth dropped open as he stared at me in horror. I let his hand fall. I clasped both arms around my shaking body as I paced the room. 'My baby – our baby – *died*, Joel. Another one! Can you believe what that felt like?' I pointed a trembling finger. 'To have lost *three* babies in as many years? It's enough to destroy any woman.'

'And you never told me! You've kept it secret all this *time*?' Joel's face was incredulous, hurt, accusing.

I paced the room again, unable to keep still. 'You were *away*!' I cried, 'hundreds of miles away! You can't even begin to imagine what a state I was in. What I was going through. I was nearly out of my mind, Joel. I think for a short period I really was deranged.' I hung my head. 'Then by the time you came home – I . . . I just couldn't do it.'

'Then what . . . where . . . whose is he?' Joel floundered, deep in shock. He spread his big hands in bewilderment.

'Davy's a foundling,' I whispered. Joel was silent for so long that I looked up in alarm. His face was brick-red now and his eyes bulging.

He seized me roughly by the shoulders and shook me. 'You mean to say,' he spluttered. 'You went to the orphanage and brought home a strange child. You passed him off as mine. And you didn't even mention it?' He gave a roar that turned into a sob and pushed me away.

I staggered and clutched at the mantelpiece. My elbow knocked the pink jug into the hearth. It immediately shattered into a dozen shards. It was the last straw. My fraught nerves snapped at last. Scalding tears poured down my face and I wept as I had never wept before.

Joel thumped one fist into his palm and swore under his breath. He went back to pacing the room. 'I suppose the whole world knows this?' His voice was dangerously quiet. 'Everyone except me?' I shook my head, but was beyond speech. 'So I'm the laughing stock of the village, am I. . . ?'

The sudden lowering of his tone and the cutting sarcasm were worse than his ranting had been. I trembled and tried to speak, but it came out as a croak.

Joel's voice rose to fever pitch now. He let out a cry. Half-groan, half scream. Then raising his fists high, he plunged from the room.

'Joel – please – just *listen* to me!' I ran after him. But he had already wrenched open the front door. It slammed behind him and the echo of his footsteps pounded down the street and away.

I slumped against the back of the door and buried my face in my hands. The great unburdening of my conscience had turned to dust and ashes. Now I was in a worse mess than before. Where had Joel gone? And more important, would he come back? Icy fingers squeezed my soul. I wrapped both arms about myself for comfort as the unanswerable questions churned round and round in my head.

Joel did not return that night. I waited at the window until the early hours, staring out at the way he would have to come, my eyes stinging with concentration, my limbs stiff and cold from inactivity. When darkness defeated me I dragged myself reluctantly up to bed and a sleepless night.

But by the time dawn was breaking over the sea and the first rays of pearl-pink light were streaking the horizon, I'd made a tentative plan. I arose before Davy was stirring and crept downstairs to find pen, ink and paper.

I had decided to write out the whole story in a letter to Joel. Leave it for him to find when . . . or if? Oh, no, not if . . . he came home. Putting it on paper would make sure that this time I said exactly what I meant. I turned up the wick of the oil lamp and began to write. An hour passed, then another. I spent long periods agonizing over what to say and how to say it, chewing the end of the pen and gazing into space.

By the time the sun was up I'd filled a sheaf of pages with blots, crossings-out and alterations. It was smudged where my tears had fallen and dampened the paper. I turned back to the beginning and read the whole thing through. It was the best I could do.

I'd poured out my heart on to the page, telling the story exactly as it had happened. I had included my own unwavering love for him and my feelings of insecurity at the time. I'd written all about Abe Russell's blackmail, and how with the new baby coming I had to clear my conscience at last.

He *must* understand. I painstakingly re-wrote the whole thing and folded it neatly. I would take Davy and go up to Pengarth for the day, leaving the letter for him to find. Maybe by the time I came back he would be home. He would have read it. Would have understood. Please God. I sent up a silent prayer and prepared to face the day.

The weather had not lived up to the promise of first light. It had turned depressingly dull and threatened rain, it was completely in tune with my state of mind as Davy and I set off for the farm. 'We'll have to walk as far as the main road, then the omnibus will take us the rest of the way,' I told the excited little boy.

I looked tenderly down at the top of his head, at the new little quiff of hair sticking straight up from his crown, for he'd recently been breeched. He had left off the frilly smocks of baby-hood and had his long curls cut.

It had been heart-rending to do so, but Davy was fast growing up. He was a little boy now and an infant no longer. And he was so proud of his new knickerbockers and sturdy boots. My emotions see-sawed between sadness at losing my baby and fierce pride in my little son.

'Will Grandpa let me feed the hens, Mama?' Davy was swinging on my hand, his new boots scuffing the dust as he skipped along, 'and pick up the eggs? And can I have a ride on Snowball?'

'I expect so, if you're a good boy.' My reply was automatic. I'd left the letter propped on the kitchen dresser where Joel couldn't fail to see it. My stomach was churning so much I felt physically sick and the whole day had taken on a tinge of unreality. How I was going to get through it, I couldn't imagine.

I was going to have to sit in Mama's kitchen and make small-talk as if nothing had happened. Although my whole world was falling apart. Perhaps I could use my 'interesting condition' as a cover for any lapses.

The day seemed never-ending. I caught myself glancing at the clock so often that I felt Ma would soon notice and make some comment. We'd hardly seen Davy at all, he'd spent all the time outside "helping" around the farm with his grandfather.

My stomach heaved again. I could not imagine how these two were going to live through the shock when the news broke. That the grandson they adored was nothing of the kind. I already knew how Ma felt, and Pa would take it equally hard.

Consequences like this would spread outwards like ripples in a pool. Since I'd tossed in the stone of my misguided actions, they would suck in more and more innocent people. And once the story got around, as it surely would in a small place like Porthleven, we *would* be the target of village gossip, as Joel had already pointed out. It would be *the* story of the year. I bit back a sob of hysteria. We'd knock the doings of the Russells for six. Oh Joel, what have I done to you? My throat constricted and my mouth was dry.

It was mid-afternoon by the time I'd collected Davy and made our farewells. We walked down the farm lane to wait for the bus back to the village. The passage of time, conversely, now seemed to have speeded up and we arrived in what seemed like only minutes.

A stiff wind was blowing in from the sea, sending huge purple bruises of rain-clouds shore-wards whipping up the water into angry white crests that were already spraying high over the wall of the quay; we were in for a summer squall.

My gaze however was fixed on the spot of green that was the front door of our home. Surely it was standing partly open? My stomach turned over as we reached the gate, and my heart began to thump in double-time. Joel was back!

'Papa! We've been to the farm.' Davy ran to his side. 'I saw some baby—' Joel was sitting slumped in a chair, both elbows on the kitchen table and had been staring into space. He had looked up, dull-eyed, as we entered. His face was pinched and his cheeks sunk into hollows in his pale face.

I gasped and my jaw dropped. It seemed unbelievable that the man I loved most in the world could have turned in the space of a few hours into this stranger.

As Davy spoke and tugged at his arm, Joel rose to his feet, his gaze fixed on my face. Without looking at the child he placed a hand on the little boy's head. 'Later, Davy,' he said gently. 'Go and play in the other room for a while. Mama and I have some talking to do.' Davy's face fell and his mouth turned down at the corners, but he did as he was told and trudged from the room.

'How could you *do* such a thing?' Joel's voice was dangerously quiet. I faced my husband's shocked and horrified face and wished I were dead. I felt smaller than the lowest crawling creature upon the earth. If it had opened at that moment and swallowed me up I would have been grateful.

Joel's voice was hoarse with either grief or anger. It was hard to tell which. He spread his hands in bewilderment, his eyes boring into mine. Then he gripped the back of a wooden kitchen chair with white-knuckled hands.

'You're telling me that for nearly three years we've been living a *lie*? All of us? That all the time I thought we were a happy, ordinary little family, it was only a sham?'

Joel glowered at me in fury. But to me, knowing him so well, his quivering mouth indicated that the bitter hurt I'd caused him had gone deeper than anger.

'A sham founded on *your* lies, *your* hypocrisy, *your* deceit. . . .' He pounded on the table with a fist. The hammer-blows thudded into my head like nails in my coffin.

Shivering with a bone-aching cold that had nothing to do with the storm now raging outside, I backed towards the range. My whole body was shaking. Holding my hands out behind me for its warmth and comfort, I hung my head.

With a roar, Joel suddenly snatched up a pot of bright red geraniums from the table and with an oath, hurled it straight towards me.

I screamed in fright and twisted away. But Joel was not aiming it at me, only giving vent to his own feelings. The flower-pot landed in the hearth with a resounding crash and shattered. A myriad shards of broken china and blood red petals fell at my feet.

I covered my face with my hands. Lacerating guilt overwhelmed me like a flood tide drowning me in a crushing wall of water. Just like the huge breakers washing over the quay wall outside, their awesome power hurling clouds of foam high into the air.

'I did it because I loved you so,' I sobbed. 'I – I couldn't bear to think of losing your love for me. I was afraid for our marriage, Joel!' I raised tear-filled eyes and held out imploring hands to him. 'I knew how much you wanted a child. And ours was dead!'

I was shouting at him now. 'I was out of my mind with worry – I told you. And then when . . . when Davy turned up it was like a miracle. . . .' My voice broke and I hung my head, holding a corner of my apron to my streaming eyes.

Joel took a step forward and thrust a hand under my chin, forcing me to look up at him. 'So I'm such a monster that you were terrified of me.' His face was expressionless. But his eyes ... oh his sunken, haunted eyes!

'That says a lot for the trust I thought there was between us!' He pushed me from him and I staggered, clutching at the brass rail of the range.

Joel was pacing up and down again, his hands balled into fists. 'What did you think I'd do to you, for heaven's sake – knock you about or something?' He rounded on me and I flinched. '*Me*?' He jabbed his chest with a finger.

'Have you ever seen me lay a hand on anybody? Least of all a woman. You were afraid that I'd beat my own *wife*? You disappoint me, Loveday, you really do.' Joel's voice was cold now, flat and cold, his face twisted.

'It wasn't *like* that,' I whispered, wrapping my shaking arms around my body. He didn't understand. How could I ever have expected him to? I fought against another rising tide of bitter tears. But tears were useless, however much his words had wounded me.

'Pah!' he spat, 'what else could it have been like, woman? You've just admitted that you're afraid of me.'

How haggard he looked. There were worry lines I'd never seen before etched on his forehead. And it was all my fault. The hammer in my head started up again. I reached for the back of a chair to support my trembling legs. For I *would* remain standing. I felt less vulnerable that way than if he were looming over me.

'And this,' Joel slumped into a chair, 'is only the beginning of our problems. You do realize that, don't you?'

I nodded, too full of suffocating misery to speak. 'Where do we go from here?' Joel spread his palms. 'What do we do about Davy? Do we try to trace his family? We can't just go on as if nothing's happened.' He rubbed a weary hand over his face and a silence fell as we both became sunk in our own thoughts.

'It's very quiet in the other room.' At last I came back to earth. 'I wonder what he's up to?'

'I'll go and see,' Joel dragged himself to his feet. 'Poor little tacker, it's none of his fault. None of it.' He slowly shook his head. 'Although I reckon he'll be the one to suffer most in the end.'

I fell into a chair at last and bit my lip until it bled, but I hardly felt it. At that moment I wouldn't have cared if I'd bled to death.

But no! I started and placed both hands to my stomach. For a moment I'd actually forgotten about the new little one. Poor little soul – what a situation he or she would be born into.

A moment later, Joel was back, a puzzled expression on his face. 'He's not in there. And I've been upstairs as well. He's not there either.'

I sprang to my feet. 'What? But there's nowhere else he *can* be.' One hand flew to my mouth as my stomach gave a sickening lurch. I glanced out of the window at the heaving sea and rain-drenched windows. 'He wouldn't have gone outside in *this*.'

I turned frightened eyes to Joel. 'Quickly, look in all the cupboards – under the stairs, everywhere!'

It took only minutes to search the tiny cottage. And to find that Davy was nowhere to be seen.

'But he can't just have *disappeared* Joel! He must have gone outside. Oh, no – in all this storm! Quick, go after him. I can't run in my state. . . .'

But Joel had already snatched a waterproof from behind the door and was racing down the path, shouting Davy's name as he went. Uselessly, for his voice was whipped far away over the rooftops by the howling gale.

I snatched a cloak and followed him along the quayside. It was slick with the water pouring over it with every wave that smashed against the harbour wall. Rain sliced in sharp needles into my face so I could hardly see. I tried to keep my eyes on Joel's yellow oilskin and went as fast as I was able.

No one else was about in this maelstrom of heaving water, why would they be? My breathing became more laboured as I limped along. Joel was making for the higher ground on the far side of the harbour.

I shook my head to clear the water from my eyes. A knot of people were silhouetted against the skyline outside a group of cottages. Something was wrong! They were waving their arms and pointing as Joel approached.

Panting heavily, I reached them at last. Joel with a coil of rope over his arm, went racing away over the clifftop now. Some other men shouting as they pounded along in his wake.

'What's happening? Where are they going? Is it Davy. . . ? Oh, *Meg*! What's going on?' I seized my sister-in-law's arm and shook it.

Meg had just opened her door and was staring out, a shawl thrown over her head. 'Loveday! Oh, my dear lord. 'Tis never Davy, is it?'

She clutched my elbow and peered into my face. Gasping for breath, I nodded miserably. Speech was beyond me.

'Come inside, my dear maid. You d'look fair done in. Shouldn't be out in your condition, my handsome. Leave it to they men.' Stout and motherly, Meg tried to drag me over the threshold.

I wrenched myself free, though. '*Tell me*, just tell me what's happening. . . .' I staggered, whimpering as I clutched at the doorframe to keep myself upright.

'Poor little tacker's out there in a boat . . . all on his awn . . . broke its moorings see, and 'tis drifting. . . . The men are trying to get a line on board and head un off from the rocks, see. Come us on, you must come in out of this rain!'

Meg tried again to guide me into the warmth and comfort of her home. But I was screaming now and shook myself free, scrambling over the slippery turf after the men.

I reached a vantage point and stood helplessly watching the scene below. Drifting at the mercy of the wind and tide and heading for the rocks – oh, dear God, those same rocks – again! – was Joel's dinghy. Crouched in the bow I could see a tiny, hunched figure gripping the sides screaming in terror. *Davy!*

My screams joined with his. Both became one with the raucous cries of the gulls wheeling like scraps of flotsam below me. I clutched my arms about my body and willed myelf not to collapse.

It was now obvious that the rope was useless in such a gale. As if in slow-motion, I saw with horror that Joel was throwing off his oilskin and boots. Then he dived headfirst into the roiling water.

I bit my knuckles until they bled, my eyes riveted on the two people I loved most in the world – my husband and child.

Slowly Joel was gaining on the tossing boat, wasn't he? I narrowed my eyes against the wind. The swell of the sea and the driving rain were making it almost impossible to be sure.

One of the men was scrambling down the cliff carrying a coil of rope around his shoulder and as he reached the rocky shelf, braced himself and threw it as far as he could towards Joel. A shout went up from the watchers as Joel's hand came up for a brief moment and grabbed it. 'He've got un, oh, praise the Lord,' shouted another.

But Joel was leaning over the side of the boat, half in and half out. He seemed unable to heave himself into it. My hands flew to my face in horror as he lost his grip and fell backwards into the water again.

He must have managed to attach the rope though. The man on the rocks was hauling it in. Oh God, thank you, thank you, I whispered. The boat although still bucketing about in the swell, was slowly but surely being drawn to safety.

And yes, there was Joel beside it, clutching at the nearest rock. Dragging himself out of the water.

Then strong arms were cradling Davy, bringing him up to me. My precious little son. He was blue with cold and bawling hysterically, but safe. Oh, safe! Opening wide my arms I clasped him to me, both of us wet through, the rain streaming from my hair mingling with our tears.

Two more brawny fishermen clasped their hands together and formed a make-shift seat. A third lifted us on to it and hurried us towards the village.

'In here – my missus'll see to them,' one said as we reached the first cottage.

'Related we are.' I realized it was Matt and tried to smile my thanks. Meg flung open the door. Over her arm at the ready were two thick towels.

She took Davy from my reluctant arms and guided me into her tiny parlour. Between us we stripped the little boy of his sodden clothing. Meg wrapped him tenderly in a blanket and thrust him into an armchair before her glowing fire.

'Now you, my handsome,' she turned to me. I was standing helplessly, shaking in every limb, my teeth chattering. Looking in dismay at the rivulets of water dripping from my hair and clothing.

'Never mind that there, I'll wipe un up soon enough. Here, take this and strip down. I'll be back in a minute.' Meg left the room and shouted up the stairs. 'Jessie! Bring down some dry clothes of mine and another blanket – quick as you can – there's a good girl. I'm going to put the kettle on.'

Wrapped in the towel, I knelt down beside Davy and stroked his hair. 'Mama!' he said drowsily as I cuddled him close. I noticed with relief that his face was losing its bluish tinge as he warmed through. He was fast drifting away into sleep. Apart from a few scratches and a bruise under one eye the little boy seemed blessedly unhurt. I sent up another silent prayer of thanks.

Then jumped as a discreet knock came at the door. Meg returned with a bundle of clothing. 'Here you are, my handsome, put these on while I'd go and make the tea.'

'Oh, *Meg*.' I laid a trembling hand on her arm. 'Thank you. Thank you so much.'

'Aw, gus on!' Meg bustled away, the old Cornish expression denoting her embarrassment at any show of emotion. 'Tidden nothing.'

She was soon back with hot drinks for us. I raised grateful eyes as she thrust a steaming mug into my cold hands.

'Oh, I'm so thankful he's all right, dear of him.' Meg looked fondly at the little bundle in the chair. I took a sip of tea and put the mug down to slip on the underclothes and dress. 'They do fit you right enough, too,' Meg said with a nod. 'Being that you're nearly so big as I am now!' She crossed the room on her way back to the kitchen.

I smiled weakly, recognizing that Meg was trying to comfort me with normal chatter. I bent down to Davy and held a mug of warm milk to his mouth. His eyes although heavy with sleep, were following my every movement as if he were afraid to let me out of his sight.

'Why did you do it, darling?' I whispered, smoothing his soft hair. 'Why did you run out in all that rain?'

Davy wriggled and squirmed away from my hand. 'You and Papa were shouting,' he pouted his bottom lip. 'You were cross and I . . . I didn't like it. I was afraid. So I thought . . . Papa would like it . . . if . . . if I went out in his b-boat.' Davy's voice trembled. He stuck a thumb in his mouth in a baby gesture he had outgrown months ago.

Guilt pierced me like a sword-thrust. I put both arms round him and hugged him close. 'Oh Davy, darling,' I rocked him like a baby, 'we weren't cross with you, Papa and I! We both love you so much. . . .' Before I could finish the sentence Davy gave a huge yawn and was instantly asleep.

I stayed on my knees beside the slumbering child. Oh Davy, what have we – what have *I* done to you? I smothered a sob and rose to my feet as I heard the door open and Meg returned carrying a tray loaded with food.

I'd never felt less like eating. But out of politeness I nibbled on a bun and drank the comforting tea as we sat around the fire. Then I frowned. 'Joel's taking a long time coming up, isn't he?'

I turned anxious eyes towards the window. The rain seemed to have eased off now and subsided into a thin drizzle. 'I hope he's all right.'

'He'll have gone home to your place to dry off, I expect,' Meg replied. 'He don't know you're in here, see, do he?'

'Oh, yes, of course.' I glanced at the sleeping child. 'I must get back there as soon as Davy wakes up.' I finished my tea and went over to look down at him.

'He'll be out for a long time yet, dear of un, after what he's been through.' Meg came and stood beside me. 'How don't you leave him here with me and I'll bring him back later? Tidden more than a step round the harbour.'

I gave her a grateful smile. 'Well, if you're sure you don't mind, Meg. Thanks. I could change and give you back your clothes then, too.'

There was nothing I wanted more than to be back in my own home. I must still be in shock, and so tired. I could hardly keep my eyes open.

Joel was lying on top of the bed when I dragged myself up the stairs and looked in on him. Fully dressed in dry clothes, his hands behind his head and a mug of tea at his side.

'Took your time, didn't you?" he growled. 'Thought at least you might have come straight home to see if I was dead or alive.' He picked up the mug and glowered at me over the rim.

My heart sank. 'I would have,' I protested, 'but Meg insisted on taking us in, as her house was nearest and Davy—'

'*Davy*!' Joel spat out the word. I flinched, 'it's always Davy first with you. Never your husband, is it? Never give me a thought, did you?'

He thumped his chest and sat up, pointing an accusing finger. 'I come home exhausted, battered, soaked to the skin, to an empty house. I could hardly stand, but I had to poke the range up, search for towels, dry clothes, even had to make my own tea.' He swung his legs over the edge of the bed. 'While you and he were being pampered and petted by *my* sister!'

'Oh Joel!' I came closer and took his hand. But apologize? No, I wouldn't – that would be to admit I'd been in the wrong. And I hadn't. So, I'd put my child first – but what mother wouldn't have? My tiredness lifted as a surge of adrenalin pumped through me.

I stiffened my jaw and met my husband's stormy eyes. Not once had he asked how I was feeling after the living nightmare I'd been through. Or was Davy all right. No, I reasoned coolly, he was trying to pile more guilt on to me, hitting back because of his shock and hurt over my confession.

All this went through my head as Joel's big hand lay unmoving in mine. I could have been holding a block of wood for all the reaction there was from him. I looked closely into his face.

'That was a really brave thing you did, diving in like that.' I paused. 'And I'll tell you what Davy said when I asked him why he'd gone out in the storm.'

I swallowed hard and held Joel's gaze. His eyes were fixed unwaveringly on my face now and he was listening. 'He ran out in all that weather, because he thought we were rowing about *him*!' My eyes filled. 'And Joel, he thought you'd be proud of him if he went down to the boat! A little lad like that!'

I felt the slightest pressure of Joel's fingers on mine for a moment. Then he drew his hand away and rasped it across his face. 'God, what a mess!' he said under his breath He sunk his head in both hands. 'Poor little beggar. Where's he too, anyhow?'

'Asleep. Meg's bringing him back later, when he wakes up.' I moved across the room. 'I must change out of these clothes.' I opened the press and took out some garments of my own.

'You haven't forgotten we're sailing out on the first tide in the morning, have you?' Joel abruptly sat up. 'For the long trip, too. We shall have to leave things as they are until I come home. Then I suppose we'll have to try and trace his family. He must have relatives somewhere. . . .'

He sighed and rose wearily to his feet, changing the subject. I understood instinctively how he needed the comfort of familiar things at such a time. He had to put aside the unimaginable. Give himself time to take in all its implications. Hide behind everyday routine like this.

'So I shall need some croust. And plenty of it. You know how hungry a man d'get out to sea.'

He left the room. I heard his heavy tread go down the stairs and out to the shed where he kept his gear. I sank down on to the bed and eased my aching legs. Tomorrow he would be off again for months, with nothing resolved between us.

And I was meant to carry on as before throughout all the lonely weeks until he came back? As if nothing had changed? I sighed. I supposed I would have to.

In bed that night we talked of mundane matters. Although we lay as close together as usual with Joel's long warm body pressed the length mine, I was very aware of the acres of emotionally chilly space between us.

In the morning, Joel made his departure outwardly in the same way as usual, holding Davy high above his head, exhorting him to 'be a good boy and look after Mama' until he came back. Then put the little boy on his feet and turned to me.

We gazed awkwardly at each other for a long moment, each wondering whether the other was going to make the first move. Then as we both moved together, my kiss just missed Joel's cheek as he bent to me, and his mouth grazed my ear. Joel smiled and gave me a perfunctory hug, but I was very conscious of the lack of real warmth in the smile and of the blankness in his cold blue eyes.

How very alone I felt after I'd waved him off and turned my back on the quay. I wrapped my arms around my swelling body. 'Oh, Joel, I need you. Come back to me,' I whispered into the wind, but the words were snatched away and lost among the sea-birds' crying.

CHAPTER NINE

KATE

Dr Roberts called at mid-morning on the day after Loveday's visit. By then, I'd made an effort to get out of bed. I was sitting in a chair again and welcomed him with a broad smile. I had to tell him right away.

He laid his bag down and came across to measure my pulse. 'I haven't taken it! I managed not to, just as you advised me.' There was triumph in my voice and his face crinkled into a smile.

'Well done!' He reached in a waistcoat pocket for his watch. 'That must have taken a great deal of willpower. Did you find it very hard to resist?'

The smile slid from my face. 'To be honest, yes. But pride kept me from giving in.' I looked down at my hands. 'And also the thought of what you would say.' How could I explain that I wanted to please him, when I could not explain it to myself?

'Am I such an ogre, then?' He laughed, producing a bottle of liquid from his bag. 'Here's your alternative medicine. If you find that you must have something to take, it will do you no harm.' His eyes met mine. 'Although of course if you can manage without taking anything at all, so much the better.' He lifted my hand and began checking my pulse.

'No – oh, no – Dr Roberts, I didn't mean. . . . But thank you for this.' I found myself stammering and felt a perfect fool. What on earth was the matter with me?

'Oh, I know some of my patients do think of me as an ogre.' The smile left his face for a moment. 'Especially when I refuse to supply them with the stuff you were taking.' He relinquished my hand and the smile was back on his face.

'Thank you, everything seems to be fine.' He straightened up. 'You're doing very well, Mrs Rosewarne.' He stowed away his watch, then cleared his throat. 'Ah – er—' he began. 'I just want to apologize for flying off the handle yesterday. I hope you'll forgive me.' He glanced up and quirked an eyebrow.

'Of course I will,' I replied with a smile.

'The fact is,' he went on, 'that until fairly recently I was an Army doctor and I'm not really used to standing on ceremony.' His eyes darkened. 'I was in South Africa during the Boer War, in the Medical Corps. When you're dealing with soldiers and their horrific injuries you get used to speaking your mind. There's no time for any thing else. I haven't yet become used to the accepted "bedside manner".' His eyes twinkled as he snapped his bag shut and turned to go.

So *that* accounts for the tan. My face cleared. What a surprising man this was and how interesting. Truthfully I said, 'I'd like to hear more about your experiences. I know so little of the world, you see.'

'You would?' His eyes widened. He regarded me thoughtfully. 'Well now, Mrs Rosewarne, that brings me to something I've been thinking about for a few days.' Instead of leaving, to my surprise he pulled up another chair and sat down beside me.

'Oh?' My brows rose as I wondered what was coming.

The doctor cleared his throat and he gave me a steady look. 'Yes. You see, I feel you would benefit from a period of convalescence before you return to your home.'

My spirits gave a little lift. It was almost as if he knew how much I was dreading going back to Rosewarne Villa and Arthur. I was aware I would soon be well enough to leave the Infirmary. It sounded as if I might be able to put if off a little longer.

He must have seen my face brighten, for he smiled. 'I know of just the place for you. A small convalescent home not far from where you live. It's in Penzance, and I can thoroughly recommend it, as it's run by my own sister.'

His eyes twinkled. 'I visit there quite often to keep an eye on my former patients. If you were staying there, we could have an informal chat. I could tell you all you want to know about my experiences in South Africa.'

'Oh that would be wonderful! What a lovely idea.' The remark was intentionally ambiguous – I could have been alluding to the idea of the home, or to his visit. That way I managed not to sound too eager to see him again.

'I'm glad you're pleased. I shall be seeing Anne at the weekend. I know she has a vacancy as I recently discharged another lady. I'll tell her the place will soon be filled.' He rose to his feet and replaced the chair. 'And now I must go. I've several other patients to see to before I go off duty.'

'Where do you live?' I asked. I wanted to know more about this interesting man, and to keep him talking a little longer.

'I have a small flat attached to the hospital. There's a gas ring and the basic necessities; I don't need much.' He spread his palms. 'I can eat in the staffroom when I want to, and I spend so much time over here anyway, I use the flat mainly just for sleeping in.'

It sounded a lonely life. And I wanted to know something else. Deliberately fishing, I said lightly, 'So I take it there's no Mrs Roberts?'

His face darkened for a second and he paused. Then he replied in the same laughing tone I'd just used. 'Oh, I've never met a lady yet who's prepared to put up with a crusty old bachelor like me!' With a smile and a wave he walked away down the length of the ward.

Arthur had been to visit me in the hospital several times. I had sensed right away a change in him. It was in the way he looked me up and down, how his nose wrinkled at the antiseptic air of the place. How he looked around the ward and at me, with distaste.

He dropped a dutiful kiss on my cheek for the benefit of the other people around and asked me how I was. He listened while I told him and I watched his expression. His eyes were raking me up and down.

'You're looking so . . . drab,' he said with a frown, seating himself beside me. I was sitting out in my robe, my hair hung loose down my back. I was aware my face had lost its colour, understandably, from being indoors so long, but it was hardly a tactful remark to make, and I glowered at him.

'Arthur, I *have* been very ill. You can hardly expect me to look glamorous.'

He grunted. 'How long before they discharge you?' He twisted the soft hat on his knees. 'We're going to Paris next week, don't forget. There's no question of putting it off. I can't be away from the office except for that particular fortnight I've arranged.'

My jaw dropped. 'Arthur, of *course* I shan't be fit to go next week. You'll *have* to postpone it. How on earth do you expect me to be well enough to travel? Look at me! I've been in bed for a month!'

He glared. 'Huh. You look well enough to me. If you put on some decent clothes and did your hair properly, that is.'

His callous selfishness pierced me to the heart. Where was the loving concern, the flowers, the consideration one would expect from a normal husband? I'd seen other people's partners coming and going at visiting times, their faces drawn with worry.

I'd seen how they gripped each other's hands, whispered closely together, dragged themselves reluctantly away when the bell went for the end of visiting. And all he could do was sit there like a brooding black shadow, thinking only of himself. My throat constricted.

However, Dr Roberts appeared at that moment and, as good as his word, introduced himself and took Arthur away into his office. Although I had no idea what he said, I could see when Arthur returned he wasn't very pleased. His face was brick-red, I presumed with embarrassment as well as anger, and his eyes cold as black pebbles.

'How dare he!' he spluttered, resuming his seat with a face like thunder. 'The jumped-up, impertinent young rascal. Calls himself a doctor! Do you know what he had the cheek to tell me. . . ? I can hardly believe the sheer *nerve* of it.' He thumped his chest. . . . 'To tell *me*, your husband, that I must leave you alone . . . er . . . in bed in future.' His fury was all the greater for having to be conducted in an undertone.

'If I listened to him, he would have me deny my marital *rights*.' His hot eyes bored into my skull and I cringed. 'How could he presume to. . . . What *gentleman* would even mention such a subject! Of course I shan't take any notice of him.' He sat back, fuming, and folded his arms.

My heart sank. Top marks for trying, Dr Roberts, I thought sadly, but you don't know what you're up against.

'So, apparently you're to have a period of *convalescence*, too.' Arthur spat the word with disgust. 'Being pampered and petted at my expense.' His lips narrowed. 'Because of course, *I* shall have to pay the exorbitant fees at this place.'

He turned on a heel, then bent down to my level and hissed in my ear. 'And what Mother will say when I tell her what a weakling you are, I can't imagine. In her day, young women were expected to put their husbands and families before themselves. But then, your parents always did spoil you, and now it shows.'

I didn't know whether to laugh or cry at this. But by the time he left, I was feeling drained, tearful and thoroughly despondent.

The next day he came to take me to Penzance. We hardly spoke for the entire journey.

The convalescent home was set in a wooded slope above Penzance, looking over the magnificent view of St Michael's Mount.

I loved 'Sea Winds' as soon as I set eyes on it. And found an unexpected friend in Anne Barrington. 'My sister's a widow' Jonathan Roberts had said, and for no reason, I had been prepared to see an elderly, grey-haired lady.

I couldn't have been more wrong. Mrs Barrington was about my own age, petite, bubbly, with sparkling green eyes and a mass of rich curly brown hair. 'Come in, come in,' she said, throwing the door wide. She must have seen the carriage approaching up the short drive that led to the house.

Arthur brought in my bag, and left as soon as he could, hardly bothering to be civil. I was shown to a pleasant, comfortably furnished room on the first floor. 'What a glorious view!' I exclaimed, going to the bay window. From here I could see beyond the wide stretch of Marazion beach, to the eastern headland that just hid Porthleven from sight. Westward, obscured by the next point in that direction, lay Newlyn and Mousehole.

'You're seeing it at its best today.' Mrs Barrington smiled. 'It's a different picture in the winter.'

'But I think I'd love it then, just as much. We live in an exposed spot ourselves, so I can imagine the waves pounding against the Mount and the wind wailing around your chimneys.'

'That's right. Hence the name of the house!' She nodded and turned away. 'Here we are.' She was opening cupboards and showing me shelves and drawers. 'There's plenty of room for your things.'

I hadn't brought much. I'd told Arthur strictly not to bring any of my grand clothes. Simple day gowns, plain fabrics, I'd said. His lip had curled and he'd looked at me with disdain, but for once he'd kept his mouth shut. Sadly I'd come to realize what I'd instinctively known all along: I was little more than a walking demonstration of his wealth and position – an animated toy, subservient to his will.

Mrs Barrington turned back to me. 'There are four other patients here besides yourself. I keep a cook-housekeeper, Mrs Laity; a gardener and a woman who comes in daily to do the "rough". And of course, my brother drops in frequently to keep an eye on us all. I hope you'll be comfortable here, Mrs Rosewarne.'

'I'm sure I shall, thank you. It all looks wonderful. And please call me Kate. If you don't mind, that is?'

She smiled broadly. 'Of course not. And I'm Anne. We try to be informal here, to make it seem as near as possible like a home and family.'

Grimly I thought it was far more homely than the circumstances I was used to. But I could hardly say so.

'I'll leave you to settle in, then. Dinner's at seven. If you need anything just ring the bell.'

I drew off my boots and sank down on to the feather bed with my feet up, suddenly tired out. I'd done very little, but obviously I was still a 'weakling' as Arthur had cruelly pointed out.

But as the days rolled by, relaxed and peaceful, with plentiful nourishing meals put in front of me three times a day, I began to regain my strength, and to put on the weight I'd lost in hospital. In the mirror I saw that my cheeks were becoming round and rosy and my hair began to regain its lustre. I felt better than I'd done for years.

I realized after a while this was because, for the first time since my marriage, I was actually happy. I strolled in the rose garden, read my way through the interesting novels thoughtfully provided and chatted to the other patients.

I dreaded returning to Rosewarne Villa. The thought of it hung over me like a small black cloud on the horizon. I tried to put it out of my mind, but of course, the day would come when I'd have to leave this heavenly place.

I was becoming more than ever drawn to Anne; her open nature and simple friendliness made me want to know more about her. So one day when she joined me under a spreading horse chestnut tree on the lawn behind the house, I asked her about herself.

'What gave you the idea of running a convalescent home, Anne? Was it your idea, or your brother's?'

Putting aside the newspaper she'd been reading, a shadow passed over her usually lively face. She twisted the wedding band on her finger. 'It was after Richard died,' she said. 'Four years ago.' She raised her head and her gaze rested on the pink and white flowering candles of the tree above us.

'He was a soldier. His regiment was stationed in India, and he caught a fever. He was dead within a week.' She spread her hands and her eyes met mine.

I gasped. 'Oh, Anne, how tragic! What a shock it must have been for you.' She lowered her head and nodded.

'This was our home when we were in England. We rented it out when we went abroad. I came back here then.' She shrugged. 'There was no shortage of money; Richard's pension and the rents saw to that, but I knew it wouldn't last for ever. I had to do something.'

She picked at a loose thread of her blue linen skirt. 'Besides, I was lonely in this huge place on my own.' She turned her head. 'It was Jonathan's suggestion I make it into a half-way house for his patients. He's been very good to me. I don't know what I'd have done without him in the early days.' She paused for a moment. 'But of course, he had his problems too. It was a bad time for us both.'

I didn't like to ask what problems Jonathan had for fear of seeming to pry, but I was intrigued all the same. Anne had picked up her paper again.

But I was enjoying the chat. 'Did you like India when you were there?' I changed the subject.

'Oh, yes.' Her face lit up. 'The heat, the colours, the bustle. And I've never seen so many people. The sheer number took my breath away.

But I was never really happy with the regimental life.'

'Oh?' My brows rose and I leaned closer. 'In what way?'

Anne's brow furrowed. 'Well, you see, I wasn't born into the middle classes. Jonathan and I come from quite a poor background, actually. He worked very hard to get through medical school and I married "up" as they say.'

'Really?' I was slightly surprised. 'How did you cope?'

Anne's expression was unreadable, but the narrowing of her lips spoke volumes. 'Well, I was lucky in one way, because I'd been in service at a large hotel before I met Richard, and I was a fast learner.' She leaned back in her chair, remembering.

'I learned about etiquette and manners during my time there. But, yes, it was very hard at first.'

She paused, lost in reminiscence, then gave a sigh. 'Richard was marvellous of course. He made sure I didn't make a fool of myself at their social gatherings. Officers wives were expected to support their husbands at the endless dinner-parties, tea-parties, tennis-parties, picnics . . . you name it. . . .

'But when he was on duty and I was left in the garrison bungalow with just the servants, I felt so alone. No-one came calling.'

She gave a rueful smile. 'I'd never been used to having servants either. It wasn't so long ago I'd been one myself! It took me a long time to get used to giving orders.' She smoothed her hands over her skirt. 'But I like to think that as my self-confidence increased, I did gradually gain their respect.'

My respect was growing too, for this brave woman who looked as if she'd never had a care in the world.

'The turning point came when I saved a woman's life after she was bitten by a snake,' Anne said in a casual manner.

My head jerked round as I gaped at her in amazement. '*What?*'

She made a dismissive gesture. 'Oh, it was nothing much, but nobody else seemed to know what to do.' She paused.

'Well, what *happened?*' I urged her. She came back to earth with a smile.

'Oh, we were out riding, a group of us, when this person dismounted to tighten her horse's girth, and stepped on a snake. She screamed, saying it had bitten her, and the other women all seemed to be screaming too and just wringing their hands.' Anne shrugged her slim shoulders.

'So I jumped down and made a makeshift tourniquet out of a white silk scarf I was wearing, and tied it tightly above the puncture. Then I managed to suck the poison out. They seemed to be quite impressed, and the woman was so grateful that she saw to it I was properly accepted as one of them from that day.'

'That was a pretty brave thing to do.' I looked at her with admiration. 'I doubt if I would have had such presence of mind.'

Anne laughed. 'Well, you see, during all that lonely time at home I had plenty of time to study the first aid manual that was issued to us all. I suppose I must have been the only one who actually read it, and it certainly came in useful that day.

'When I realized *how* useful it was, I went on to study first aid and home nursing to certificate level.' She paused and the smile slid from her face. 'Soon after that Richard was taken ill. And all my new-found skills couldn't save him.'

'Oh, Anne, I'm so sorry.' I laid a hand on her arm.

She nodded. 'He died on my twenty-first birthday. We'd been married for exactly two years – such a short time. I still miss him, Kate.' There was a dampness about her eyes as I gently squeezed her arm.

'At least you had a happy marriage, if only a brief one.' I spoke softly, almost to myself. 'Not like – me. . . .' I hadn't meant it to slip out, but Anne had obviously caught what I said, for she turned to me with sympathy in her expressive eyes.

'I know . . . um . . . something of it,' she murmured. 'Jonathan did tell me a little of the position you're in. He mentioned your illness you see, and how it was caused. He had to explain why you were coming here to stay. I hope you don't think I was prying, or that he was being unprofessional, but—'

'Of course not,' I broke in. 'I'm very glad you do know. It's too embarrassing a subject for *me* to bring up. The only other person I've ever told is my sister.'

Anne gave me a level look. 'Kate, isn't there some way you could leave Arthur? You don't owe him anything after the way he's treated you.'

'We did talk about it, Loveday and I.' I nibbled my bottom lip. 'Although that was before my illness. But it's such a huge step to take, Anne. I don't know if I could actually do it. Stand up to Arthur, I mean. He's such a well . . . bully is the only word to describe him.' I bent my head and twisted my fingers in my lap.

'I hoped the situation might change since Jonathan . . . Dr Roberts I mean . . . I know he spoke to Arthur in private before I left the hospital, but Arthur was just so livid with rage at what he called his "presumption" that he fully intends to ignore his warning.' I couldn't prevent my voice from trembling as I imagined my first night at home, and Arthur's wrath.

'We'll see what Jonathan has to say next time he calls in.' Anne tossed her head and nodded, full of determination. I saw a flash of the spirit that had got her through her own tragedy, and thought what a remarkable woman she was.

A silence fell as I tried to read a few pages of my book, then found I hadn't taken in a word of it. As I raised my head, I caught sight of the headlines in Anne's newspaper.

The suffragettes were at it again: chaining themselves to railings outside the Houses of Parliament, getting themselves imprisoned; going on hunger strike; being force-fed in the most degrading way. I shuddered.

Anne noticed me looking over her shoulder and pointed a finger. 'You've got to give them credit for their courage and their convictions,' she remarked. 'I'm sure I couldn't do it.'

I took a breath and sat back. 'Do you know, I was thinking about those women when I was in hospital with nothing else to do. I read a similar article then. And yes, I do admire them too. Although, Anne,' I half-turned to meet her steady gaze, 'I did wonder how much better off we shall all be if and when, we ever get this vote. It seems such a remote possibility, don't you think so?'

'Well, yes. They don't seem to have actually achieved very much yet. I suppose in time, maybe. . . .'

'But meanwhile, women all over the country continue to be beaten up, and worse, by their drunken husbands.' I drummed my fingers on the wooden arm of my deckchair.

My eyes were focused far away across the sparkling water below us, but I took in none of it. 'Anne,' I said, 'what I would dearly like to do is to open a refuge for battered and abused women like me, married to brutal husbands, trapped by their marital vows with no way out of their suffering.'

'How wonderful!' Anne's eyes were warm and interested. 'I'm sure there's nowhere like that around here. I think it's a marvellous idea.'

'And so do I.' We both jumped, then laughed together. Neither of us had heard Jonathan approaching across the grass. Confused, I felt my cheeks redden and my heart began to beat a little faster. 'That sounded as if you were speaking straight from the heart, Kate.'

'Oh, believe me, I am.' I met his sympathetic eyes. I could feel my own sparking with anger.

'Yes. Now. . . .' he folded his long legs and sank into a basket chair beside us. 'We need to have a long talk, you and I. And I'm sure you won't mind if Anne hears this too; she's fully aware of your position.'

'Actually I must go in,' Anne said, folding her paper and rising. 'Tell me later. I have some urgent letters to write before lunch. It's so lovely out here I tend to forget the time.'

'Oh, all right. We'll see you later on.' Jonathan turned back to me.

Before he could speak I broke in, 'Jonathan, I would just like to thank you for speaking to Arthur as you did. I'm really grateful. Not that it's made any difference, I'm afraid, but I appreciate your trying.' I bent my head and brushed a falling petal from my lap.

'He's determined to ignore all you said,' I continued, 'He didn't even seem very embarrassed. He believes that I'm his property, you see, so he can do what he likes with me.' I raised my head to meet Jonathan's steely expression.

He narrowed his lips. 'I gathered as much from his reaction. However, we'll see about that.' He pulled his chair closer and bent forward, his hands resting on his knees.

'Now, Kate. This is going to come as a bit of a shock, so prepare yourself.'

My hand went to my throat and I felt my eyes widen with apprehension. A shock? Good or bad? How could I be ready if I didn't know which to expect?

'I've been talking to someone I know in the legal profession and making a few enquiries. I can tell you that it is perfectly possible for you to apply for an annulment of your marriage: a divorce in other words.'

The word hit me with the force of a sledge-hammer. '*Divorce*?' I gasped as the ground tilted. 'Could I *really*? B-but . . . how . . . how . . . what. . . ?' I couldn't string a simple sentence together without stammering. The blood pounded in my head and my stomach was turning somersaults.

Jonathan's gaze met mine. 'Forgive me for being so blunt about this, Kate. It's the only way.' He cleared his throat. 'I imagine that, given your husband's habits, your marriage has not been . . . er . . . consummated in the normal way?' He quirked an eyebrow.

My head was still swimming. 'Y-yes. I mean no. No! That's right. Absolutely. It hasn't.' I felt my face flame.

And what depths of despair it had brought me to. Especially watching Loveday's delight in her little boy. For saddled to Arthur as I was, I faced the prospect of remaining childless all my life.

Oh yes, as the years passed I'd come to understand better what had led my sister to behave the way she'd done regarding Davy. But now. . . ! I felt as if a window had been opened in my mind, letting air and light come streaming in.

'Well, then, you definitely have a watertight reason for taking him to court.' Jonathan nodded decisively.

It couldn't be true. Could it? No, there must be a catch somewhere. 'But . . . are you sure?' I whispered.

'I'm sure.' He looked steadily back at me. 'Our uncle, Anne's and mine, was a lawyer. He was very good to us and spent a lot of time at our house. I think he must even have helped my parents with funds when I was a struggling student. But never told me.' He paused, apparently back in the past.

'Anyway, we grew up hearing bits and pieces of his cases. Some of his legal knowledge stuck in my mind and rubbed off on me.'

'So, it's true all right.' He smiled and patted my arm. 'I know the idea takes a bit of getting used to, but you could do it, Kate. You would never have to worry about him again.'

Overcome, I felt foolish tears welling up. I swallowed impatiently, now was not the time to give way to tears. Jonathan was saying something else.

'The only thing is, I'm afraid you'd be required to undergo a medical examination.' His face was sober.

My heart sank. 'In front of strangers?' Both hands flew to my mouth. 'Oh, no!'

Jonathan nodded slowly. 'Now, it's possible that as your doctor, I might be able to submit a statement saying I've conducted it myself.' He drummed his fingers on the arm of the chair. 'Which would let you off that unpleasantness. Of course, I can't guarantee they'll accept my word, but they just might.'

'You would? Oh, wonderful.' I could only goggle at him as I tried to take it all in. Oh, Jonathan. I could have sunk to my knees and worshipped him. It was reassuring beyond measure to have someone on *my* side.

'What would I have to do? I wouldn't know where to begin.' The vastness of the idea had robbed me of my power of rational thought.

Excitement and trepidation were combining in a hard knot in my stomach. But my soul was singing. For there was a way! Light at the end of the long, dark tunnel of my marriage. The dream might become reality after all.

'The first thing is to get a good solicitor.' Jonathan's expression was thoughtful. 'And as it happens, I can help you there, too. My cousin, the son of the uncle I mentioned, followed his father into the profession. We're on friendly terms although I rarely see him.'

He pulled out his watch and glanced at it. 'But I'm afraid it's time for me to go. Duty calls.' He smiled. 'I have to do the rounds of the other convalescents before lunch. After that I go back to the Infirmary.'

He rummaged in a top pocket and pulled out a piece of pasteboard. 'Now, Kate, you get yourself an appointment with Ernest as soon as you're well enough. Here's his card. Tell him I sent you and you shouldn't have any trouble.'

I took it and held it to me as if it were a lifeline. 'Oh, Jonathan, I can never thank you enough.'

I think my heart must have been in my eyes as our glances met and held. For a long moment we gazed at each other. He gently pressed my arm as he rose to his feet.

'No thanks needed,' he said softly. 'I only hope it all turns out well for you. If anyone deserves a bit of good fortune, Kate, it's you.' He turned away. 'I'll see you at lunch.' With a wave of his hand he crossed the lawn and disappeared round the corner of the house.

I sat on lost in my thoughts. Telling myself not to get excited, not to raise my hopes too high. The whole idea could well crumble into dust and ashes around me. But try as I might to look on the dark side, I couldn't prevent the corners of my mouth lifting, and I knew a broad smile was spreading across my face.

Roused by the gong sounding for lunch. I jumped to my feet and hurried inside. Most of the residents were already seated and throughout the meal as we chatted and made polite small talk, I felt as if I was only half present. Especially as I caught Jonathan's eye across the table and he smiled as if he knew exactly what I was thinking.

When the meal was over we took our coffee out into the conservatory, as did a couple of other people. The room was a vast glass semi-circle with stunning views of the bay. Potted plants stood around, revelling in the warmth and humidity; some of the climbers had reached the roof and nodded down at us, releasing clouds of perfume to fill the already scented air.

There was no opportunity to talk privately of the matter on both our minds, so as we seated ourselves in a couple of cane chairs partly screened by a huge potted palm, I remarked, 'Jonathan, do you remember you promised to tell me about South Africa?'

'Oh, so I did.' He took a sip of his coffee and put the cup down on a small glass-topped table between us.

'I know so little of the world, you see and you've travelled abroad. As well as being in the thick of a war.' I leaned forward. 'I'd love to hear your experiences. What's the country actually like? Why were we fighting out there in the first place? Who exactly are these Boers and why—?'

Jonathan laughingly held up a hand to stem my flow of questions. 'Whoa! One thing at a time.' He crossed one leg and its gleaming boot over the other. 'South Africa is a beautiful land.' There was a far away expression on his face.

'With its vast open spaces and clear, clean air, it teems with the most amazing animal life. It's bakingly hot and dusty in the summer. In the spring, sudden storms turn everything to mud.' He spread his hands.

'As for the Boers, they are mostly farmers. Originally they were Dutch settlers who believed that God had directed them to South Africa as their "promised land".'

I lifted the coffee pot and refilled my tiny cup. Jonathan declined with a shake of the head. 'Yes?' I waited for him to continue.

'Oh, they'd been harassed by the British and have been fighting us on and off for years.' He drained his cup and replaced it on its saucer. He paused, his eyes on my face. 'But this is boring talk for such a lovely day. War is never pleasant, so I'll spare you the gory details.'

'But Kate,' Jonathan's face darkened. 'I've seen sights that I wouldn't wish to share with anybody. The full might of the British Army deployed against a handful of farmers armed with pitchforks was not exactly fun. I just helped to pick up the pieces.'

He was about to go on when my attention was distracted by a movement outside. Someone, a woman, was walking down the drive towards the house and as she came closer I recognized the familiar figure. 'Oh, there's Loveday!' I turned to Jonathan in surprise. 'My sister. I didn't know she was coming today. Oh, I'm so sorry, but you'll have to excuse me.'

'Don't worry. It's time I wasn't here, anyway.' He uncurled his long legs and rose. 'I'll go out the back way to collect the pony and trap. Have a pleasant talk together,' he said over his shoulder as he turned to leave.

I went outside to meet Loveday as she reached the house. 'Oh, it's good to see you!' I hugged her. It was only as she drew away I noticed her distraught expression. My heart began to flutter. Something was obviously wrong.

CHAPTER TEN

LOVEDAY

I saw Kate sitting in the conservatory as I walked up the drive. This time I'd had to bring Davy with me as Meg was out for the day. The drive sloped upwards and with him dragging on my hand it took a while before I reached the house. My body was getting heavier as well and I couldn't walk as fast as I used to.

I could not shake off my depression. Although I knew Joel wouldn't be back for several months, the unresolved problem was ever present in my mind. Maybe it was being made worse by my present condition; women carrying a child were notoriously prone to extravagant fancies. My problem, though, was more than mere fancy.

I sighed, paused to draw breath and wiped the back of my hand across my brow. The sun was very warm, a lovely summer day in early July.

'Loveday!' Kate was at the door to meet me. 'And Davy too. It's lovely to see you.'

'We had a ride in a *train*, Aunt Kate!' The little boy's eyes were shining. Kate picked him up and dropped a kiss on his rosy face.

'You've never walked all the way from Marazion station, have you?' Her brows rose as she turned to me.

'No, Davy couldn't manage that. It's as much as I could do to get him up the drive. We waited for the bus.'

Kate must have seen how warm I was for she gave me a look of concern. 'Shall we sit in the garden where it's cool?' She pointed towards a stretch of lawn shaded by a huge horse chestnut tree laden with blossom.

I nodded gratefully. 'You go and sit down then.' She put Davy on his feet. 'I'll ask someone to bring us a cold drink.'

I sat down with a sigh of relief. Kate was back in a minute and settled herself beside me. I'd brought a couple of Davy's toys in my bag, but he was quite happy to go off and explore the garden. 'He won't come to any harm,' Kate said, 'he can't get out. The fence is quite secure all round.'

At that moment a buxom woman in cap and apron brought out a tray and laid it on the small table nearby. There was a big jug of home-made lemonade. Wonderful, I thought.

'Thank you, Mrs Laity.' Kate nodded to her.

'I put a mug there for the little one.' She pointed. 'I reckoned it'd be easier for him than one of the tall glasses.' She smiled at me.

'Oh, that was thoughtful of you. It certainly will be.'

I lifted the jug and helped myself before she'd reached the house. I took a sip, leaned back and tried to relax. 'It is delicious and I was *so* thirsty.' I rubbed a hand across my tired eyes; 'we had an early start.'

Kate drew her chair closer and gave me a level look. 'Loveday, there's something wrong, isn't there? Is Abe Russell still bothering you? Is that it?'

'No – well, no. But there's something else.' I laid down my glass. 'Kate, I'm going to have another child.'

'Oh, that's wonderful!' Then the smile slid from her face as she stared at me and frowned. 'Isn't it? You don't seem to be very pleased.'

'Oh, yes, I am. That's not it . . . well, only partly.' I fiddled with the buttons down the front of my bodice.

'Loveday,' Kate looked sternly into my face, 'you're not making any sense. *Talk* to me.'

I lowered my head and twisted my hands in my lap. 'It's . . . what with the new baby coming . . . and Abe's demands . . . I couldn't take any more. So . . . Kate. . . .' I raised my head and our eyes met. 'I've told Joel.'

Her jaw dropped. '*Told* him? You don't mean . . . you haven't told him about. . . .' She jerked her head towards Davy, happily playing some imaginary game. I nodded miserably.

'Loveday! How *could* you?' Her eyes blazed. 'After all this time! After you've – we've, both of us – been so careful, watching every word in case something should slip out. How could you *do* such a thing?' Her voice rose further up the scale as the tale unfolded.

With a flash of temper I snapped at her. My overstretched nerves couldn't take any more. 'I've just *told* you why! I couldn't live with myself any more. Kate, you've no idea what I've been going through!' I glared at her and spread my hands for emphasis.

'If you only knew how it's been weighing on my conscience. The longer it went on the worse it became. It was the only way to free myself, you see.' I thumped a fist on the arm of my chair.

'For nearly three years I've been jumping at every shadow, and as you said, watching every word I uttered in case something should slip out. I was living a life of lies and falsehood.' I drew in a breath.

'That business with Abe Russell brought it all to a head. He was the last straw. I couldn't risk it, Kate.' I shook my head and held her gaze, willing her to understand. 'I'd rather Joel heard the truth from me than from that lout, whatever the consequences. I felt I owed him that much at least. I couldn't see any other way.'

'Oh, my dear life!' Kate raised both hands to her face and her eyes were huge at the enormity of what I'd done. 'So how did Joel take it? What did he say? What did he do?'

I couldn't stop the tears from coming then. When I'd recovered enough to speak, I told her the whole story. How Joel had totally misunderstood me and stormed out. How we'd had a monumental row. And how it had all culminated in Davy's dramatic rescue. How even after I'd written it all down, he still hadn't understood.

'Now nothing's right between us. He's going to be way at s-sea for months. And we didn't have time to make up, to talk about what to do next, or anything.' Tears were streaming down my face, but I hastily wiped them away as I caught sight of Davy anxiously watching.

'Oh, my goodness.' Kate had fallen silent, her gaze far away. Then she pulled herself together. 'So where do we go from here?' Her brows rose. 'What are you going to do now?'

Wearily I shook my head. 'Nothing. Until Joel comes home. We'll have a few months before the storm breaks. After that, Kate, I just do not know.' I sank my chin in my hands. 'The future's too awful to contemplate.' A silence fell.

I heaved a sigh. 'As for Abe Russell, I told him never to come near me again. That I'd had a heart-to-heart talk with Joel. That Joel said if Abe ever bothered me in future he'd knock him in the harbour again and this time he'd hold him under.' I gave a bleak smile.

Then I placed a hand on my stomach and sighed. 'What a start in life this one's going to have.' I paused and drew in a breath. 'I worry about that, too, Kate. In case it . . . happens again. . . .' I nibbled my bottom lip and reached for a handkerchief.

Kate squeezed my hand. Then leaned back and folded her arms. 'When's it due?'

'Sometime in October. Joel will be back by then, of course. And we shall have to sort everything out. I'm not looking forward to it.'

She nodded slowly. Her attention seemed to have wandered, and she was gazing into space, preoccupied. I stared at her. 'Kate, are you all right?'

With a start she came back and smiled. 'Oh, yes, sorry. It's just that I've got some news as well.'

'Have you really?' With a stab of guilt I apologized for my selfishness. 'Oh, Kate, I'm sorry. I've been rattling on about my own troubles for far too long. I haven't even asked you how you're feeling now.'

She shrugged. 'All right, I think. I should be leaving here soon. And Loveday, there's something I want to ask you.' She bent her head and twisted her wedding ring round and round. 'You may think this a strange thing to say, but do you think I could possibly come and stay with you when I come back?'

'With *me*? Yes, of course you can. I'd love to have your company.' I looked at her in surprise. 'But why? Why aren't you going back to the villa? Is it . . . is it because of Arthur?'

She nodded. 'It is, in a way, but you'll never guess how.' She leaned forward, wide-eyed. 'You know that nice Doctor Roberts I told you about – um – Jonathan?'

I nodded. 'Yes. I saw him in the distance when I came to visit you in the Infirmary. You pointed him out to me. What about him?'

'Well, he was furiously angry when he found out how Arthur had been treating me. In fact he told him off, but you know what Arthur's like. He refused to take any notice.'

She lowered her voice and her eyes were sparkling with suppressed excitement. 'Loveday, Jonathan told me I could actually *divorce* Arthur. That I've got grounds because the marriage has never been – um – *consummated*. Do you know what I mean?'

I stared at her, thunderstruck. '*Really?*' My voice came out in a high-pitched squeak. 'Oh, how wonderful! And you're going to, of course, aren't you?'

'Yes. I'm going to see a solicitor just as soon as I leave here.' She nodded, her face aglow. 'Now can you see why I don't want to go home? Or up to the farm? Can you imagine my trying to tell Mama and Papa?'

'Of course I can. Oh, Kate, I'm so thrilled for you. It's the best thing that could ever happen.'

'I haven't done it yet, don't forget. And I'm dreading facing Arthur when he finds out.' Her face fell. 'I just hope I'm strong enough to stand up to him.'

'But he won't be able to do anything, will he? If the law is involved.' I frowned.

'Once it gets under way, no. But I'm going to have to speak to him face to face sometime. If I'm in your house it'll be much easier. Do you see what I mean?'

'Oh, yes. Kate, I'm getting as excited as you are!' I smiled and gripped her hands.

We were interrupted at that point by a pleasant-faced young woman who was walking across the grass towards us. Wearing a gown of white-trimmed emerald poplin, I saw as she came closer how the colour exactly matched her twinkling green eyes. Davy was clinging to her hand.

I jumped up in alarm. I hadn't missed him. We had been so deep in our conversation I hadn't noticed him wander off. How could I have been so careless!

'Oh, Davy, you naughty boy, where have you been?' Quite unfairly, I tried to cover my own guilt by scolding the child. His bottom lip pouted and he glowered rebelliously.

'I'm so sorry you've been troubled, Mrs . . . um. . . ?' I looked at Kate who had also risen.

'This is Anne Barrington, Jonathan's sister and the owner of the home. Anne, my sister, Loveday.' We shook hands.

'Don't be sorry.' She smiled. 'I came across Davy digging in the flowerbed with a piece of stick. He told me his name and said he was looking for worms. Then we found one, didn't we?' Davy brightened and nodded.

I noticed then how grubby he was, with grass and soil stains all over his hands and knees. He came closer to me. 'And I saw a ladybird, Mama. A baby one.'

'Lovely,' I said, then turned to Anne. 'Thank you so much for bringing him back. I didn't realize he'd wandered off so far. My sister and I were chatting and the time just flew. In fact, it's time we were getting back.'

'Did you come by train?' Anne enquired and I nodded. 'Just wait where you are for a moment.' She went running back towards the house. My brows rose, wondering what she was doing. I heard her call to someone inside, they exchanged a few words then she returned.

'I just wanted to catch my brother.' She was breathing heavily and put her hand to her side. 'A stitch!' she laughed. 'Jonathan's just leaving. He was detained by a patient, otherwise he would have gone an hour ago. He'll give you and Davy a lift to the station in the trap.'

'Oh, that's too kind,' I felt my cheeks flush, 'but I couldn't be such a bother. He must be in a hurry to get back.'

'Nonsense,' Anne said stoutly. 'It's on his way. Come along and don't think any more about it.' She took Davy's hand and moved towards the house.

'Well, if you're sure, then. Thank you very much.' I turned to say goodbye to Kate. 'Drop me a line when you're coming. And good luck with everything.' She pressed my hand and I followed Anne across the lawn.

Kate arrived in Porthleven the following week. She'd been with me for a couple of days, when I remember on one blessedly peaceful evening, just after I'd put Davy to bed, I was gazing thoughtfully out of the landing window.

I was idly watching the play of light and shadow over the sea; a haze had developed with the approach of evening, smudging the division of sky and water at the horizon and enveloping both in a swathe of milky-blue.

My thoughts had drifted back to the fateful day of the storm. It seemed like a kind of watershed for so much that had happened since. The web-like consequences of the wreck had spread far and wide. It had affected the families of the drowned seamen and the men who had tried to rescue them. Foremost, however for me, my own life had changed dramatically overnight. Kate's too, for she had been drawn into these events and had become a vital part of my secret.

It was lovely to have her staying here; her company kept me from brooding too much. I glanced out over the sea again. The setting sun was fighting through the haze now to poke a last few fingers of gold through the thickening veil. The sky around it that had been swathed in opalescent shades of pink and pearl, was rapidly darkening as twilight took over.

I snapped out of my reverie and was about to draw the curtains when a movement outside caught my attention.

Bill Mitchell the harbourmaster, in a dark brass-buttoned uniform and peaked cap, was rounding the quay. I watched as he approached along the road. The way he stode purposefully, with his head bent made me look twice. I wondered where he was going. But he had slowed outside *my* house and was opening the gate.

A shiver of apprehension feathered down my spine. An official visit? For me? Something must be wrong. Joel, I thought. My heart began to flutter. It could be about anything, of course it could. Nevertheless my legs had begun to shake, and my hands felt clammy. I wiped them down the sides of my apron, stumbled downstairs and went to meet him. I was trembling so much I could hardly open the door.

'Mrs Penrose.' The man nodded and tipped his cap. I stammered a greeting in return. 'May I come inside for a moment?' He removed his cap and took a step forward.

'Of course.' I ushered him into the parlour. He stood in the middle of the room and regarded me anxiously.

'I think you should sit down, my dear.' There was concern in his eyes. 'And prepare yourself for a shock.' My hand flew to my throat. My heart began to thump madly. 'Are you alone in the house?'

'M-my sister's in the kitchen.' It came out as a croak. I licked dry lips and sank into a chair as Kate, who must have heard our voices, put a head around the door.

'Come in, Kate,' I said flatly. 'Do you know Mr Mitchell?' Courtesy came automatically, even under stress. She nodded and murmured a greeting, then came across the room and joined me on the settee.

The harbourmaster reached into the pocket of his coat. 'I'm afraid I have – um – some disturbing news for you.' I felt all the blood drain from my face. He was pulling out a buff envelope. A telegram! Something must be badly wrong. 'About – about Joel?' I whispered. He nodded slowly. I reached for Kate's hand and clutched it hard.

He lowered himself into a chair and cleared his throat. 'Mrs Penrose. I'm more sorry than I can say to have to bring you this news. I've received this telegram from Jack Tamblyn, the skipper of the *Sea-Mew*. He drew it out of the envelope and scanned the single sheet.

'It says, REGRET PENROSE LOST OVERBOARD STOP PRESUMED DROWNED STOP LETTER FOLLOWING STOP.'

I gasped. 'Oh, *no*! No-o!' A groan rose from deep within me. 'Not Joel – it can't be!' Not my big, capable husband with his strong arms and boundless vitality.

'*Drowned?*' My hands fluttered uselessly. 'But he'd spent the whole of his life at sea – how could he have drowned? Surely there must be some mistake?' I felt icy-cold. Then sick as my stomach began to churn.

The man's eyes were full of sympathy. 'Believe me, my dear, I only wish there were. But Jack wouldn't have sent this message if he hadn't been certain. He sent the telegram to me, see. To make sure I'd break the news to you. And soften the shock a little.'

One part of my mind registered the thoughtfulness of the man while my body turned numb; the deep penetrating cold began to filter into my very bones.

'Are you staying with your sister, Mrs Rosewarne?' He turned to Kate. Her face was white with shock, too.

She nodded. 'Yes, yes, I am.'

He looked relieved. 'Oh, that's good. I'll leave you now. You'll want to be by yourselves for a time. But if there's anything I can do, for either of you. . . .'

Kate rose to her feet. 'Thank you, Mr Mitchell, you're very kind. I'll see you out, shall I?'

Stunned, I stayed where I was. I felt as if I'd never move again. I was riveted to the chair, my mind repeating over and over again the words of the dreadful telegram. I knew them by heart, as if they had been engraved there in letters of fire.

I could hear Kate rattling about in the kitchen. Soon she returned, passed me a steaming mug of tea and resumed her seat. I silently sipped it and as the welcome warmth seeped into my frozen body, some measure of feeling returned to my limbs.

And with the return of feeling, I began to weep. Great dry sobs wracked my body, without the relief of tears.

'Loveday, listen to me.' Kate was looking anxiously into my face. 'It did only say "presumed drowned", didn't it? They haven't found a . . . a body, dear. Don't give up hope yet. Joel's a strong swimmer. And very fit.' She put both arms round me and I rested my head on her shoulder.

'Oh, Kate! I know you're trying to comfort me. But inside myself I know Joel's dead. Think about it. It's only common sense. The crew would have made a thorough search before sending such dreadful news. They'd make sure.'

'What I think, is that you should wait for that letter to come.' She gave a determined nod. 'Because that'll give you more details of what's happened.'

I looked up at her. 'I suppose you're right.' I was too weary to argue.

'Of course I am.' She rose to her feet. 'Now I'm going to boil up some water and put the stone "pig" in your bed to warm it through. Then I think you should go up. You're so cold.'

I passed a sleepless night during which my racing mind would give me no rest. Images of Joel and our life together continually unrolled behind my eyelids as if written on an endless scroll.

I was haunted by the memory of our parting. Of how distant we'd been with each other. Now I might never see Joel again to tell him how much I loved him. Or how sorry I was about what I'd done. Or to ask his forgiveness.

Then an avalanche of hot tears began to pour down my face. Soaking my nightgown and pillow as if they'd never stop. But eventually of course my sobbing eased, and I felt better for the release which tears had brought. I dozed fitfully for what was left of the night.

*

It was a crisp, invigorating day. One of high skies and clear, extensive views. Huge waves the colour of jade were rolling in on to the beach. Laced with caps of pure white, they ran up the shingle in long tongues of hissing foam. I hardly noticed its beauty as I walked with head bent, locked in my own thoughts.

I was on my way to see if Meg was back. She might not have been told yet. She'd been away visiting her sister when the news came. Davy was with me, because Kate had a dental appointment that morning. She'd offered to cancel it for my sake. But I wouldn't hear of it, I knew she'd been in pain for several days.

As we approached Meg's cottage, Davy ran on ahead and banged importantly on the knocker. 'Davy! Loveday! How nice to see you.' Meg's face broke into a broad smile as she opened the door. She hadn't heard, then. I dragged myself up the steps.

'Come in, come in. My word, how he's growing, aren't you my handsome?' She ruffled the child's hair.

'In here,' she said. I followed the dumpy little figure into the parlour. Meg chattered on about the weather and things domestic. 'There you are, you make yourself comfortable.' She tipped a tabby cat from the chair and plumped up a cushion.

'Out, Misty,' Meg ordered. 'Do you want to go with her, Davy? George and Henry are out in the back playing on the swing.' The little boy grinned and scampered off.

Meg seated herself and smoothed down her skirt of dark blue cotton. 'Well, how are you keeping, Loveday?' She glanced at my swelling figure and back to my face. I saw her eyes narrow as a frown creased her brow. 'You're not looking too good, my handsome, if you don't mind me saying so. Feeling a bit whisht are you?'

I nodded and swallowed. 'Meg, I came over to see if anyone's told you the news. Obviously they haven't.'

Meg's brows shot up. 'News? No – what news?' She bent closer.

'You have to prepare yourself for a shock.' I paused and took a deep breath. 'Bill Mitchell came to see me last night. He b-brought a te-telegram.' My shoulders began to shake. I fought against the huge sobs threatening to choke me.

'Oh, my dear life! Oh, Loveday, what is it?' Meg jumped out of her chair. She knelt down and placed both arms around me. 'Joel? It's Joel, isn't it? Oh, tell me – tell me quickly!' She clutched at my hand.

'Oh Meg, he's m – missing, believed dead.' I raised streaming eyes.

'*Dead?* Joel *dead?*' Through a mist of tears I saw all the colour drain from Meg's rosy cheeks. 'But he can't be! Not Joel . . . not my brother!' She clutched my arm and her fingernails dug into my flesh. She looked into my face, silently pleading for denial.

'That's all I know.' My voice broke. 'There's a letter coming.' I reached for a handkerchief. Meg awkwardly pushed herself to her feet like an old woman.

'He can't be. . . ! Not like this – not gone so – so *suddenly*!' Meg's haunted eyes met mine. I knew exactly what she meant. There was a dreadful finality about it. He was gone forever with no chance for us to say goodbye – with none of the warning which we would have had with illness, or an accident on land where we could have braced ourselves for tragedy.

But for someone we both loved so much just to vanish out of our lives! How were we ever going to come to terms with such a loss? We gripped each others hands. Then fiercely clung together, but could give each other scant comfort.

I spent the next few days in a kind of limbo. The expected letter when it came was no real comfort. The men had been fishing in extremely rough conditions. The deck had been slippery. It was dark and blowing up a gale. A rope had snapped without warning, catching Joel behind the knees and sweeping him instantly overboard.

They had circled all night searching for him, but the waters of the North Sea were icy-cold, even in summer. He had been wearing his full kit of gum-boots and heavy oilskins. There was nothing more they could have done. Condolences followed.

And that was all. There was nothing I could do either. There was not even a funeral to plan. It would have been better in a way if there had. At least it would have been conclusive. I could have seen Joel for one last time and mourned him in a normal way.

*

Through the endless days that followed, Kate was a tower of strength, despite being preoccupied to a great extent with her own affairs. I tried to take in what she told me about the legal process, but my head could have been stuffed with cotton for all I understood of it.

Meg and Susan frequently came and went. They took Davy to play with his cousins or the neighbours' children. They brought food I could hardly stomach, but I was grateful and dutifully ate what I could. 'For the sake of the little one', as I was told.

So the time dragged by. I was left to cobble together some sort of life for myself and Davy. And for the soon-to-be-born new baby.

I spent some days at the farm. Ma came down to Porthleven to visit when she could spare the time. I think Kate told her some kind of half-truth to explain why she was staying with me for such a long time. I seemed to be living a kind of a half-life. It was as though I was in a world of my own, behind a pane of glass, through which I noticed these things, but was distanced from them.

Having a child around helped me pull myself together eventually. I became more and more thankful to have Davy for comfort. He acted as a buffer against the darkest times when depression would descend all at once, like a grey fog – sapping my energy and isolating me in a world of my own.

My child had to be cared for. I had to feed him, play with him, talk, and even laugh, with him, however much I felt like crawling into bed and staying there. Several weeks passed after Joel's disappearance, but if anyone had asked me what I'd done in that time, I could not have said.

CHAPTER ELEVEN

KATE

I'd told Arthur I was going to finish my recuperation by staying with Loveday for a few days. She was expecting another child, I said. We would be mutually supportive. He'd made some cutting remark and was obviously fuming, but he could hardly remove me by force.

Then when the news about Joel came through, naturally I stayed on with my sister for comfort and companionship. The neighbours accepted the situation as only natural, there was no gossip Arthur could object to, so again he could do nothing. He didn't know I was planning never to come back.

So I watched Loveday going quietly about the house and I worried about her. The black of her mourning gown did nothing for her complexion and she drifted about like a small, white ghost.

She was *too* quiet. Too obedient. She simply ate what was put in front of her and went through the motions of normal life. She looked after Davy as devotedly as she'd always done and we celebrated his second birthday with a family tea-party. But there was something missing. She never seemed quite present, but dwelt in a place apart where I could not reach her. I'd no real idea what was going on behind the façade, in that small, neat head. I felt helplessly at a loss, and I began to fear for her mental state of health.

I also began to feel increasingly rootless myself, in my position of being neither married nor single. I drifted about on the fringes of Loveday's life, waiting for the bomb to drop, as it would when Arthur heard from the solicitor and discovered what I was doing.

I was beginning to wonder how long the whole business of the divorce would take, because I had very little money. I desperately wanted to go up to the villa and fetch all my expensive jewellery. Then I could pawn or sell it, and live on the proceeds.

There was no reason why I shouldn't just call in and take what I needed. I could do with some more clothes as well. So, what was stopping me? I realized when I thought about it, that it was a superstitious notion that if I set foot in that place again, something would happen to trap me there.

Stuff and nonsense! I told myself sternly. But even so, I chose a Wednesday morning when Maud would be at her meeting, and Arthur at work. I dragged myself up there, heart in my mouth in case I bumped into one of them after all. Then I scurried in, bundled up what I wanted and scurried out again, feeling like a thief.

One day however, the long-awaited letter arrived for me from Ernest Pascoe, the solicitor. My heart lurched as I opened it, for this was the first step in the momentous business that was about to change my entire life. I scanned the stiff, headed notepaper. It was offering me an appointment at his office in Truro.

Two days later I was hurrying up Lemon Street, scanning all the brass plaques for one bearing the right name. It was an elegant Georgian street, the businesses situated at its lower end gave way as it climbed the hill, to town houses of the well-to-do.

I was only vaguely aware of noise coming from the quay to my left, where ships from all around the world were disgorging their cargo with much shouting and clanging. I passed it without a second glance. Under normal circumstances I would have stopped and watched with interest. Instead, I was concentrating so hard on where I was going that I almost bumped into the man coming towards me.

'Whoa there, Kate Rosewarne!' A familiar voice hailed me. I jumped, startled, and spun round as a restraining hand was placed on my arm.

'*Jonathan*! Oh my goodness. I didn't expect to meet *you*.'

He tipped his hat and his eyes twinkled. 'Kate, you wouldn't have seen a coach and four if it came rattling towards you. What are you doing?'

I told him. 'Oh, it's on the other side of the street.' He pointed. 'The one on the corner with the green door.'

'Oh, right, thank you.' I looked up at him and smiled, but I hardly knew what to say next. His appearance had been such a surprise, I was still feeling flustered. However, he was saying something, so it didn't matter.

'Look, I'm free for a couple of hours. I've just come off duty.' Of course. I realized then, the Infirmary was only a stone's throw away. 'How would it be if we met for lunch after you've seen Ernest? Then you can tell me all about it.'

I felt a little lift of my spirits, and nodded vigorously. 'That would be lovely,' I answered. 'I'm sure I shall have a lot of questions to ask you. I feel so out of my depth about this whole thing, Jonathan.' I shrugged and spread my hands.

'Right then. I'll meet you at the Red Lion at one o'clock. I'll wait outside until you come.' He turned away with a smile and a nod as I paused to cross the road. 'Wait though,' he turned on his heel. 'Take my arm while you cross. There's so much traffic and it comes so fast down the hill.'

He looked right and left as I lifted my skirt to avoid the worst of the horse droppings. Then we threaded our away through the clamorous stream of carriages, delivery wagons, cabs and omnibuses to the other side.

Here we parted and I approached the solicitor's door with a spring in my step and extra colour in my cheeks.

I came out bursting with excitement and so glad there was going to be someone I could talk to. It was a couple of minutes after one, and when I arrived at the hotel I found Jonathan as promised, standing outside its impressive gabled frontage.

Sometimes when I stopped to think about it, I was amazed at how comfortable I always felt in Jonathan's company. And the ease with which our friendship progressed. As he crooked his arm and I placed my hand on it to go up the steps, I stole a sideways look at him.

He wore a three piece suit of charcoal grey today, with a gleaming watch-chain leading from the buttonhole of his lapel across to the waistcoat pocket. His stiffly-starched wing collar was a pristine white, as was the shirt. Absently, I wondered who did his washing for him. Maybe he used the steam laundry.

The initial impression I'd formed when I'd seen him in the hospital for the very first time, hadn't changed. I knew I could trust him totally. I felt I'd been looking for him all my life. I stole another glance at his profile. The narrow intelligent face with its straight nose, firm, determined jaw and neat moustache. He had a boyish flop of wavy brown hair which I saw as he removed his soft hat.

It looked so soft, his hair. I imagined how it would feel beneath my fingers. It would be silky to the touch . . . smooth. . . . Hastily I jerked my gaze away as Jonathan turned round. Had he seen me staring at him? Oh, how embarrassing. I felt my cheeks burning and lowered my head to unfasten my cloak as we were ushered to a table. Jonathan took it from me and hung it up.

I was wearing a slim costume of sage-green gaberdine, and had slipped on a light cloak of pale grey over it as it had looked like raining.

I was saving my news until we'd been served and the hovering waiter had taken himself off. Meanwhile we passed the time in small talk.

I was thinking how little I actually knew about his background, so I seized the opportunity to ask. 'What part of Surrey do you come from, Jonathan? And I don't know anything at all about your family, either.'

He drew in a breath. 'Well, I was brought up in Guildford. My father still lives there. He's a widower. My mother died while I was in Africa.'

He paused and his expression sobered. 'I've always regretted not seeing her once more. But it was a heart attack, very sudden. There was nothing I could have done even if I'd been there.' He paused.

'I also have a brother, George, married to Ellen. They live not far away from father, and have three children. Of course when Mama died, the shock for Papa was immense. He still refuses to leave the family home, although it's too big for him. It's because of the memories. He copes very well, considering.'

Our order arrived at that moment and Jonathan brought up the subject on both our minds before I did.

'Well then, how did you get on with Ernest?' He opened his napkin and picked up his spoon.

So over our mushroom soup and fresh crusty bread I told him the events of the morning. And how 'earnest' the man had been. I smiled as I recalled the solemn, dark-suited figure and his gloomy office.

'Well, he's not much like you, is he? Considering he's your relation. He seemed old-fashioned, I thought. Ernest by name and earnest by nature.' I laughed as I put down my spoon and broke a piece of bread.

'He struck me as rather – um – *disapproving*, too. In fact, he reminded me slightly of Arthur.' I wrinkled my nose in distaste.

Jonathan chuckled. 'You're right. Ernest's always been old. He was like that even as a small boy. I think he was *born* old.' He pushed aside his empty soup-plate and dabbed his mouth 'But he's a good solicitor. So, what did he say?'

I felt my face darken with annoyance. 'Well, at first he just looked down his long nose at me. As if I was something that had crawled out of the woodwork.' I glowered. 'I don't think he likes women much. He made it very clear that he was doing me a favour, and had only agreed to see me because of your request.' I finished my soup and sat back.

'Then he pulled out all these dusty great legal tomes and pored over them for ages, humming and hawing to himself. The room stank of tobacco fumes and it was full of fusty old furniture. I couldn't wait to get outside again.' I waved an imaginary fan under my nose.

'*But*,' I felt my face brighten, 'Jonathan, he did grudgingly admit that I had a case! Oh, he was as embarrassed as I was concerning the root cause.' I giggled. 'But he fluffed his way round it. And, bless his heart, he's going to start proceedings at once!' I clasped my hands together in delight. 'Oh Jonathan, I forgave him everything after that. I could even have hugged him, pipe smoke and all!'

'That's wonderful! So what's he going to do – write to Arthur?' Jonathan's eyes met mine.

'Yes, I gave him the address. Also Loveday's, so he can write to me there. Oh, I can't believe it's actually happening. It seems too much to hope for.' I shook my head and nibbled my bottom lip.

'And part of me is apprehensive too. It sounds too good to be true. I keep telling myself there's so much that could go wrong.' I lifted my eyes to his face. 'And now I've just got to wait.' I spread my hands wide. 'That's the hardest part!'

Then, amazingly, Jonathan reached for my hand and gave it a gentle squeeze. It was so fleeting, and over so quickly I might have imagined it. But, the tingling in my cheeks proved it hadn't been imagination.

'I'm sure it'll be worth the wait.' He nodded. 'I do have every confidence in Ernest, as I said.'

But I had another worry on my mind as well. I bent my head and began to pleat my napkin. 'Kate, what's the matter?' Amazing as it was, Jonathan had sensed my anxiety in a second.

'Oh, I was just thinking that – um – if he's that good a solicitor, I-I expect his fees are tremendous. I might have to look for some kind of . . . employment to cover the cost.' I bit my lip. 'I don't have very much money of my own, you see.' I was speaking almost to myself. Thinking aloud. 'Only what I could get for my jewellery.'

'Your *jewellery*?' Jonathan's eyes widened. 'You don't mean you've had to sell that to . . . to *live* on? Doesn't Arthur. . . ?'

My chin came up. 'I wouldn't lower myself to beg from him.' I felt my eyes flash with anger. 'I want to avoid all contact between us. And the jewellery means nothing to me. It was blood-money, Jonathan, expensive gifts to make him feel better about what he was doing to me.'

'How preposterous! The man's a monster!' Jonathan's face was thunderous. I nodded. 'Leave the fees to me, Kate.' He patted my hand. 'I can lend you what you need to tide you over. I'm not hard up – I've very little to spend my money on.' For an instant his expression was bleak. 'I would willingly *give* it to you, but I know you would hate to feel beholden.'

How understanding he was. How well he knew my character. I raised my eyes to his face. 'I can't tell you what that means to me, Jonathan.' I heaved a sigh of relief. 'Thank you so much.' I smiled as I added, 'And you're absolutely right, of course.'

His eyes twinkled and we sat back as our second course arrived. Then over the fresh fillets of Dover sole, I confided in him my worry over Loveday.

Jonathan squeezed lemon juice over his fish and listened closely.

'The grieving process takes time,' he replied. 'And the length of time varies with each individual.' He wiped his fingers and picked up his knife and fork.

'From what you've told me, I gather Loveday's getting plenty of support from relatives and neighbours. And having you staying with her must be the best comfort of all. She has someone to talk to if and when, she needs it. And she will do, Kate, once she's come to terms with her loss.' He nodded decisively. 'As I said, you just have to give her time.'

'I see. Thank you. That's very reassuring.' I toyed with my fish. 'I'm hoping they'll find Joel's body soon. So there can be a funeral. A proper goodbye, and an ending.'

'Absolutely. I entirely agree.' He pushed back his plate and reached for the menu card. 'Would you like a dessert?'

'Oh, no. No thank you.' I shook my head. 'I couldn't manage anything more. That was a delicious meal.'

He smiled. 'It was. A meal out with an attractive companion is a rare treat.'

I felt colour creeping up my neck at the unexpected compliment. I kept my eyes on my empty plate and fiddled with the cutlery, straightening it until it lay just so. 'And is there no – um – *regular* attractive companion?'

There, I'd said it. I had to ask. He was a good-looking man, and by his own admission, comfortably off. Such men didn't remain single except for a reason. I'd soon discovered that with Arthur to my cost. Now I wanted to find out where I stood with Jonathan. To *know*. Because I'd come to look upon him as a good friend. And lately, as someone to turn to for advice and guidance. Someone to lean on.

Jonathan's head was lowered, his napkin scrunched in his hand. 'There was someone once.' His voice was so low I had to strain to hear it. 'I thought – er – I thought she loved me. I thought I was in love with her.' He tossed aside the napkin and traced a pattern on the damask tablecloth with a fingernail.

'One day we became caught up in a street accident. A woman was knocked down by a horse as she was crossing the road. The animal's hoof caught her on the head. There was a huge gash. She was bleeding badly. I ran across to help. I urgently needed something to staunch the flow. I asked my – um – lady friend for the silk scarf she was wearing.'

He frowned and his lips narrowed. 'But she refused point blank. She clutched it to her and ran off, screaming. The woman died in the street where she lay.' Jonathan's shoulders heaved in a huge sigh.

'Later I received a letter telling me she could never live with a doctor. Her delicate constitution would be unable to withstand all the "unpleasantness" that went with my calling. I never saw her again.'

He looked up and smiled bleakly. 'So there we are. Since then I've lived the life of a bachelor. I have friends. I get by.' His face sobered.

I gazed at him with sympathy, my mind full of tumbling thoughts. A silence fell. Until I caught sight of a clock on the wall above Jonathan's head and gasped.

'Oh, look at the time! Jonathan, I must go. If I miss this train there's ever such a long wait for the next.' I moved to get up but Jonathan caught hold of my wrist.

'Just a minute, Kate. I've been thinking.' My brows rose and he met my eyes. 'We'd better not be seen together in public for the time being, you and I.'

My jaw dropped. 'Why ever not?' I frowned at him.

He smiled and shook his head. 'Not because I don't want to, believe me, but think about it.' He grasped both my hands and this time held them firmly as he looked fully into my face. 'If you're going through the divorce process we don't want to give Arthur any ammunition he can use against you, do we?'

He paused. 'For example, an occasion when you've been seen out with another man, a meeting which might suggest you're having an affair. If you were seen, who's to say you haven't been committing – um – adultery? Forgive me for being so blunt, Kate, but do you see what I mean?' He shook my hands, to drive home his point, then dropped them. He turned away to reach my cloak.

I held both hands to my burning cheeks. 'Oh, yes! Yes, of course. I hadn't thought of that.' More good advice. How would I have managed without him?

It was going to be hard. For Jonathan had become such a part of my life in the short time I'd known him. I knew how much I would miss his friendly company.

He leaned closer and whispered in my ear. 'But we can write to each other, remember? As often as we like. You will write, won't you? I shall be itching to know how things turn out for you.'

'Oh, yes, of *course* I will.' My mood lightened and I smiled broadly up at him as we parted and I hurried away.

A few days later, I was in Loveday's little kitchen, attempting to make a casserole. She'd taken Davy up to Pengarth for the day. I'd told her not to hurry back, hoping the visit would take her out of herself. It would certainly keep Davy occupied for a few hours. Then we could have the casserole later, when they came back. I was really enjoying trying my hand at cookery. I'd never had so much freedom to experiment before and I was totally absorbed in what I was doing.

Until a knock on the front door broke my thread of concentration. I made a gesture of annoyance, put the dish in the oven and wrenched off my apron. I would tell whoever it was that Loveday was out, and that would be it. Glancing at the clock as I went, I made a mental note of the time it would need to cook. And thinking of this made me totally unprepared for the visitor.

Arthur! My heart leapt and began drumming at my ribs. I felt all the colour drain from my face and my knees slackened. He could have been the devil incarnate. Standing on the threshold, his face brick-red, his eyes bulging, in his hand he was brandishing a large white envelope.

I gasped and recoiled. This was it, then. The confrontation I'd been waiting for and dreading.

Arthur pushed his way past me and entered the house. 'You hussy, you slut,' he spat, rounding on me, eyes blazing. 'What the hell's the meaning of this?' He stabbed the letter with a finger. '*Divorce* indeed! How *dare* you!'

I straightened my spine and lifted my chin high. Not by the slightest degree would I let him see how my legs were shaking. When I spoke, my voice was ice. 'Good morning, Arthur,' I managed. 'Do come inside, won't you?'

For an instant he looked taken aback. I noted with satisfaction the way his jaw dropped. He'd expected me to cringe. To cower. To plead. Hadn't he? My mouth tightened, and I glared at him.

He followed me into the sitting-room, still blustering. 'Without the slightest hint to me, with no consultation whatever, you take it into your head to go and . . . and . . . see a *solicitor*! You've discussed our personal, private life with a strange *man*?'

He took a step forward and reared menacingly over me. 'You must be out of your mind. You can't seriously imagine for one moment I would agree to such a thing?' He turned, his black eyes flashing sparks, and began to pace up and down.

'I shall tear this up of course, and explain that my wife has been very ill. That she's been suffering from delusions and is not responsible for her actions.'

'I don't think you will, Arthur.' My quiet, level tone was in direct contrast to his shouting and bluster.

I'd seated myself, ramrod straight, my hands folded in my lap, a picture of composure. I was determined to remain, at least outwardly, calm and collected. I knew my husband through and through. This would annoy him much more than a full-scale row.

'If you read the letter properly, you will see that my doctor is willing to speak for me, and that the medical evidence he can give, holds sufficient grounds to bring proceedings against you.'

'And what *grounds* are these, pray?' His lip curled in a sneer.

I drew in a breath. 'In case it has not already been made plain to you, the grounds are non-consummation of the marriage.'

Arthur sank heavily into a chair as if his legs would no longer support him. 'You wouldn't . . . you couldn't . . . you'd drag our private life out . . . to be picked over in *public*?'

His face had paled, and for the first time I saw fear in his eyes. It gave me the confidence to carry on. 'That would only happen if you choose to contest it, Arthur.'

He leaned closer, the black eyes boring into my skull. I steeled myself not to flinch. 'Don't think for a minute you can get away with this!' Flecks of spittle sprayed his moustache as he hissed at me.

'Oh, no. I'll bring all my influence to bear on you. That of my friends and associates too. I'll make damned sure this doesn't go any further.

'Anyway,' he smirked with an attempt at bravado, 'how do you think you're going to prove it, eh? Everything must have – um – healed up by now.'

'Oh, I can prove it.' I stared him down. 'I've already had the medical examination. Some months ago. And I've got a doctor's written report to back me up. Solid proof, Arthur. Besides a few other things it mentions.' I rose and stepped across the room, my hands raised, my fingers counting.

'Like grievous bodily harm. Like mental cruelty. Like denying me my natural desire – my marital right in fact – to have children.' I ticked the points off one by one. 'Do I have to go on?'

Arthur jumped up with a howl. 'You . . . you. . . .' He reached out an arm as if to grab me. I faced him down, unmoving. The arm fell helplessly to his side. He raised a fist instead and shook it in front of my face. I remained outwardly implacable.

'You bitch! You'll be the ruin of me!' He was snarling now, his face contorted with fury. 'After all I've done for you!' He jabbed a finger. 'You were a nobody until I married you. I raised you up in the world. As my wife you were somebody in the village.' He turned on a heel.

'And I gave you everything money could buy! Jewellery, beautiful clothes – I lavished them all on you. No expense spared. And *this* is how you treat me!' He was almost sobbing with self-pity. I threw him a look of contempt. What a pitiful, whining *coward!*

Then fury welled up and shattered my fragile composure at last. 'And I suppose you've forgotten how you made me suffer for it!' I blazed at him. 'Night after night for your perverted pleasure! My whole body raw and racked with pain. My flesh broken and bleeding.' I flung away with a swirl of skirts, balling my hands into fists.

'I put up with all of it because I thought I had no choice! That there was no other way. But now I *do* have that choice. And nothing is going stop me. Nothing. Do you understand?' I jabbed a finger under his nose.

'I'm not your *property* any longer, Arthur. You'll soon be receiving official papers stating the terms of the divorce. From now on our only communication is going to be through legal channels.'

He was pacing the room again. Running his hands through his hair as he went. 'But I'll never be able to hold up my head in the village again when this gets round,' he wailed. 'What am I going to *do*?'

He turned and spread his hands wide. 'And have you thought for one moment about what this will do to mother?' His eyes widened as his brows rose. 'The shock and disgrace could kill her.'

I almost burst out laughing. How *pathetic* the man was. The bully brought low – given a taste of his own medicine. Although he would never suffer half the pain I'd been made to suffer, whether physical or mental. I would carry the scars of both for the rest of my life.

Arthur carried on pacing the room. 'I shall be a laughing stock everywhere I go! I've just been accepted at a highly respectable gentlemen's club as well. I shall have to resign from that! Oh, you . . . you. . . . You've got a lot to answer for.' His face only inches from mine, he ground out the words through gritted teeth.

I tried to stare him down and not recoil from the blast of his hot breath. I was feeling sick to my stomach, but I must remain firm if I were to be free of him for ever. And surely anything was worth that. I drew a deep breath willing myself to keep calm.

'None of this need happen if you agree to go along with the divorce, Arthur.' I managed to retain my haughty stare. 'Yes you'll have to face the ignominy. But if you don't contest it, the *grounds* need never be made public.'

'Pah!' He flashed me a look of pure hatred. I could see the struggle he was having with himself. How he loathed the idea that I had the upper hand, that he'd lost control of me, for ever.

Without another word, he crammed his hat on his head and made for the door. He was halfway down the street before I recovered myself and stopped shaking in every limb.

I leaned against the back of the door after I'd closed it behind him, suddenly full of doubts. What if I had, as the old expression went, 'bitten off more than I could chew'? I imagined the unthinkable, that Arthur by some means would somehow manage to get the upper hand after all.

What if he could crush my pathetic bid for freedom. What if my case were thrown out and I had to go back to him and Rosewarne Villa. My stomach churned at the very thought. I would rather kill myself.

Then in the distant recesses of my mind I saw an image of Jonathan's smiling face – like a shining beacon in the distance. He was standing up for me. He believed in my case. I was *not* fighting this battle alone. Together, we would win through. I raised my head, straightened my spine and made my way down the passage.

Then I realized I could smell burning coming from the kitchen. My casserole! It was ruined. That was the last straw. My over-stretched nerves could take no more. I sank into a chair and burst into tears.

CHAPTER TWELVE

LOVEDAY

The fleet returned to port in early October, but there was no husband for me to welcome home this time. I stayed indoors and drew the curtains. I busied myself at the back of the house. Aching with loss as the shouts of joyful reunions rang through the street.

I knew that the village women whose husbands had returned safely in the normal way, felt awkward with me. They didn't know what to say when they met me in the street. People who formerly would have stopped and had a good chat, now passed the time of day politely enough, asked after my health, and scurried away.

For I was bereft, but not officially widowed. In a similar way, Kate was neither married nor single. Our lives weren't like anyone else's. Only Susan remained as supportive and cheerful as she'd always been, and I was grateful for it. And what it meant to have Kate living with me, I could not have put into words.

We must have seemed an unusual pair, 'they Trevarthen sisters', as I'm sure we were being called. The village was no doubt wondering why Kate was still with me, when her own home was so close. I'd been alone for long enough now to have come to terms with my loss. She could quite easily have gone to and fro on visits.

Mama too, was going to find Kate's position hard to understand. 'I shall have to tell her sooner or later,' Kate said one morning. 'Will you come with me, Loveday? Please? I shall need some moral support!' So the three of us went up to Pengarth together on the bus.

Arriving at the farm I was struck as I always was, by how little it had changed since we'd been children. It was a bright morning in mid-October, Pa was ploughing the lower field and I could hear his gentle voice encouraging the horses as he turned them on a bend. There was something restful about living close to the land, hard work though it was.

Rooks were squawking in the grove of sycamores beside the gate as they always had. The familiar sound took me straight back to childhood. I turned my face into the clean, fresh air of this windswept upland and sniffed appreciatively. It was a far cry from the fishy miasma that hovered around Porthleven.

A couple of Border collies came bounding out to meet us, followed by Ma coming to see what all the noise was about. There was the usual chatter and exchange of news as we gathered in the kitchen. Ma fussed over Davy, then me, making sure I was, yes really, thank you, all right. And Kate as well.

Then Davy trotted off to find Pa and we three women gathered round the big, brown teapot. I heard Kate beside me draw in a deep breath. With her eyes on the spoon as she stirred her tea, she broke the brief silence that had fallen.

'Ma, there's something I have to tell you.' I could feel the tension radiating from her. Her body was rigid and the spoon trembled slightly.

'Mm?' Ma put a steaming cup in front of me and sat down in her rocker, smoothing her apron.

'It's about Arthur. You see, I'm leaving him. I'm not going back to Rosewarne Villa. Ever. I've petitioned for a divorce. It's all going through.' Out it poured in a jerky, staccato tone.

'*What?*' Ma's eyebrows disappeared into her hairline. Her jaw dropped. Then she frowned. 'You wouldn't! I can't believe it. *Divorce?* Your own *husband?* What ever gave you such a preposterous idea!'

Kate's mouth tightened. 'Pure desperation, Ma. That's what drove me to it.' She glared. 'For years I've been trying to pretend, to cover up the true state of our marriage. For the sake of appearances. He damaged me, Ma. I almost died. I'm not going back to him. Ever.' She shook her head vigorously. 'And that's that.'

'B-but. . . .' Ma's mouth was opening and closing, but Kate hadn't finished.

'Arthur was a brute, Ma. And I mean that in the literal sense. I've been suffering from his brutality all this time. You know it was the cause of my illness, don't you?'

Ma stared at her and folded her arms. 'He knocked you around, you mean? But lots of husbands, I'm afraid . . . in drink. . . . Women just have to accept it as part of marriage.'

I broke in then. 'No, Ma, you don't understand. It was more than just beating. When Kate said "brutality" she meant just that. Think about it. And as for meekly "accepting" it, what would *you* do in the same circumstances?' Kate shot me a look of gratitude.

I watched as Ma's face turned bright red, then paled. Then she shook her head. 'But even so – to break your vows like that. Vows made before God. . . .' She pursed her lips and tutted. Kate and I exchanged glances and there was exasperation in her eyes. We both knew that, even now, Ma had not fully understood. Maybe such behaviour was totally outside her comprehension.

Incensed, Kate slammed a fist on the table. 'And what about the vows *he* made? After Arthur Rosewarne broke every rule in the book – you still condemn *me* for leaving him?' Eyes blazing, she rounded on Ma.

'But the scandal of it!' She sniffed and there was a dampness about her eyes. 'The shame! What will people think?' She fumbled for a handkerchief.

'And what about *me*, Ma?' Kate thumped her chest. 'Who matters most to you? Outside people or your own daughter?' Her mouth trembled.

Ma bridled and pursed her lips. 'Well, there's no need to take it like that. Of course families always stick together.' She lifted her chin. 'But what your father'll say I can't imagine.' She shook her head. 'It's going to take us both a long time to get over this.'

She stared at Kate as if she were a creature from another planet. Sadly I realized our mother's attitude towards 'appearances' was not so far removed from that of Maud Rosewarne. Maybe it was something peculiar to that generation of women. The way they'd been brought up by their parents. Who would have been early Victorians of course.

Ma's bosom was heaving with indignation. 'And how . . . how did you set about getting this – um – *divorce*?' She spoke the word with distaste. 'Arthur may be a solicitor, but *you* know nothing of legal matters.'

'I have a friend I met in the hospital.' Kate lowered her head and stirred her tea round and round. So far, none of us had drunk any of it. 'The doctor who was attending me. His name's Jonathan Roberts. It was he who told me I had grounds – because of my injuries. He's been immensely helpful. I could never have gone through with this if it hadn't been for Jonathan.'

Ma's brows rose. 'Hmm. Jonathan, is it? A new friend, eh?' She gave Kate a long look. The words, 'It didn't take you long to find another man, did it?' hung unspoken in the air. 'A doctor?' She nodded. 'That's a very respectable position.'

We exchanged knowing glances, Kate and I, and she quirked an eyebrow. 'You'd like him, Ma. He's a perfect gentleman. A genuine one. Not like Arthur, all charm on the surface and rotten underneath. And he's just a friend.' Kate threw her a warning look.

'Hmm.' Ma fell silent and picked up her tea, obviously mulling it all over. She was just drawing breath to say something when the door flew open and Davy came running in. Full of excitement and chatter about what he'd seen on the farm. So the subject changed and soon afterwards we left.

A few days later, Kate and I were sitting in the parlour chatting one afternoon. She was asking me a question, but the reply died on my lips as my attention was distracted by a movement outside.

Bill Mitchell. My heart began to thud. For the harbourmaster was heading up the path towards my door. Memories of the last time he'd called came flooding back and I swallowed on a throat gone suddenly dry.

'Loveday?' I heard Kate's voice, but I was already on my way down the passage.

'There's been some news?' I asked. Just a glance at his grave expression and I felt all the colour draining from my face. Automatically I led him into the kitchen, the most comforting room in the house. I sensed I was going to need comfort. For the man's visit could only mean one thing. Kate came out of the parlour and on seeing who it was, followed behind us.

'Yes,' he said briefly, 'I'm afraid so. Mrs Penrose. I'm so sorry.' He pulled out a bentwood chair and sat down, nodding towards Kate as he did so. I sank down in my rocker by the range. My knees had turned to jelly.

'I'm glad you're here, Miss Kate. I'm sure you can both guess why I've come.' He placed his hat on the table and glanced at me.

'Joel's been found, hasn't he?' I whispered.

Bill Mitchell pulled his chair nearer and nodded. 'His body's been washed up off Lowestoft, my dear. I can't tell you how sorry I am.' Awkwardly he patted my shoulder. I'd known all along he wasn't coming back, hadn't I? So this news shouldn't have come as a shock, but it did; the finality of it hit me like a hammer blow. I covered my face with my hands and bent my head as huge sobs threatened to choke me.

Kate knelt down on the hearth-rug and placed both arms around me. 'You're – you're quite sure it is Joel?' She stared up at the man. 'There's no mistake?

'Quite certain.' He nodded. 'I had it from one of the men Joel did business with at the fish market. He's known him for years. They were very friendly and always had a drink together, you know?' He spread his palms. 'He formally identified Joel and he's seeing to all the arrangements at that end. He's also offered to escort the – um – body home.'

'That's really kind of him,' Kate said, as the man rose to his feet. 'I'm sure my sister will thank him personally when he gets here.'

I raised my head as she glanced towards me. 'I knew he was dead.' My voice broke. 'Right from the beginning, I knew. But I'm so *glad* he's been found. Now we can lay him properly to rest.' I turned my heaving shoulders into Kate's embrace again.

But I could hear Davy calling me from the other room. If I didn't answer he would come to find me. Not wanting him to see me like this, I pulled myself together, wiped my eyes and straightened up.

I dragged myself to my feet and held out a hand to the harbourmaster. 'Thank you so much for coming, Mr Mitchell, and for all your kindness. You'll be in touch when – when. . . ?'

'My condolences, Mrs Penrose.' He bowed over my hand. 'And you know if there's anything further I can do, you have only to ask.' I nodded dumbly.

'I'll see you out.' Kate followed him down the passage and I heard the door close. It seemed to close a chapter of my life.

What was I to do now? How could I go on without him? Joel had been my prop and mainstay. My reason for living. All I'd ever wanted. I felt like a small, vulnerable creature whose protective shell has been ripped away. True, he had always been absent for long periods, but not like this. This was the final absence. If it hadn't been for Davy and the coming little one I would gladly have followed him into the sea.

I was back in the rocker when Kate returned to the kitchen. Davy had taken himself off to play outside. Tears were streaming silently down my face, there seemed to be no end to them. Kate knelt down and took my cold hands in hers, squeezed them, then rose to her feet.

'You just stay there, Loveday, and don't worry about a thing.' She opened the door of the range, poked up the coals and pulled the big, black kettle across to boil.

'Tea, I think. Then I suppose we must think about ... um ... arrangements.' Kate bustled about the kitchen, rattling dishes, talking over her shoulder. 'After that I'll go up to Pengarth and tell Ma and Pa.'

She was all action and chatter. I suppose she thought it would help, would take me out of myself, but I scarcely heard her.

Kate placed a steaming mug on the hearth at my feet. I followed the move and caught sight of Joel's pipe and spill jar he always kept there, ready to hand. The familiar, homely objects set me off again and a fresh rain of tears poured down.

Kate was pacing the room, talking as she went. 'We'll have to ask the undertaker to call when you're strong enough. And remember to put up a card outside the Fisherman's Rest when we know the details. And a notification in the newspaper. There's such a lot to think about, but the undertaker'll see to most of it, of course.'

I dried my eyes and tried to think straight. 'I'm so glad you are here, Kate,' I whispered. 'I'm really going to need your help, and everybody else's, to get over the next few weeks.'

She gave me a quick hug. 'That's what sisters are for.' She smiled tenderly. 'It won't be the first time we've weathered a storm together, will it?'

*

A few days later the undertaker called. The coffin had arrived safely and he was awaiting my instructions for the funeral service.

Our eyes met. 'First of all, I want to see Joel. For the last time. To say goodbye,' I told him.

The man took a step back and frowned, looking ill at ease. I gestured him towards a chair. He sat down, twisting his black hat in his hands for a moment, then cleared his throat.

'No, Mrs Penrose.' He slowly shook his head. 'I'm afraid that's not possible. You wouldn't want to see him, um, as he is now.' He raised his head. 'After being in the water so long, you understand? Better to remember him as you knew him in life.'

My stomach turned over as his meaning suddenly hit me. Somehow the reality of it had passed me by. I imagined Joel would be lying peacefully as if asleep. As I'd always known him, but cold. He would be lying in a padded box like a bed, his beard and moustache neatly combed and his hair likewise – his thick and lovely blond hair. I would lay my hand on his forehead and gently stroke it back from his eyes. He would be looking as if at any moment he would wake up, smile and speak to me.

If only . . . I bit down hard on my bottom lip, but I would not weep now. I had the rest of my life in which to weep.

I thought of his big hands. I wanted to hold them in mine. They'd been such capable hands, tender enough to stroke my face, strong enough to haul in a net full of fish and yet clever enough to chisel wood into useful articles for our home.

He was now as cool and smooth as marble. 'Oh Joel, I'm sorry,' I whispered in my head. 'Sorry for everything I did: about Davy and that I deceived you so. I'm sorry I ever doubted your love for me.'

Then I felt the baby move inside me. 'And now you'll never have a chance to see your own child.' I started and came back to the present moment, fighting against the lump in my throat.

Like an automaton I dealt with the undertaker's questions. What I couldn't manage, Kate filled in for me. And after the man had gone I gave way to the tears which flowed relentlessly down my face. I lacerated myself with grief, guilt and anguish.

'Oh, Joel!' I sobbed. 'Kate, he never knew how much I loved him!'

I felt her hand on my shoulder. 'He knew,' she whispered, and rocked me in her arms. 'Of course he did. I always envied you the love you shared. It shone out of him, Loveday, out of you both. Did you truly never know?'

'But we never made it up between us . . . we parted in coldness . . . in anger. I never had time to ask his forgiveness . . . or for him to give it. Now I shall never know!' I looked at her in despair.

'Loveday, listen to me.' She pulled me round to face her and looked steadily into my eyes. 'Joel would have forgiven you *anything*. I know he would. So does Meg. Ask her if you don't believe me.'

'B-but she doesn't know about Davy.' I lifted my shoulders and spread out my palms in frustration. 'Nobody knows. Not any more. Only you.' I sank my face into my hands and nothing could comfort me.

I had imagined that Joel's funeral would be a quiet family affair, but I'd been quite wrong. It was nothing of the kind. Most of the village turned out to pay their respects to one of their own. The fleet stayed in port that day, and an air of unusual solemnity hung over Porthleven.

As I stepped out from home and the cortege left for the service there was a crowd lining the quay. Several familiar faces caught my eye; with their heads bent they were silent witnesses showing how popular Joel had been. Even in my distress, however, I started and drew in a quick breath as I caught sight of two figures standing apart from the rest, watching.

Abe Russell and Billy. Even through my heavy veil, I knew for a split second that our eyes had met. What had brought *them* here? Conscience? Guilt? Regret? I would never know, but I felt strangely heartened. Our old enemies, Joel's and mine, must have had a touch of compassion in them somewhere after all. I saw Abe snatch off his greasy cap and give his brother a nudge to do the same. Then we moved on and left them behind in the crowd.

'I hadn't realized how popular Joel was,' I remarked to Meg. My sister-in-law and Kate were seeing to the refreshments that followed the service. We were holding the reception in the Sunday School room of the Methodist chapel. Davy was being looked after by Susan

Trembath, whose husband was one of the bearers.

'That's like 'tis when you've been born and raised in the village.' Meg's eyes were red-ringed and tearful. 'People think of him as one of their own, you see. They do know the same thing could happen to any of them just as suddenly.'

I nodded and looked around at them all. My eyes filled at the quiet kindness of these people. Now I was actually widowed, all the former awkwardness had vanished. Some of them I hardly knew, but they were constantly coming forward with condolences and offers of help.

Then Kate materialized at my elbow with a plate of saffron buns in one hand. In the other were slices of the Cornish fishermen's traditional 'hevva' cake, with its criss-cross decoration of fishing net. 'Do you want something to eat, Loveday?'

I shook my head. I felt as if food would choke me. 'No thanks. But Kate, I really appreciate all you're doing.'

She shrugged and smiled. She was about to turn away when our attention was drawn to two old ladies who were sitting in a nearby corner. With their backs to us, the black plumes on their hats bobbing as they sipped their tea, they were obviously enjoying a good gossip. Then we overheard some of what they were saying.

'Here, I heard that Maud Rosewarne have passed away,' one said. The plate in Kate's hand jerked. A couple of buns fell unheeded to the floor.

'Never! Have she?' came the reply. The tea-cups tinkled.

'Ess. Last night, so they say. But she been in hospital a day or two.'

'That's right.' The plumes nodded. 'She were took sudden. With a h'apoplexy, so they said.'

'Come to think of it, I seen her daughter-in-law in here just now. 'Tis her sister's husband's funeral, see.'

Her companion took a mouthful of tea. 'Hard luck on she, then. Two deaths in one week, poor soul.'

'Ess,' chimed in a third voice. 'But know, did you,' her voice lowered an octave and she raised a hand to shield her mouth. I craned my neck to hear better. Beside me, Kate was rigid, a frozen expression on her white face. 'I heard a rumour that she've left her husband.'

'Left him! What – Mr Rosewarne you mean?'

'Ess. Him. With all his money and that great house too.' The plumes nodded faster.

'She never have! Oh, my dear life. The woman off her head is she?'

The plumes closed together in a huddle. 'Whatever's the world coming to?' Then someone spoke to me and the rest of the conversation was lost.

Kate clutched my arm and jerked her head to indicate the back room. She meant we could talk privately there behind the great tea-urn. I nodded as I rose to my feet. Then all of a sudden I seemed to be dizzy. The room began to float around me. I was making my way towards a chair when suddenly I gasped.

'Loveday! What's the matter?' Kate turned to me in concern.

'I felt a . . . pain.' I flinched and put a hand to my lower back.

Kate's brows disappeared into her hairline. 'No! You mean – the *baby*?'

I nodded, biting my lip. The flash of pain had receded to a dull ache. Fear clenched my stomach and I grasped the back of the chair to steady myself. 'I think it might be.'

CHAPTER THIRTEEN

KATE

Loveday had arranged some time ago that she would go up to Pengarth to have the baby there. It seemed the most sensible thing, Ma said, so that she could look after both her and Davy.

So she went with them directly from the funeral. I went back to the cottage and collected what Loveday would need. Fortunately she had prepared well in advance, packing for herself and Davy as well as baby-clothes for the new-born infant. So I collected up the bags and followed on the omnibus.

There was no reason why I shouldn't stay up there as well. I was feeling completely rootless, my life on hold, like a soul in limbo while I waited for news. If I could make myself useful, so much the better. I would serve a purpose and the time would pass all the quicker.

But after the first few warning pains, there was a lull in Loveday's condition. Relaxed and resting in bed, she had got over the initial shock. Now we were all just waiting for what was to come.

I was sitting at her side, talking over the events of the morning. And of my astonishment at Maud's death. 'That's one funeral I *shan't* be going to,' I remarked. 'Do you know, I can't remember Maud ever saying a kind word to me? In all the time I lived there.'

'That's really sad.' Loveday's pale face was solemn. 'That a person should only be remembered for their nastiness.'

I nodded and there was a pause. But there was something on my mind that was giving me no peace and I had to talk about it. 'Loveday,' I looked down at my lap and twisted my hands, 'I can't help thinking I was partly responsible for Maud's death.'

'*What?*' A look of amazement crossed her face. 'Why on earth should you be?'

'You heard what those old biddies said. She died of apoplexy. And that could have been from shock. Shock of hearing about me. . . .' I frowned.

'You remember what Arthur said, don't you?' I leaned closer and clutched her arm. 'Something about . . . "what this will do to mother" . . . and I laughed at him, Loveday!' I bit my lip as I gazed at her. 'It *must* have been because of me, the more I think about it. Maud never had a day's illness in her life.'

Loveday's eyes flashed with indignation and she sat up straighter. 'For goodness sake, Kate, you can't *really* blame yourself? Don't get so wound up! Maud was an old woman. She could have died for any number of reasons.'

I wanted to believe her, but I was finding it hard to convince myself. I nibbled a thumbnail. Loveday must have seen my dubious expression for she leaned over and placed a hand on mine.

'Listen. You haven't the slightest shred of evidence that Arthur even *told* his mother.' Her eyes bored into mine. 'I can't imagine he would have been in a hurry to do so, would you? He's got too much to lose once the news gets round.' She shook my arm for emphasis.

I gave her a long look. I suppose what she was saying did make sense. I felt a bit better. Loveday must have noticed, for she repeated her assurance. 'Get it into your head that it's not *your fault*. None of it is, Kate. Believe it.'

I sighed. Then shrugged and gave a rueful smile. 'I was just thinking . . . here we both are, look at us. Flaying ourselves with guilt over things which were never our fault in the first place.

You were like that over Joel, when what you did was only ever out of love, and to spare his feelings. And I'm taking the blame for Arthur Rosewarne's innate perversions, aren't I?'

'Absolutely.' Loveday nodded vigorously. Then her eyes widened and she took in a sharp breath.

'What's the matter? A pain?' I jerked myself back to the present.

She bit her lip. 'Yes. A sharp one. I think it's really starting now.' She shifted uncomfortably.

I jumped to my feet and made for the door. 'I'll go and tell Ma. We must send for the midwife.'

Loveday's labour went on all that night. The following day dawned with still no relief from her agony. More hours passed. The doctor came and went. The midwife came and stayed. Ma and I hovered around, feeling helpless, watching the writhing figure on the bed and willing it all to be over soon.

Loveday seemed to be trapped in some hideous nightmare as she thrashed about, shouting and crying. Another scything pain left her gasping for breath. Then, as her body contorted with another spasm, she gave a shriek. The shriek turned into a pitiful sob, then a groan. At last with one long shuddering breath, the baby came plunging forth.

Loveday slumped back on to the pillow, exhausted. But instead of relaxing after her ordeal, she began to writhe and flail her arms. Clutch at the bedcovers, mutter to herself. The midwife put a hand to my sister's hot forehead. Then shook her head in concern.

We stood helplessly by while the fever mounted. The doctor was recalled. Delirious, Loveday thrashed from side to side. Through her muttering and shouting, I caught the words, '. . . dead . . . another. . . .' Then she screamed, 'Kate!'

I bent to her and clasped her hot, dry hands; she was burning up. 'I'm here darling, I'm here. Loveday, open your eyes.'

But she was heedless of everything from the cooling cloths we placed on her forehead to the words of comfort and encouragement we uttered. Then at last the thrashing ceased and, exhausted by her struggling, she lay motionless.

'I'm so worried about her, doctor.' Ma said, with me at her elbow, looking down at the bed. Loveday was as limp as a rag doll, her rasping breath the only sign of life.

'Mm.' The doctor put away the stethoscope he'd been using. 'Your daughter's suffering from puerperal fever, ma'am. Sometimes it does follow childbirth, you know? Where there's been an infection.' He snapped shut the clasp of his black bag, and stood up.

'But,' I broke in, 'this seems to have affected her mind as well.' I gained his attention. 'She doesn't recognize us or respond to our voices. Is that usual?'

'Fever leads to delirium, madam. Your sister's been under a lot of strain, of course. From the shock of her husband's death. She was probably in a run-down state of health even before the actual birth. She would have had little stamina for such a difficult delivery.'

He reached for his bag. 'You must keep her cool. Sips of water – as much as she'll take. Wipe her down with damp cloths. And wait for the fever to break. When it does, she should be over the worst. That's all we can do, I'm afraid. Just wait.'

He picked up his hat. 'I'll call in again tomorrow.' He looked worn out himself as he turned to Ma. 'The baby's all right, I trust?'

'Oh yes, he's a fine little fellow. But with his mother like this. . . .' She spread her hands and sighed, 'we shall have to engage a wet-nurse. Not knowing how long Loveday will be . . . or if she'll be able. . . .'

She raised sunken eyes to his face; the strain was telling on her as well. 'Anyway, thank you for coming, doctor. I'll see you out.' She followed him down the stairs.

I sat on the edge of the bed and took Loveday's flaccid hand in my own. I put my face on the pillow close to my sister and whispered in her ear. 'Loveday, it's Kate. Wake up. Open your eyes. Speak to me.'

But she only began her restless tossing and turning again – moaning and crying pitifully. She muttered weakly to herself. 'Punishment! Dead! No! Another one. My fault!'

Then suddenly she jerked her head from the pillow. Her eyes snapped open, but they were blank and unseeing. 'Kate. Where's Kate? I want Kate!' Tears came pouring down her haggard face. She sank back again.

I tried once more. 'Loveday darling, I'm here.' I squeezed her hand. 'Feel me. I'm right beside you. Look at me. Please.'

But she was somewhere else, locked in her nightmare world. It was heartbreaking. I was almost in tears myself.

It went on all night. I sent Ma to bed. She needed the rest more than I did. I stayed in the chair at the bedside, occasionally dozing off for a while, then jerking awake to change the damp flannel I'd placed on Loveday's brow.

In the early hours of the morning I rose, stiff from being in one position. I must have slept for a longer stretch that time. I went across to the wash-stand for some more cool water, and as I paused to wring out the cloth I glanced towards the window. There, through a crack in the curtains, I could see that dawn was breaking. I pulled them wider apart and leaned on the sill to look out.

In the distance, the twin hills of Godolphin and Tregoning still hunched darkly to the west. Towards the east however, I could just see a bar of pearly-grey light that was gradually gaining strength and moving up the sky. The long night was over. I rested my face against the cool glass and watched it for a while.

I returned to the bedside to lay the cloth on my sister's hot brow and gave a start – Loveday was feeling cooler. Wasn't she? I laid a hand on her cheek. It was cooler. Her skin was moist. The fever must have broken! Oh, thank you God, thank you!

'Ma! Quick. Come quickly.' I was across the room and calling down the stairs. Ma's face appeared at the bottom, white and frightened. 'No, don't worry.' I hastened to reassure her. 'It's good news. The fever's broken. Loveday's going to get better!'

'Oh, thank the dear lord for that!' She bunched her skirts and came hurrying up the stairs.

'She's sleeping, look.' I pointed. 'Peacefully. Normally.' As Ma's face lit up with joy, I threw my arms around her neck and we hugged each other close. All our former animosity had vanished in the light of what had so nearly happened in this room. At least, I felt like that and I'm pretty sure Mama did too. The thin line between life and death had put our differences in perspective.

We left the room together and quietly shut the door. Over breakfast we chatted normally, comfortable with each other. Later on Ma looked at me with real gratitude in her eyes and said, 'Oh, Kate, I can't tell you how good it is to have you here.'

Slumped in a chair at the kitchen table, she leaned her face on her hand. 'I feel exhausted enough as it is. I should have been run ragged without you, what with looking after Davy and the baby, and tending to Loveday too. Even if she hadn't been taken so ill.' She smiled wearily.

'And thank you so much for sitting up with her last night. Even so,

I couldn't sleep for worry, even when I was in bed.' She smiled wanly and passed a hand over her forehead.

'That's all right, Ma. I'll stay until she's strong enough to go back home.' I rose to my feet. 'And right now I'll see to that pile of ironing.' I'd caught sight of the big wicker flasket brimming with clean washing.

Ma gave me a grateful smile. 'Where's Davy now?' I asked as I put the flat iron to heat on the range.

'Pa's taken him to see the new piglets. He's been very good with taking Davy off my hands, but we're neither of us getting any younger. Davy's been fractious too, not understanding what's wrong with his mother.' As I shook out a shirt ready for ironing, Ma stood up to unroll the old blanket she used to protect the table.

'He's very taken with the baby, though.' I wiped the plate of the iron and began to smooth the shirt. 'I took him in again last evening, and he was talking away to it like anything.'

'Poor little mite.' Ma's face fell. 'He keeps asking when he can go home.' She sniffed. 'He seems to think Joel will be there when they get back.'

I changed the cooling iron for another from the range. 'It's a good thing in a way that he's used to Joel being away at sea for long periods.'

Ma nodded. 'I suppose so.' She crossed the room. 'I'll look in on Loveday again and see if she's awake yet.'

'No, you stay here. I'll go while the iron's re-heating.' I hung up a nightgown to air on the rack above the range. 'You're worn out from trailing up and down those stairs.' And the way that she meekly did as she was told, proved to me how right I'd been.

When I returned to the bedroom, Loveday was lying on her back, her eyes wide open, staring at the ceiling. With tears running down her face and soaking into her hair.

'Loveday, darling, you're awake! But what is it?' I knelt at the bedside and took her hand.

She grasped it like a lifeline and half raised her head. 'Oh, Kate,' she sobbed.' My baby. Tell me the truth. It *is* dead, isn't it?'

'Dead?' I frowned. A spasm of fear ripped through me. Had the fever damaged her mind? I stared at her, horrified, as the words brought back a fleeting memory of the shipwreck. I passed her a handkerchief and she wiped her eyes with a shaking hand. 'Loveday, dear, you've got a little son.'

'Yes, yes. I know. Davy.' Her voice was fretful. 'I'm not out of my wits, Kate. I mean the baby I've just given birth to.' She spoke slowly as if to an imbecile. 'The one who should be here, beside me in his crib. The one who d-died.'

I put a finger under her chin and turned her so that we were eye to eye. 'Loveday, listen to me. You gave birth to a healthy little son. Since then you've been very ill for several days, with a fever.

Ma and Pa and I have been looking after you, Davy and the new baby. I've been staying here to help. Until you were better. Until now. Do you understand?' I spoke slowly as if to a child.

Loveday's eyes widened. 'But I heard . . . I felt . . . it was horrible! Oh, Kate, do you really mean it?' A trembling smile crossed her face through the tears, like a rainbow through a sun-shower.

I nodded. 'You were delirious, Loveday. You had nightmares. It sounds as if you thought you were back in that other time . . . when Davy. . . .' I pressed her hand and withdrew it. 'Wait there, I'll be back in a second.'

As if she were going anywhere! I laughed at myself, with relief as much as anything, as I went to fetch the baby. I laid the small white bundle gently in her arms and stood back. 'Here he is, Loveday, your new little baby. Your very own son.' Our eyes met in mutual understanding. There was no need for words.

Loveday's face was transformed as she gazed and gazed at the infant. At last she turned to me, and all her soul was in her eyes.

'Look at him, Kate, just look.' Her voice was scarcely above a whisper. 'Isn't he exactly like Joel?' She stroked the tiny head. 'See that tuft of blond hair? Those sea-blue eyes? He's the image of him!' She cuddled the baby close.

'And I'll tell you something.' Her eyes were huge in her pale face. 'All through the birth, through all those hours of pain and agony, I could feel Joel close to me. Urging me to carry on when all I wanted to do was give in and join him.

All through the nightmares, and the hallucinations while I was dreaming that this little one had died, I saw it as my punishment for deceiving Joel so. But he came to me, Kate, truly, I know he did. He was watching over me. I could feel the warmth of his love.' Her voice trembled. 'And of his forgiveness.' She laid a gentle hand against the baby's cheek. 'And now I can see why. Because look, he's been brought back to me!'

A silence fell, broken only by the baby's soft snuffling breath. I turned away, my eyes full of unshed tears. I couldn't bear to watch any longer. However much she'd suffered for it, I couldn't help but envy my sister her little family.

'Have you thought yet what you're going to call him?' I swallowed and straightened the covers, then busied myself about the room.

Loveday's voice was dreamy and she seemed half-asleep. 'I shall call him after his father.' She paused. 'But as there could never be another Joel for me, he'll be known as Joe.'

I went back to the cottage later to make sure everything was all right there, and to pick up the post. There was only one letter, and it was addressed to me. It was from Stephens, Rosewarne and Vigus: Arthur's firm!

My heart was thudding as I picked it up off the mat. I turned it over and hastily slit the envelope. Several sheets of heavy cream notepaper crackled as I drew them out. I scanned the long-winded legal jargon, not understanding half of the Latin terms with which it was peppered. Then took it with me into the parlour where I sat down and read it more closely.

It concerned conditions of settlement. I could make out that much. Then I drew in a swift breath and clapped a hand to my mouth. I couldn't believe what I was reading. . . .

I needed advice. I couldn't cope with this on my own. My mind was in a whirl – Jonathan. I would write to Jonathan. I glanced at the clock. If I posted a letter to him right away he would get it in the morning. I hastened off in search of pen, ink and paper.

I hadn't expected him to turn up in person. My jaw dropped in amazement when I saw his familiar figure standing on the doorstep. Then as our eyes met I felt the magnetic current of his personality. I both marvelled at, and was irritated by the power this man had to pull me towards him without either of us moving an inch.

'For the sake of the neighbours,' he jerked his head towards a knot of interested women on the quayside, 'I'm your doctor. I was visiting "Sea Winds", my sister's home in Penzance, and I've called in to give you a final check-up.'

I laughed and relaxed. 'I'm so *glad* to see you.' He removed his soft hat and bent his head under the low lintel. 'Come through.'

'It's very quiet.' He looked around. 'Where's your sister?' He lifted one of Davy's toys from the sofa in the parlour and sat down.

'Oh, Jonathan,' I sank into my former seat, beside him. 'I've such a lot to tell you I hardly know where to begin. I know I told you about Joel in my last letter, didn't I?' He nodded slowly. 'A sad business. How is Loveday now?'

I proceeded to give him a brief account of all that had happened. For he knew nothing of Loveday's baby, or her illness. And certainly not that Maud had died.

'Goodness, I see what you mean.' His eyes widened in surprise, then with sympathy. He leaned across the space between us and clasped my hand. 'Oh, Kate, you poor little thing! I thought how tired you were looking. Now I can see why.'

I nodded, my gaze on our linked hands. His kindly concern had brought a lump to my throat. In another moment I would be weeping on that comforting tweed-clad shoulder so close to mine. I turned away before he saw how affected I was.

I cleared my throat and picked up the letter. 'Look what I've just had from Arthur's firm.' I waved it under his nose. 'Do you think it's legal for him to represent himself?'

Jonathan shrugged. 'I don't really know, but it would certainly be more ethical to use one of the other partners.' He looked over my shoulder as I opened the envelope and handed him the document.

'This is laying out Arthur's terms for the settlement. But it's so wrapped up in legal jargon I wanted you to read it. To make sure I've understood it.'

'You look very excited about it,' Jonathan remarked with a wry smile. I knew my eyes were sparkling and I was fidgeting in my seat and he must have noticed. He was sharply observant, it was part of his character. Being a doctor he needed to be, I suppose. I knew those steady brown eyes rarely missed anything.

'I am. Look at this paragraph here,' I pointed.

'Wait. I must start at the beginning.' Jonathan was painfully methodical. Another aspect of his medical training, presumably. I had to control myself while he turned back to the first page. He read every word slowly and meticulously, he would not be hurried. Eventually he came to the clause I'd mentioned.

'This is why I'm so excited. Look.' I pointed. 'Jonathan, is he *really* offering me Rosewarne Villa as part of the settlement? He is, isn't he?'

Jonathan frowned, then scanned the clause a second time. Then he nodded. 'Oh yes, that's right enough. And a fairly hefty sum of money, too. I didn't realize he was such a wealthy man.' He looked up from the page and our eyes met.

'Oh, believe me, he is.' I glanced away. I was only half-listening, nibbling my lip as my mind raced. This was momentous news and I was thinking of the implications of it.

'So that means Arthur must be planning to leave Porthleven for good.' My brows rose. 'Loveday said she thought he would. Because of the scandal. And of course, now Maud's gone there's nothing to keep him here.'

'That's right.' Jonathan grunted, still deeply absorbed. He turned a page. 'Mm. The condition he makes, is that the divorce should be settled out of court and nothing made public.' He looked up and smiled. 'All this generosity is to tempt you, or bribe you, whichever way you look at it, into accepting his terms.'

'Actually they were *my* terms.' I said firmly, pointing a finger at myself. 'I told him he could save face by not contesting it. So he obviously decided in the end to give in quietly. Then sneak away and start a new life.'

I paused to think about it. 'I can imagine the struggle he must have had with himself.' I didn't know whether to laugh or cry at the poignancy of it. 'It must have been a real blow to his pride. Letting me get my own way!'

Any sense of triumph I felt though was tinged with bitterness: how very different our marriage could have been if my husband hadn't been such a warped individual!

Jonathan had obviously noticed my change of expression. 'Is something the matter, Kate?' He looked at me with concern.

'I was just wondering what made Arthur into the person he is.' I nibbled a a thumbnail and my gaze was far away, trying to imagine him as a small boy. 'Do you think he was just born with an evil streak in him?'

'Unlikely, I'd say.' Jonathan shook his head. 'In my experience, children are born innocent; it's the way the world treats them that forms character.'

'Well, going to boarding school at the age of seven may have contributed a lot to that.' I'd learned that much from Arthur in the early days when he was courting me. In a rare moment of closeness, he told me too about a nanny who'd been dismissed without a reference. He'd cut the story off short, and refused to be drawn further, but I'd wondered then why she had been.

'Oh, boarding school, was it?' Jonathan's face darkened. 'I've met men who have told me horrific tales of what can go on in some schools. And Arthur I imagine, was a cherished only child. To be thrown to the wolves as it were, must have been shattering at that age.'

'He *was* severely bullied there, I know.' I nodded slowly. 'Then his father died when he was thirteen, you see. He told me that, during one of the few normal conversations we had. I had the impression Arthur had idolized his father.'

Jonathan grunted, 'Mm. Not that anything condones his adult behaviour, I've nothing but outrage for a man who behaved as he did. But you can see in his background reasons for why he grew up as he did. Bullying begets more bullies.'

A small silence fell as we both sank into our own thoughts. Then I glanced towards Jonathan to find him gazing steadily at me. 'So, not only will you soon be a free woman, but one of means as well.'

I held his gaze. My outward calm gave away nothing of the turmoil inside me. For the villa was mine! I could do what I liked with it! What I wanted! A surge of excitement swept through me and I felt my eyes begin to sparkle. For I knew exactly what I wanted.

'Of course, you'll sell the place,' Jonathan remarked. 'It must be worth a small fortune to the right person. With that fabulous view. You'll be extremely well off then, Kate.'

I came back to earth with a bump. Jonathan had risen and crossed the room. He was looking out of the window at the boats bobbing in the harbour on the incoming tide.

He half-turned. 'It's really nothing more than a great white elephant. You'd never dream of going back to live in that great place on your own, would you?' He smiled and came back into the room. 'I don't suppose you ever want to see it again. It must be so full of painful memories.'

'No, Jonathan. I'm not going to put it up for sale.' I kept my eyes downcast so he should not see my excitement.

'*Wh-what*? But . . . you're never keeping it! You're *not* going back there to live, are you?' He goggled at me as if I were mad. I decided to tease him a little. It had been a long time since I'd had any fun.

'Oh, but I am, you see.' I jumped up and did a little twirl as I crossed the room towards him. I was so full of excitement I could hardly keep still.

'You *are*?' Jonathan's brows disappeared into his hair. 'B-but. . . .'

I could not suppress the twinkle I knew was in my eyes, and of course he noticed.

'Come on, what are you not telling me?' He gave a boyish grin and his whole face lit up. 'Out with it, woman, share the secret.' He grabbed hold of my wrist and held me still. 'I know you're hiding something. You look far too devious.'

'Of course I am.' I looked up into that familiar face and sobered as our eyes met. He was looking intensely at me. I released my wrist from his grip and turned away. 'And I can't keep this to myself any longer.'

I danced across the room, swept up my skirt and he followed me back to the sofa. 'Jonathan, do you remember when I was in hospital, I said I would love to open a women's refuge one day?'

His face cleared. 'Yes! Yes, I do. I thought then what a good idea it was. I told you so, didn't I?' I nodded. 'Oh, of course,' he squeezed my hand and withdrew, 'I can see it all now.'

'Jonathan,' I was on the edge of my seat and I half-turned towards him, 'it's a chance to make my dream come true. I now have a large house,' I flourished a hand in the air, 'and capital as well. Exactly the two things I need. Handed to me on a plate.' I smiled. 'Although I would never in a million years have guessed that Arthur would be the one to make it happen!'

'It's almost like some kind of divine retribution.' He chuckled. 'But seriously Kate, it's no more than you deserve.'

I nodded, and lost myself in my dreams for a moment. Then I came back with a start. 'But Jonathan,' I spread my hands helplessly, 'I've actually no idea *where* to begin.'

Our eyes met. His were dark and serious as they looked deeply into mine. 'I'm willing to help you in any way I can, if you'd like me to.'

'Of *course* I would. That would be marvellous!' I clasped my hands together in delight. Then I realized how often I seemed to be turning to this man for support. More and more. Me, who had been so looking forward to being independent! But Jonathan was such a tower of strength. And I was so unused to standing on my own two feet.

'Good.' He nodded vigorously. 'And I happen to know too, that Anne is very interested in the idea. We were talking about it the other day, after you'd left.' My eyes widened.

'Yes. She says there isn't anywhere like that in Cornwall, as far as she knows. And it would fill a need, you know? She said she's had other injured women at "Sea-Winds" before you, who've been treated badly by their husbands.'

He glanced up at the clock and started. 'My goodness, I must go, or your neighbours will start thinking there's something going on between us!' He rose to his feet. 'Now, Kate, we'll meet again soon and discuss the whole business, but it had better be in Truro next time, I think.'

As we made arrangements to do so, he picked up his hat and hesitated for a moment. Then clasping my hand, he drew me towards him and dropped a soft kiss on my cheek.

I followed him down the passage and quietly closed the door. Then I put my fingers to the warm place where his lips had been. It seemed to tingle with a life of its own, until long after he was out of sight.

I was longing to go and look over my newly acquired property. And I wanted to go alone to face whatever demons of the past still lurked there, and banish them for ever. But in another way I was dreading it and found all sorts of excuses to put off doing so.

However, I could not prevaricate much longer. So, one bright but cold day in early December I seized my courage in both hands and searched out my key, which had been unused for so long. This was a day for action. Lace-trimmed waves, one after the other, were sweeping up the beach. Each one like a bolt of shot-silk fabric in greens and blues, unrolled on a draper's counter for approval. They came with a hiss of foam on shingle, the air was crisp and exhilarating and I walked with a spring in my step.

As I approached Rosewarne Villa, however, my feet slowed and faltered. There it stood, grim, shuttered and forbidding. Oh, for goodness sake! I told myself, it's only a *house*.

Even so I hesitated on the top step before turning the key. I pushed open the door in trepidation. Would I find the memories too painful? Would the house be peopled with ghosts, and resonate with echoes of my past suffering? Don't be such a fool, I said again to myself, and forced my feet over the threshold. This is *your* house now.

But as I walked down the hall, my footsteps echoing eerily on the patterned tiles, I was constantly looking over my shoulder. I could not shake off the feeling that at any moment Arthur would appear from his study, or Maud would call down over the banisters with some snide remark.

The house was silent of course. It smelt of old dust and closed in stuffiness. But even so, the place seemed to loom threateningly above and around me. It hemmed me in as I glanced into each room, trapping me in the memories of past torments. The atmosphere was so oppressive I could scarcely breathe.

Pieces of furniture swathed in dust sheets loomed like monsters in the gloom of the shuttered windows. It required a supreme effort of will not to take to my heels and run. But I pulled back my shoulders and steeled myself to remain calm.

I forced my feet to go in and out of every room, and into the shadows, I whispered, 'You're *mine* now.' But even so I couldn't get out fast enough.

I skittered back along the passage and slammed the door behind me. Then I leaned my back against it for a long moment. And filled my lungs with the hugely welcome fresh air.

But the first steps had been taken and now I couldn't wait to start work on it. I would transform it from a mausoleum and place of nightmares into something positively good. I would use this house to make my dream come true.

CHAPTER FOURTEEN

LOVEDAY

Lying in the warmth, cuddling my baby close while Davy ran happily about the farm, I had plenty of time to think about the future. What would we do? What would we live on? A cold finger travelled down my spine. I would certainly have my hands full with two little sons to care for. But I would have to earn money somehow, which meant going out to work. And I must go home soon.

I was miles away when Ma came bustling in with a bowl of soup on a tray. 'Here, give him to me, the dear of him, and you get this down you. Good and strengthening this is – I boiled up that ham-bone for stock this morning and put plenty of vegetables in it.' She sat down in the cane chair next to the bed, taking the baby from me and cradling him in the crook of her arm.

'I've been thinking, maid.' She broke off to croon to the infant and rock him tenderly. 'Why don't you come back here to live with we now. Permanently I mean?' She raised her head and looked at me with a direct gaze.

'You're going to have to find some way of paying the rent, else.' An echo of my own thoughts. 'You could help out in the dairy like you used to. Round outside a bit too. Pa and me, we aren't getting no younger, you know. You could pay for your keep that way. And we'd have plenty of time with the children.'

Her gaze rested wistfully on the face of the sleeping baby as she hugged him to her. I realized I would have to handle this with a good deal of tact.

Genuinely touched as I was, I could hardly tell my mother it was not something I wanted to do. Having been mistress of my own home for so long, there was no way I could face coming back here as if I'd never been away.

I leaned over and squeezed her arm. 'Ma, I appreciate that more than I can say.' I slowly shook my head. 'But I really couldn't give up the cottage. It's Davy's home. And mine and Joel's family are in the village, too.'

As the light left Ma's eyes, I felt a stab of guilt. 'But as for the children,' I patted the arm I was still holding, 'I'd really be more grateful than I can say if I *could* leave them with you. If I can find some work. I want to keep my independence if I can, you see.'

Ma nodded. 'I thought that's what you'd say.' She smiled briefly. 'And I think I'd do the same in your position.' Our eyes met. 'We're more alike in character than you might think, maid. I never was one for being beholden to people neither. Not even my own family.'

She stood up to place the baby in his crib. 'But if we can have these dear children up here running about, it'll be wonderful. Like having our own family small all over again.' This time her smile was radiant. 'And the offer's always open my handsome, if you can't find no work elsewhere.' I held out both arms to her and as we embraced, my heart was too full to speak.

After she left the room, my thoughts drifted again as I looked dreamily out of the window. In the far distance I could see Pa mending a fence. The hammer would fall, then a few seconds passed before I heard the sound of it. Davy was trotting about importantly, never still. One minute he was handing nails up to Pa, the next, scampering after the dog.

The soil was a rich deep brown, the hills in the distance a hazy purple. Shades of ochre and lighter brown tinted the woods beyond the fields. The muted, pastel shades of late autumn pervaded the scene. Rooks were squabbling in the elm trees as usual and unseen, another dog was barking after rabbits.

It all seemed a world away from Porthleven and the fishing community, but that was the birthright of my children and where I wanted them to live.

*

A couple of weeks passed. Now I was no longer an invalid. I had rapidly recovered my strength due to Ma's care and the nourishing meals she pressed on me. Davy had been taken off my hands to a large degree, and I had had Kate for company, too. But this period of cosy warmth and security had to end. I'd been up and about for a week. My 'lying-in' was over. It was time to go home.

I felt cold at the prospect of going back to the cottage and taking up life again without Joel. But that was what I'd decided to do. I must face it. Then, practical worries set in once more.

'I'm going to have to find some kind of work, Kate,' I remarked when we'd been back in Porthleven for a few days. I was sitting by the range, feeding Joe. 'There's the rent to pay if we're to go on living here.' I glanced up at her. 'You know Ma wanted me to go back home to live, don't you? And I declined?'

'Yes.' Kate paused. She was sweeping the kitchen floor. I was amazed at how she seemed to really enjoy housework. But of course, she'd never been allowed to do any when she lived with Arthur. She leaned on the broom and looked towards me. 'I can understand your wanting to be independent, but I think you'll find it hard going.' Her face was dubious.

'Of course,' she returned to her task, 'if you could manage to begin with, when I get the refuge set up, you could come and work for me!' She looked over her shoulder and smiled, her face bright and lively at the prospect.

I knew how fully occupied she was with her own plans, and completely understood. I'd noticed how she would get lost sometimes in a daydream, in the middle of baking, or whatever she was doing. Then she would forget the milk put on to heat, or the pie in the oven, until the milk had boiled all over the stove and the contents of the oven began to smoke.

'Thank you, that's a lovely idea.' I smiled. 'But it's a long way in the future. You see I have to support us until then.' While she was living here, Kate was, of course, contributing to the household expenses. So that, along with a little I had saved, would keep us going for a short while. Soon, though, Kate would be leaving, and I had to look ahead.

'I thought I might work in one of the village shops perhaps. Or as a cleaner in one of the big houses. Maybe yours, when you get it! And I would have to rely on Ma to help with the children. But she'd like that.' I nibbled my bottom lip.

Failing all else, there were the fish-cellars. My throat tightened. I recalled the row I'd had with Joel about working down there. I could hear his voice quite clearly ... 'You don't know what you'd be letting yourself in for – your hands would be chapped and raw from the salt in five minutes. You'd be in agonies, my handsome' ... Oh well, hopefully it wouldn't come to that.

Eventually I had to face the heartrending task of clearing out Joel's belongings. Not that he had a great deal. Some tools and his fishing gear which I could easily give to one of his friends, the rest was mainly clothes.

I put it off for as long as I could, then one morning Kate took Davy off my hands and I forced myself into action. It felt as if I was clearing out all the memories of Joel. But I didn't need material things to remember him by. He would always be in my heart. He was part of me in the same way our little Joe was part of us both.

But while Joel's clothes still hung in the cupboard and the smell of him was there every time I opened it, I could not move forward as I must do. I wept long and bitterly into one of the navy blue guernseys I'd spent long hours knitting for him. It wrapped its sleeves around me like a pair of comforting arms.

It still held a faint tang of fish and salt, well-washed though it was, and a hint of Joel's own distinctive smell, a mix of soap and tar and the open-air. I folded it carefully and laid it in the basket beside me. Some other fisherman would welcome its oiled warmth and it would not be wasted.

I gradually became accustomed to my widowed state. I no longer felt my heart turn over when a storm at sea threatened the fishing boats; they were no part of my life now. I stopped listening for the tread of Joel's heavy boots coming up the path, for his blond head appearing round the door and the way that the room would be suddenly full of him.

I cleared my head of all thought of the way we'd parted. He'd come to me in the dream and that was enough. I felt forgiven. Now my dreams of him were of happier times, but always left me with tears in my eyes when I awoke to the lonely reality and the empty bed.

Kate spent a lot of her time coming and going to Truro to meet Jonathan and also to see the solicitor. I was beginning to wonder whether her friendship with Jonathan was becoming something more than just friendship. But as she never brought up the subject, I couldn't really ask without appearing to pry.

I was coming back from the shop one day when I was caught up in a knot of my neighbours by the harbour wall. I had to stop as they all wanted to see the baby, make a fuss over Davy, and enquire how I was.

Then after a while the subject changed. 'Something funny going on up to Rosewarne, is there?' Jane Polglase peered closely into my face, her brows rising. 'We seen your sister down here some lot. Still living with you, is she?' There was a pause while all eyes were turned on me.

What should I say? I tried to skirt around the absolute truth. 'Oh, Kate's been a tower of strength to me all this time. I don't know what I'd have done without her.' A few sympathetic nods and murmurs followed.

Then a voice piped up. 'We heard that she idden going home no more. That she've left her husband. That right, is it, Loveday?' One, bolder than the rest, was looking avidly into my face.

They knew. Of course they did. 'Um. . . .' While I stalled, another voice broke in.

' 'Course she have. Mr Arthur have left Porthleven for good. Know that, did you?' The woman nodded and pursed her lips as she looked around the group. She paused for their reaction.

'What? How do *you* know so sure?' Jane bridled and lifted one shoulder.

'I *do* know,' the other woman nodded vigorously. 'My Ben – you know he's a carpenter?' She looked around at her audience. 'Well, he been up there on a job, *boarding up the windows*, see?' This was news to me, and would be to Kate as well.

All eyes were on the speaker. 'Anyway, he had a good look in, and he said the furniture and stuff's all still in there. And the house all bolted and barred up.'

'Sure enough?' The eyes widened. ' 'Course, nobody haven't seen Mr Arthur since his ma's funeral. Reckon he's left for good, we do.'

'Ooh, my lor. Look like it, don't it?' As the heads drew together to digest this latest bit of gossip and its implications, I saw my chance. I turned the baby carriage away with some excuse about it being Joe's feeding time, and left.

I was preparing to tell Kate all this when she came back from Truro. However, she forestalled me by dancing in, beaming all over her face.

'Loveday, it's come through!' She dragged a piece of paper out of her bag and waved it under my nose. 'The decree absolute! I'm a free woman!' Laughing and crying at the same time, she seized me in a bear-hug and waltzed me round the kitchen.

'Oh, Kate, I'm so *glad* for you!' I said when I'd got my breath back.

It took Kate some time to come down to earth. When most of her euphoria was over and she'd settled in a chair, I said, 'So what are you going to do first with all this new-found freedom?'

'Jonathan's coming down tomorrow. He's got a day off and we're going round to the villa. They've given me the keys, look!' She reached in her bag and jangled them as proof. 'You can come too – you've never been further than the parlour, have you?'

Then her face sobered. 'It's wrong I know, and I'm not gloating, really, but I can't help enjoying the feeling that justice has now been done and that Arthur has got exactly what he deserves.'

She was twisting her wedding ring round on her finger as she spoke. All at once she raised her hand, looked at it and realized what she was doing. Then her face lit up with a beaming smile. 'Oh, Loveday, I don't have to wear *this* any more!' She drew it off and put it away in her bag. 'How strange my hand seems without it.' She examined it closely.

I smiled and touched my own ring – I'd no intention of removing that, ever. 'According to the grapevine, Arthur's left Porthleven for good. Do you know that?'

Kate nodded. 'Ernest Pascoe told me. He received notification of Arthur's new address. Apparently he's given up his share in the firm, left Cornwall completely and gone up to London.' My brows rose at this.

'He's staying in lodgings at the moment, presumably while he sorts himself out.' She paused and gazed at me. 'I can't really see him ever coming back down here, can you?'

I shook my head. 'No, he wouldn't run the risk of being humiliated having to face the pointing fingers and wagging tongues.'

'Anyway,' Kate shifted in her chair and tilted her chin, 'I was saying to Jonathan earlier, if that house of horror can be transformed into something good, and positive . . . if women can find a safe haven there . . . well, it'll be a kind of, um, *redemption*, for all I suffered. Do you see what I mean, Loveday?'

Our eyes met and I nodded. It wasn't often Kate opened her heart and talked so seriously. She was coming into her own at last. An independent woman and a 'doll-wife' no more. I'd noticed for a long time that she no longer wore the elaborate gowns and hats she used to, even when going to Truro, and she seemed the happier for it.

Then a plaintive wail from upstairs alerted me to the fact that my baby was awake and hungry again. I rose to my feet. 'Now it's all over the village that you and Arthur have separated,' I said over my shoulder, 'you know when they see you with Jonathan you'll be branded a scarlet woman, don't you?'

Kate tossed her head. 'I don't care what they think any more. I've got more important things on my mind.'

I slowly climbed the stairs. Yes, she certainly had. There was much to be done if she were to make her precious dream come true.

Jonathan turned up next morning casually dressed in a dark blazer and grey flannels. Kate's face lit up when she saw him, giving fuel to the suspicions I already had. Then we all trooped up to the villa, Jonathan pushing the baby carriage up the steep hill for me.

He looked as if he'd been doing it all his life, and was quite oblivious to the open stares of the women we passed. He raised his hat and passed the time of day with a natural courtesy that won them all over and left them smiling in his wake.

He and I intuitively hung back as we reached the house and let Kate enter first. I could only guess at her feelings and wanted to give her time alone to compose herself.

She vanished into the darkness of the shuttered rooms and after a while I heard her voice echoing up the passage, saying something I couldn't catch. Then she came back towards us with amazement on her face.

'Everything's still here,' she spread her hands and shrugged. 'Just as it was. Even Maud's clothes are still hanging in the wardrobe. Arthur's only taken his clothes and personal stuff. We're going to have a terrific amount of work to clear it all out.'

'We'll manage it between us,' Jonathan said firmly.

I nodded. 'Yes. I'll help as well, if you like.' I offered hesitantly, as I didn't want to come between them if they'd rather be alone.

'And me, and me!' Not to be left out, Davy piped up without the least idea what we were talking about. We all burst out laughing and the situation that could have been a little awkward, passed instead in merriment.

'First of all we'll have those windows opened up,' Kate said. 'We can't creep about in here in the dark like moles.'

'I know who put in the boards. I was talking to his wife the other day. Shall I see to that?'

'Fine. Thanks, Loveday.' Kate looked preoccupied. 'I shall have to bring a notebook with me next time and make some lists. Jobs to be done . . . what we shall need to do them . . . things like that.'

Jonathan was peering into the gloomy depths of the parlour. 'We'll get an auctioneer round and send all the surplus furniture to the saleroom. Unless there are any pieces you want to keep, Kate? To use in future?'

Kate vigorously shook her head. 'No, never. I want the place completely emptied. A fresh start, new paint, new everything. No reminders of the past. Nothing.'

I nodded. I could perfectly understand how she wanted to wipe the slate clean. Rid herself of all the painful memories and start afresh. A new house for a new life.

'What I'd really love to do,' Kate went on, her face thoughtful. 'Is to do the work myself. Well, ourselves anyway,' she glanced at Jonathan as she spoke. 'As much as we can, that is. Painting all through, and cleaning. It would make me feel as if at last it's really mine.' She nodded slowly.

'And it would be fun!' Her eyes suddenly sparkled with enthusiasm. I was watching Jonathan and the way his face lit up like a beacon as his gaze rested on her.

Back at home later on we were going over the events of the day, when Kate turned to me with a thoughtful look in her eyes. 'Loveday, I've had an idea. You know we're going to work on the house ourselves?'

I nodded. 'Well, I thought about this when you offered to help.' She nibbled a lip. 'Now, don't take this the wrong way,' she gave me a long look, 'but you said you need to find a job to make ends meet. Well, would you like to work for me, and I would pay you a wage for doing it?'

I sat up straight and started to splutter. 'B-but . . . Kate, I couldn't take money from you! My own sister? I was just coming along to help you out. You've been such a help to me and I thought . . . to repay. . . .'

She held up a hand to stop my babble. 'Don't be silly, I'm not saying this out of, well, charity or something. If you don't agree I shall have to hire someone else. We need serious help. You can see it's going to be too much for Jonathan and me to handle on our own. Isn't it better that you should benefit from it than a stranger?'

Put like that I was having second thoughts. But I knew she had plenty of money and could well afford it. And it would be such a weight off my mind. I smiled and reached for her hand. 'Well, when you put it like that . . . Kate, yes, I'll be delighted. Thank you. I'd love to.'

Her face brightened. 'Oh, I'm so glad. I didn't want to offend you – but it seemed to make such perfect sense. Oh, wonderful!'

'I do know. And it's a lovely idea. I can take the children. Davy can play in the garden. And I can leave Joe out there too, in his playpen. They'll be completely safe.' Then I laughed. 'I've never used a paintbrush in my life. But neither have you. I suppose there has to be a first time for everything. And it'll be fun learning.'

'Wonderful!' She squeezed my hand. 'Jonathan's taking some leave, he says he has a couple of weeks saved up and no plans for them. So we'll start then.'

So over a period we transformed Rosewarne Villa. The ghosts of Maud and Arthur were sent packing for good, along with the old-fashioned furniture, the sombre curtains and the hideous ornaments.

We brought in light colours and muslin curtains that fluttered at the windows, let in sea air and allowed reflections of sunlight to dance on the polished floorboards. There were bright rugs, tasteful pictures on the walls and pretty china.

By the time it was finished we had had a great many laughs, learned a great deal about home decorating, and Jonathan and I had become firm friends. I had nothing but admiration for his quiet and efficient approach to any problem. There were many of these along the way, but I never saw him ruffled.

What did emerge to my observant eye was his devotion to Kate. It was in the way he watched her movements, in the air of careful attention that hovered around him when they were together. A certain look in his eyes when they were talking to each other. And if he wasn't smitten, why should a man of his standing give up his spare time in this way?

Kate gave nothing of herself away, but I gained the impression she enjoyed his company immensely. It was a delightful idea to think that maybe one day she might find happiness with this man.

I brushed away the surge of loneliness that washed over me at the thought. For I was locked into my single state, probably for the rest of my life. What man could ever compare to Joel? What man would take on two children who were not his own? But I still had Kate to keep me company for a little longer. Until the house was finished of course.

Weeks and months passed, Christmas came and went. The year turned and by late spring, Rosewarne Villa was actually finished at last. Kate had had her way and we'd done most of it ourselves, apart from some very rough outside work for which she engaged a firm of builders.

After they'd packed up and left, we sat in the sunny drawing-room and celebrated with a toast to the future. I think then we all felt a bit flat that the project that had occupied us for the best part of six months, was no more.

The money I'd earned during those months had covered the rent and our food, but now that was all over. I had to think about finding other work. Kate had de-camped to the villa to live. She was concerned at leaving it empty in case of intruders. She was also quite excited about living in her own home as she furthered her plans. Of course we saw each other frequently, but now I was living alone for the first time too.

I managed to find employment in the dairy of a nearby farm. The farmer's wife was a distant relative of Meg's. I was sure she'd put in a word for me, and was grateful for her thoughtfulness, but she swiftly changed the subject if I tried to thank her.

Beatrice, the farmer's wife, was kindness itself and had no objection to my bringing the children with me. The farm was on the fringes of Porthleven. So much nearer than Sithney, I hastened to explain to Ma, feeling awkward after the way I'd turned down her own offer. Then noticing the disappointment in her eyes, I promised to bring the children over to Pengarth every weekend to make up for it.

So each morning I churned butter and slapped it into shape with the wooden butter pats stamped with a thistle, the farm's 'trademark'. Scalded milk in the big flat pans until the clotted cream rose to the top and could be skimmed off.

Davy played happily in the fields with the children of the farm. Little Joe sat in a playpen outgrown by one of the farm children, playing with his own toys. He was a placid, happy child with a smile never far from his face. I was surprised at this, considering the trauma of his birth.

The work in itself was not particularly taxing, for I'd been doing it from childhood until my marriage. But the farm did lie up a steep hill, and as Joe became heavier, so the baby carriage was harder to push. By the time I returned home and started on my own cooking, cleaning and washing, I was tired out. Sometimes I wondered with hindsight whether I would have been better off taking up Ma's offer after all. But it was too late now.

The weeks slipped by. Summer came and soon Davy's third 'birthday' was approaching. Astonishing to think that ten months had passed since Joel's death.

Little Joe was crawling now and just beginning to pull himself to his feet. Although he promptly sat down with a bump every time. He followed the older boy's every movement with lively eyes and chortles of delight. The two were devoted to each other and Davy had never shown the slightest jealousy of his baby brother.

It was one Saturday, a mellow day in August, that I promised the children a picnic lunch on the beach while the weather lasted. Then we would go up to Pengarth in the afternoon. First of all however, I made a diversion to visit Joel's grave and change the flowers on it.

My gaze rested on Davy for a moment as he skipped over to the bin to throw away the wilted ones. I never ceased to marvel at the little boy's matter-of-fact acceptance of his father's absence, in much the same way that he had accepted Joe's arrival.

How much he understood I'd no idea, but he must remember the long periods when Joel was away fishing, for he prattled about him being up in heaven as if it were somewhere like Whitby or Lowestoft. He seemed to accept that the grave was some magical way of keeping in touch with him.

As I tipped away the stale water and went to fetch some fresh, Davy began to play with a ball among the grassy paths between the graves, while Joe gurgled encouragement from his baby carriage. Joel's grave was not far from the great cross that had been erected as a memorial to the shipwrecked sailors from the "Meervogel". Three years ago. What an age it seemed now. I skirted round it and drew some water from the pump outside the churchyard gate, which also served the village.

I was returning the way I'd come when I noticed a man standing beside the cross, his head bent in silent prayer. He held his hat in one hand, the other rested on the shoulder of a little boy of about six or seven. I hesitated, not wishing to disturb what was obviously a private moment, but I had to pass by him, it was the only way back.

At that moment, however, the man straightened, murmured something to the little boy and replaced his hat. But as he turned, Davy's ball came rolling down the path with the child chasing after it. It bounced against the stranger's leg before coming to rest at his feet, and the man bent down, retrieved it and handed it back.

'Oh, I'm so sorry,' I said to him. 'What do you say, Davy?'

'Thank you, sir.' The little boy took the ball and put it under his arm.

'You're very welcome,' said the man, looking intently at him. 'You're a fine lad. How old are you?'

Davy's gaze was on the other boy, who was peering around his father's back and returning the stare. 'I'm nearly three.' He raised his head. 'Next week it will be my birthday.' He skipped off up the path again.

I'd been looking at the children too. They were both wearing the sailor-suits which were all the fashion for small boys, and the elder boy had let his straw boater slide from his head, where it dangled by its string at the back of his neck. How alike the outfits made them seem, I thought, then gasped as an icy finger touched my heart.

For it wasn't the outfits alone. The two boys *were* alike. Astonishingly alike with their blue eyes and fair hair, which stuck up in a similar tuft at the crown of each of their heads. My heart started hammering and I felt colour flood my face.

I turned to look at the stranger. His face too seemed momentarily frozen in shock. He recovered so quickly however, I wondered if I'd been mistaken. For as I glanced at him again, he tipped his hat and smiled at me.

Then I experienced such a sense of déjà-vu that all the breath left my body. My stomach lurched and my legs began to shake. For I knew that smile. Knew it because I'd been looking at it every day for the last three years. And from that instant, there was no doubt in my mind as to his identity.

CHAPTER FIFTEEN

KATE

The next time Jonathan and I met was not in Truro at all as we'd thought, but over at 'Sea Winds'. I'd gone there to see Anne, whom I'd counted as a friend ever since my stay with her. I was eager to tell her all my news, and it so happened that Jonathan too was calling that day.

'Oh, Kate, what a lot has happened since I saw you last!' Anne paused after I'd told her my tale. 'So what's the next step in your plans for the refuge?'

We were sitting in the big conservatory that ran the full length of the front of the house. It was too cold to be in the garden today, so we were in the next best place. Although it was unheated, the rays of a pale winter sun striking on the glass gave just enough warmth for comfort.

'I'm not quite sure, actually.' I nibbled my lip. 'I need to get some helpers together, but I hardly know where to start.'

'Well,' Jonathan said, folding one long leg over the other, 'first you need to form a working committee. A treasurer, secretary, chairman' – he ticked them off on his fingers – 'you know what I mean. Then you'll have to find wealthy people who'll agree to put money into the scheme.'

'That all sounds very grand.' I turned to him with a smile. 'And very organized. But seriously, where am I going to find people who are willing to do these things?' I spread my hands wide. 'People I can rely on not to let me down?'

'Well,' Anne's green eyes twinkled, 'you're looking at one of them right now.'

My jaw dropped. '*You*? You mean it? But Anne, how can you? Where would you find the time? And what about this place?' I waved a hand to indicate the large house, the well-tended grounds, the contented residents whose chatter I could hear behind me.

'Well, I have such a reliable and devoted staff, in fact it almost runs itself. But of course I have to be here most of the time to oversee things.' She nodded and smoothed a crease out of her skirt.

'But I've been thinking a lot about your refuge, ever since I heard of it at all. It's such a wonderful idea. And this is what I came up with. Jonathan already knows most of it,' she glanced towards her brother. 'I mentioned it to him last time he was here.' She sat up straighter in the wicker chair and gazed at me.

'I haven't the time as you pointed out Kate, to sit on a committee, but there were two things I did think of. One,' she held up a finger, 'I would be willing to train up two or three girls in basic nursing care for you. I've got this diploma, remember? And I could start doing that right away, so that when you open they'll be ready. You'll need nurses, and I could teach them child-care as well. My studies covered that too. You're obviously going to have some children along with their mothers.'

I nodded. 'Oh, Anne, what a good idea! That would be marvellous.' I drew a breath to say more but she held up a hand, obviously not yet finished.

'And, two. You see, I belong to the Salvation Army.' She paused. I knew my face must be a picture of astonishment when she laughed. 'You're surprised.'

I nodded. 'Well – yes. I am really. You don't strike me as the type at all.'

Anne looked at her brother. 'We weren't born into the middle classes at all you see, were we, Jon?' With her elbows on the arms of her chair, she steepled her fingers. 'We came from quite a poor family.' I glanced at Jonathan too, as I recalled how he had told me the same thing once.

'No, I married "up" as they say, when I met Ray.' I felt my brows rise. I took in Anne's expensive-looking costume of aquamarine wool jersey. The fine lawn of her blouse, trimmed with hand-made lace.

And had a mental vision of the scruffy urchins who abounded in the poorer parts of any town and city. It was hard to reconcile this image with the poised and elegant woman sitting opposite me. But they hadn't been that poor, of course. My imagination was carrying me away.

As if she'd read my thoughts, Anne said, 'Oh, our parents managed to make ends meet. We never went hungry, did we?'

Jonathan shook his head. 'In fact we were a very happy family.'

Anne nodded and spread her hands. 'But what I'm coming to,' the hands fluttered, 'is that the Salvation Army was a big part of my growing-up. Not so much with Jonathan, but they fascinated me.'

She leaned closer. 'As I grew older I could see beyond the brass bands and the banners. Beyond the uniforms, with those ugly black bonnets the women wear. I could see how they went round to the public houses every pay-day. They persuaded the men from the factories to go home before they drank away all their wages.'

Her face was serious. 'They went into places where the established churches never would, and they were really making a difference. Providing soup-kitchens for the destitute – things like that. And I've never forgotten it.'

I was wondering what all this had to do with what we were talking about. Had she gone off the point or was this leading up to something?

'So you see,' Anne waved a finger, 'I thought they would be the people who can find the women who are most in need of a refuge. The women too scared to tell the authorities, or the doctor.' She gave a nod in Jonathan's direction.

Ah, now I understood. I began to listen more closely. 'They could send them on to you. You could use the Sally Army as a sort of bridge. And of course, some women turn up here for convalescence, like you did. Jonathan too, comes across needy cases at the hospital.'

'That's right,' he nodded, 'I shall be delighted to have somewhere to send them instead of back to their homes. It's heartrending sometimes to see them having to return to their brutal husbands to be knocked about all over again.'

'And another thing.' Anne had been deep in thought, her gaze far away. 'I'm in touch through Ray's regiment with some very wealthy and influential people.' Her eyes, serious now, met mine.

'People who are only too pleased to have their names associated with charitable causes. It gives them a little glow of self-righteousness. They can tell their dinner-party guests of the good works they're supporting. At the same time they don't actually have to do anything, you see?' She raised an eyebrow. 'Not concern themselves at all with the seamy side of life. That can be safely left to people like us, and "the Army".'

I looked steadily at her. Anne was talking a lot of sense. I felt the first stirrings of excitement and clasped my hands tightly together in my lap as I regarded her with respect. There was more to this woman than met the eye.

'What a good idea! Isn't it, Jonathan?' I turned to him to see him nodding vigorously. 'It certainly is.'

'Oh, Anne,' I gripped her hand as excitement mounted. 'I really think it could be done, don't you?'

'Of course I do,' she said stoutly. She smiled, a mischievous grin that took years off her age. 'Right. I'll pay a few calls on various people I know and sound them out. It might not be until after Christmas. We're nearly in December now. But by then, with a bit of luck, this refuge of ours will be ready to open!'

It was comforting to think that the whole idea had ceased to be solely mine, but had now become 'ours'. I was coming to like Anne more and more. I recognized the streak of toughness that lay below the surface of this remarkable woman. So there were three of us now. Already the beginnings of a team.

'Oh, yes. It'll take us that length of time anyway to furnish the house properly. At the moment I'm living in the kitchen and a corner of one bedroom.' I nibbled a fingernail. 'I must make a list of all we shall need. Several lists, in fact. . . .'

We launched into a discussion about furniture and fittings that went on so long that at last Jonathan coughed discreetly. I broke off and turned to him to see his eyes were dancing with merriment.

'Now, if I can get a word in edgeways,' he said with a laugh, 'I'd like to suggest myself as chairman. Rather than you, Kate, which would be the obvious thing.' His face became serious as he must have seen my look of surprise. 'The reason being not that I want to push myself in, but there's something important that neither of you has thought of.'

I felt my face fall as I racked my brains for something left undone. Where had we slipped up? I thought we'd covered everything between us.

Jonathan leaned closer. 'Remember, we're going to involve these "wealthy and influential" people of Anne's. People who are going to be bred in the same mould as, for instance, Arthur.' He looked steadily at me. 'Self-righteous, conventional people, mostly men. Men who believe a woman's place is at hearth and home. And nowhere else.' He leaned his elbows on his knees, held my gaze and paused.

'Now you, Kate,' he raised a finger, 'would be seen as the founder of an institution that plainly undermines the sanctity of marriage. The right of a husband to treat his wife as he pleases.' He paused. 'You would be immediately condemned and this whole venture doomed.' He gave me a searching look. 'You *do* see what I'm getting at, don't you?'

In his earnestness to make me understand, he'd taken one of my hands in his and was squeezing it hard. For my heart had sunk to my boots and my feelings must have been reflected on my face.

This was *my* venture. It had been my dream for so long. And after all this time was at last within my reach. But I was not to be acknowledged. It was too much. I straightened and drew in a deep breath to protest. Jonathan must have seen how indignant I was for he was patting my hand now. I bit my lip and turned away in disappointment as a lump rose to my throat.

'Don't be upset, Kate,' he added gently. 'It's not as bad as it sounds. Listen. You can still sit on the committee as a representative of the staff. I suggest we tell them you are the matron, manager, what ever you like to call yourself. The person in charge, certainly. So when and if they call to see the place, you'll show them around. And as far as they're concerned, the actual owner wishes to remain anonymous.'

I gave him a dubious look. Then I began to think about it. I wasn't really losing out at all, was I? I'd still be running the refuge myself. All I was losing was my personal pride in having my efforts *acknowledged*. So, what sort of charity was that? It made me no better than the people Anne was talking about, the ones who contributed to a cause in order to be seen to be magnanimous.

So I sighed, swallowed my emotions, then turned a bright face to them both. 'That's an excellent idea, Jonathan, thank you for pointing it out.' I saw his expression of relief, and also the look of sympathy in Anne's eyes, for she had understood.

'Well, it's time for me to go in and see to things.' She rose briskly to her feet. 'I can't spend all day out here chatting like you people.' She caught her brother's eye and gave a nod. 'Some of us have work to do, you know.'

Jonathan laughed and made a face at her as she bustled into the house. The serious moment was over.

'I must go too, Kate.' He uncurled himself and straightened his jacket. 'Anne's right. There's work to be done. But we'll arrange our first committee meeting as soon as she's contacted those people.'

He turned as a thought obviously struck him. 'You'll have to think of a new name for the house, won't you?' His brows rose. 'I can't imagine you'll want to go on calling it Rosewarne Villa. Now that it's not, if you see what I mean.'

'Well, I've been thinking about that, actually.' I touched my ringless finger, which seemed very bare and strange. 'And you're right. I don't ever want to be reminded of the name again. Jonathan, what do you think of it being called "The Phoenix Refuge" for obvious reasons?' I nibbled my lip. 'As it's rising out of the ashes of the house of horror, so to speak. And becoming a place of safety. Of redemption. A whole new beginning. . . .' I was stammering, worried that he would think I was overdoing it. 'How does that sound? Do you think I'm being silly?'

'No, of course you're not, my love, don't look so anxious. It sounds absolutely perfect to me. A splendid name in fact.'

My brows rose. The little endearment had slipped casually into the conversation, almost automatically. As if it was the most natural thing in the world. Perhaps to him it was, although I'd never heard him use it to anyone else. And I wondered.

I hadn't seen Loveday for some time so I paid her a visit soon after this. She opened the door with her usual smile, but as it faded, I noticed a couple of worry-lines on her brow. Those hadn't been there since she'd recovered from her almost-breakdown.

'How are you Loveday? Are you feeling all right?' I pulled off my gloves and hat and followed her down to the kitchen in the usual way.

'Yes, of course I am.' Her back was towards me and she turned the conversation by countering my enquiry. 'How are you? And your plans? I haven't seen you for quite a while.'

I began telling her as I bent down and made a fuss of the children. Davy was piling up wooden building blocks on the floor, and Joe was taking great delight in knocking them down again.

'They get on well together, don't they?' I remarked. Loveday looked fondly down at them both. 'Oh, yes, Davy's ever so patient with him. He's never been the slightest bit jealous. If he wants to play on his own he just goes upstairs where Joe can't follow him. I'm very lucky.'

I sat down and told her all that had happened since we last met. I could tell, though that Loveday was only half-listening. She had an air of preoccupation about her, and when I stopped talking, she came back with a start from some topic her mind had been engaged with. I knew my sister well enough by now to tell when something was amiss.

'Loveday, are you *sure* you're all right?' I tried again.

'Of course I am, I told you. Don't *nag*, Kate.' Her eyes flashed. 'I'm just a bit tired, that's all.' She turned away and busied herself about the room. This was so unlike her I was struck dumb in astonishment. Then she seemed to pull herself together and make an effort. She plied me with tea and biscuits and after a while I almost believed I'd imagined the whole thing.

'What I came to say as well,' I handed Joe a piece of broken biscuit, which he promptly crammed whole into his mouth, 'is whether you'd come with me to Truro one day and help me choose furniture for the house?'

Loveday turned to me with interest. 'Oh, I *would* like a day out!' Her face brightened. 'It would have to be a Saturday though, because of my job. But I could leave the children with Ma. We go up there most weekends anyway, as you know.'

I felt cheered by her response. 'Right, we'll do it.'

So we did, and enjoyed ourselves immensely, visiting the great emporia and ordering vast quantities of attractive furniture, fittings and linen. Fortunately Arthur and Maud had always had accounts with these stores. So for once I was forced to replace my wedding ring, and have all the goods charged in the name of 'Mr Rosewarne'.

Crossing my fingers that our supporters would come up with enough in donations to cover my huge outlay, we returned home in jubilation.

A few days later an enormous delivery van pulled by four horses arrived at my door and a squad of men spent the best part of half a day carrying in all my purchases. I'd told Jonathan when they were due to arrive and arranged that he would direct them from upstairs as I pointed out the various rooms where everything was to go.

When it was all done and everyone including Jonathan, had gone, I wandered from room to room, marvelling at what we had achieved.

Downstairs, the parlour had been transformed from the dark and gloomy place where I'd spent countless boring evenings listening to Arthur pontificating over the newspaper and hearing Maud's disapproving sniff if I dared venture an opinion of my own.

It had been papered in a William Morris design of birds and flowers, with curtains to match. The big window, instead of being shrouded in thick nets and heavy chenille, was now opened up to the view that was always so glorious, whether summer or winter. Today the sea was a steely grey, buffed into silver where a ray of pale sun caught it. There was next to no wind and small waves were slapping peacefully on the shingle as if in denial of the ferocious force they could raise during a storm.

Each of the bedrooms had a bright square of carpet on its polished wooden floor, a white-painted wash-stand with pretty matching china, and colourful curtains. I walked through them all, and lingered in the one I'd shared with Arthur.

I'd taken particular care here to scour away any traces of what had been. Physically it was unrecognizable, but even so a shiver of distaste ran down my spine as I looked around. I could still hear echoes of my anguished screams, as if they had become embedded in the very walls themselves.

I now slept downstairs, at the front of the house, where memories could not intrude. There was a small annexe there that had been built on for some purpose long forgotten, and I made this my domain. It had formerly been used as little more than a dumping-ground for paraphernalia that, 'might come in useful one day'. I'd made it into a pleasant apartment for myself. It was not large, but I had a bed-sitting room, a kitchen, and a den that would become my office.

The stables had been converted into quarters for those of the staff who would be living-in, which left the main part of the house for our patients. I walked the as-yet unoccupied rooms and felt a small frisson of anticipation and of pure pleasure at the way my dream was fast becoming reality.

Our first committee meeting was held in the dining-room, which looked twice as large since I'd stripped it of all its clutter. The long table was perfect for our purpose. I'd previously laid out blotters, pens and ink bottles at each place, and now my stomach did a little flip as I thought how business-like it all looked.

A ring at the front door had me on my feet. Anne was standing there beside a tall man with a magnificent waxed moustache and trim goatee beard. 'Colonel Hugo Hastings,' she said with a smile.

The man bowed over my hand. 'Call me H. H. – everybody does,' he boomed. 'Hate standing on ceremony – get enough of that in the regiment, don't you know?'

At his side was an elegant middle-aged woman, tall and slim with warm brown eyes and an engaging smile. She was dressed in the height of fashion with a fur tippet over her close-fitting costume of bottle-green wool. This had a long-line jacket, decorated at the hem with loops and swirls of black braid, as was the skirt, and her hat was a confection of green velvet roses. I couldn't take my eyes off her, the woman was the epitome of wealth and elegance.

'I've brought along one of our supporters,' he said, indicating his companion. 'She happened to call on me just as I was coming out. Apologies for not consulting you first, but there was no time. This is Lady Mary Desborough, and she has promised to help us in any way she can.'

Introductions followed. 'Do come in, Lady Mary. And you too, um – H.H. You're both very welcome.'

'Lady Mary's a great supporter of deserving causes,' said the colonel as I ushered them to a place at the table. 'Women's suffrage to name just one of them, so of course what you people are doing at the refuge appealed to her right away.'

Lady Mary held up a hand and gestured him to stop. 'H.H., 'you've said quite enough, you're holding up the meeting.' As he looked suitably abashed, and twirled his moustache with a loud 'Hurrumph', I smiled to myself, wondering if he was smitten.

Just then Jonathan appeared, accompanied by two more people. 'Kate, this is James Kingston, an old acquaintance, and his daughter Miss Alice Kingston.' I stood up and held out my hand. 'James has just retired as headmaster of a small private boys' school; I bumped into him in Truro, and he's very interested in what you're doing.'

He found seats for them then turned to me again. 'Miss Kingston is an excellent cook who has had enough of feeding little boys, James is looking for something to do in his retirement. I suggested they might like to become part of the staff.'

His eyes were sending me a message I took to mean 'hope you don't mind – too good a chance to miss', or something similar. I smiled at them both. James Kingston was a mild-mannered grey-haired man with spectacles. His daughter tall and slim with an air of authority about her.

'Lovely to meet you both. Do make yourselves comfortable. And now if we're all here, shall we get down to work?' Taking the chair at the end of the polished walnut table, with Jonathan opposite me, I settled myself and took up a folder of papers and a pen. I outlined my plans and the arrangements we'd made over the running of the refuge and then got down to details.

'Well, first of all, Mr Kingston,' I looked towards him and smiled. 'James,' he corrected me and I nodded. 'James, I think you could be the answer to my prayers!'

I'd been doing a bit of quick thinking since he came in. I needed staff and they had to be trustworthy. Here was a man who inspired immediate trust – for he'd been running a school for years, hadn't he? And he was known to Jonathan. What better recommendation could he have?

'I need a caretaker. One however, who would be willing to live on the premises.' I gave him a long look. I'd decided to get that condition laid down right away. 'And I do need a cook as well.' I turned towards his daughter. 'Now, if you both agree, from my point of view to get a caretaker and a cook at the same time would be almost too good to be true! So do think about it and talk it over among yourselves before deciding.'

By the end of the meeting it had been agreed that James, Jonathan and I should be the steering committee, responsible for any major decisions. That H.H. and Lady Mary would be 'sleeping partners' continuing to contribute financially, and he would encourage some of his fellow officers and influential contacts to do likewise.

'People like Sir Robert de Villiers, don't you know, and the Hon. Nicholas Smythe and his wife. Then there's Major Charles Fortescue. I've known him for years. All of them are people of substance, and they all like to be seen as patrons of worthy causes, haw, haw!' he chuckled.

Alice Kingston would approach the Board of Guardians with a view to employing some women and young girls to help with the day-to-day running of the place.

Anne would contact the Salvation Army and other charitable bodies. She would make sure as many people as possible learned of the new refuge and the facilities it offered. Also she would teach basic nursing to the girls Alice would find. With Jonathan as our official doctor, it seemed that everything had been covered.

'Oh, I feel absolutely exhausted!' I closed the door behind the last visitor and joined Jonathan in the kitchen. 'But exhilarated too, you know? Because it all went so well.'

Jonathan placed a mug of tea at my elbow and reached for the milk jug. 'I should think so! Only the first meeting, and it went better than I could ever have hoped.' He put his hand over mine. 'I'm so glad for you, Kate. I know how important this is to you.'

I nodded. 'If I can only help out one woman who has suffered as I have, it will be worthwhile, but I'm really optimistic about it all.' I smiled at him. 'If I believed in fate, I would say that such a good start means our venture is bound to succeed.'

Jonathan laughed and dropped a kiss on the hand he was still holding, brushing it with his soft moustache. I drew in a quick breath as I felt my body respond in a way that surprised me.

'If it does – and I'm sure you're right,' he added, 'it will have less to do with fate, my love, than sheer hard work.' I registered the 'my love' that had slipped in there again and swallowed hard. These gestures of affection were becoming more frequent and I wasn't sure how I felt about them.

'This is a massive undertaking, you know.' His serious eyes looked into mine. 'A full-time job. And Kate, as a full-time employee, don't forget you must give yourself a salary, of course, like the rest of the staff.'

'Oh, Jonathan, I couldn't!' I nibbled my lip. 'It's a labour of love. And we're going to have so many expenses.'

'But you must.' Jonathan's brow furrowed. 'This is a business we're running, remember. The donations from your wealthy supporters will cover the costs; that's what they're for. Besides which, if you don't, you'll have no income at all. What do you think you're going to live on?' He frowned.

I nodded slowly and turned away. 'Yes. You're right, of course.'

'And I hope you realize Kate, exactly what you've taken on.' Jonathan's face was still serious. 'A word of warning, as your doctor.' He looked me in the eye. 'I don't want you to exhaust yourself and putting your own health in jeopardy, mind. You don't have to be in the place all the hours there are. Remember you'll have plenty of staff and make sure you delegate the work to them.'

'Oh yes, of course I will.' I suppressed a flash of impatience that he should order me around so. 'But this is *my* enterprise, Jonathan.' I tilted my chin and looked coolly at him. 'It's the first important thing I've ever done in my useless life, and I intend to oversee every aspect of it.'

Jonathan's lips narrowed as he rose and reached for his hat. 'Just make sure you leave some time for yourself.' He looked over his shoulder as he turned to leave. And added softly, so softly I wasn't sure I'd heard him correctly '. . . and, um – for me, too.'

I closed the door behind him and leaned against the back of a chair. How did I really feel about Jonathan? Yes, he was very dear to me. Yes, his touch had my whole body responding in ways I found hard to ignore. But I'd never known plain, simple affection from a man, had I? So of course it was pleasurable.

Yes, I had come to depend on his reliable and comforting presence. But having at last achieved my hard-won independence, I was very wary about relinquishing it to any man, however attractive he might be.

Jonathan and I were due to meet for lunch in Truro. The refuge had been up and running for a couple of weeks and so far there had been no problems. At last I'd persuaded myself to relax and to realize I could have a day away from it without disaster striking. That my excellent members of staff were capable and trustworthy. And that my establishment ran on oiled wheels whether I was there to see or not.

I'd arrived before Jonathan and was sitting in a window seat over a cup of tea, my mind occupied with these thoughts. Then, feeling his eyes on me, I turned and there he was.

'I was just thinking how many more road motors there are around nowadays.' Jonathan removed his hat and gloves. He waved a hand towards the jostling traffic and sat down. 'The automobile certainly seems to be here to stay.' His eyes twinkled. 'I must say I quite fancy having a go in one myself. I'll have to start saving up my pocket money!'

'They look highly dangerous and unpredictable to me.' I frowned. 'Noisy, dirty things. You won't find me in a hurry to keep you company!'

Jonathan gave a hearty laugh and picked up the menu card. 'How are things at the refuge today?'

'Oh, I was just thinking. We've taken in six women and two children since we opened. Isn't it wonderful, Jonathan, when you think how well it's all going?'

He smiled and placed a hand over mine, giving it a gentle squeeze. 'And it's all thanks to you, my dear,' he said affectionately.

'Oh, no!' I protested. 'I couldn't possibly have managed without you – and the team. So many people have played a part.'

Jonathan lifted my hand and clasped it in both of his. 'Kate, there's something I've wanted to say to you for such a long time. You must know by now how I feel about you. . . .'

The hand he was holding trembled and I made to pull away, but he tightened his grip. 'I have to know . . . whether you could possibly return those feelings.' Melting brown eyes gazed into mine and my heart lurched.

'Because, dearest Kate, I hope that one day – and I've been waiting a long time to say this – you might consent to be . . . my wife.'

I felt my colour heighten and lowered my lashes to hide my eyes. I'd had a feeling this day would come, sooner or later. I'd rehearsed exactly what I would say. But now I sat tongue tied, my little speech flown completely out of my head.

'No . . . no . . . you won't really want to marry me, Jonathan.' I raised my eyes and anguish flooded through me. 'I think too highly of you to . . . to . . . let you do that. You're too good, too decent a person. After Arthur. . . .' I swallowed. 'I love you too,' I whispered, at last admitting what I'd being trying to deny for a long time, 'but I'm not fit to be a proper wife for any man, you see?'

Jonathan leaned across the table and put a finger under my chin, lifting my face to his. 'Kate, Kate, how many more times must I tell you that nothing of that was *your fault*. I love you, I want you for my wife, and as for anything else, I would never do anything that you didn't feel comfortable with. Do you understand me? I've got endless patience; I wouldn't be in this profession if I hadn't.' His warm brown eyes gazed into mine and I wavered.

'If you'll only agree to marry me, I'm willing to wait a lifetime for you to come to me of your own free will. And I would never, ever force you to do anything you didn't want to. Can you just promise me that you'll think about it?'

We were still looking closely into each other's eyes. At last I nodded and squeezed his hand, incapable of speech.

CHAPTER SIXTEEN

LOVEDAY

For the whole of the following week after my meeting with the stranger in the cemetery, I couldn't get him out of my mind. The incident had burned itself indelibly into my brain and I couldn't rid myself of it.

As I went about my daily business I felt all the time as if some impending disaster was hanging over me waiting to break, as I saw again and again that unsettling, so familiar, smile.

All he'd said was, 'A lovely day, ma'am', and tipped his hat as I turned to go. I'd murmured some polite platitude and tried to put as much distance between us as possible without making it obvious. When I stole a glance over my shoulder to see if he'd gone though, to my embarrassment he was still standing in the same place, staring after us.

We went to the beach and we had the promised picnic. The children romped on the sand until Davy was so tired I'd almost had to drag him home. But all the time I was thinking of that chance meeting. And had been ever since.

And what it was going to mean. After all this time, after all I'd been through, surely the ghosts I'd thought laid to rest for ever weren't coming back to haunt me now, were they?

Calm down, I told my racing heart. Just because it's so obvious to you, it doesn't necessarily mean that he noticed. He hadn't said a word, had he? No, but how he'd stared! So, he'd stared – but, well, he'd been speaking to Davy, hadn't he, and watching him playing? Perhaps he was just fond of children. Perhaps. I tossed and turned in bed all that night, and awoke weary and unrefreshed. Since then I'd dragged myself around, waiting.

I think Kate must have noticed, although I shrugged it off when she came down that morning. I did enjoy the trip to Truro though, and I went up a few days later to admire the completed house. However, the day after that, a Sunday morning, I answered a knock at the door and there he was on the step.

Just when I'd least expected him. Immediately I felt all the blood drain from my face. I knew too that caught unawares like this, I looked as guilty as I felt.

'Mrs Penrose, ma'am?' He removed the soft cloth cap he was wearing. 'Edward Rule. We met in the cemetery the other day.'

He held the cap in front of him, twisting it in both hands as he regarded me steadily from penetrating steel-blue eyes. The hands were narrow, with long tapering fingers.

'H- how did you know where I lived? And my name?' I stammered.

Tall and lean of build, with a narrow, intelligent face, he wore a tweed knicker-bocker suit of brown shades. I could see his bicycle propped against the wall inside the gate.

He turned and pointed 'Your neighbour informed me. I saw your little boy with her and recognized him.'

I looked past his shoulder and could see Susan Trembath just turning the corner. She was taking Davy to Sunday School along with her own brood. She was looking back, staring over her shoulder. So she'd be round later, asking questions. . . . But thank goodness Davy was out of the way for an hour.

'What do you want?' Fear roughened my voice.

'I think we need to talk.' He looked steadily into my eyes. 'May I come in?'

I would have to face up to it. He obviously knew – well, suspected anyway. An icy shiver of foreboding feathered down my spine and my legs trembled. Had the moment I'd been dreading for the past three years at last arrived? Was this to be the day of reckoning?

I widened the door and with a jerk of my head invited him inside. I led the way to the parlour and my visitor settled himself in an armchair. I picked up little Joe and sat on the edge of another chair, clutching the child so hard for comfort that he wriggled and cried to be put down.

I fussed with his toys as long as I could, avoiding the moment when I would have to come face to face with those piercing eyes. Eyes which were the exact colour of Davy's, as was his smooth fine hair which flopped in the same way over his forehead. With his fresh complexion and open face, I thought absently that he was the kind of person who immediately inspired trust.

He was the first to speak, in a brisk and business-like way. 'Well now, by the fact that you didn't ask me what we have to talk about, I take it you realize who I am.'

I gulped. It was a shrewd observation that immediately put me in the wrong. Tantamount to an admission of my guilt, in fact. I could have hedged, fended him off perhaps, if I'd been quick-witted enough. If I'd had time to prepare myself. But I'd panicked and given myself away! Strangely though, now that I *was* cornered, it was a kind of relief. Just as it had been a relief to tell Joel the truth at last.

'I-I think so,' I whispered.

He leaned forward, resting his hands on his knees. 'Three years ago, Mrs Penrose, my wife, Johanna, lost her life when the *Meervogel* went down off Porthleven. Just before she died I received a telegram at my office in Falmouth, saying she had given birth to our second son. I never saw her alive again, and never set eyes on my child.'

His face twisted as he blurted, 'For three years Mrs Penrose, I've never ceased to mourn them, my beloved wife and the lost little boy cruelly snatched away almost before he'd lived. Every year since then I've come here on Johanna's birthday to remember them, and to make sure that Daniel understands what happened to his Mama.'

He paused to rub a hand across his jaw, then smoothed down his blond moustache. In the background little Joe crawled about on the floor and babbled to his toys. I sat stock-still, my fingers clenched in my lap, my gaze never leaving his face.

This was even worse than I'd imagined. Davy had a brother, a father and presumably other family members. And I'd stolen him away from them. The ache inside me was too deep for tears.

'Yesterday,' he said and I jumped, startled, 'I met a little boy there who resembles Daniel, and myself, so strongly it was like seeing double. And he told me he was three years old.'

The room was very quiet now. Joe had fallen asleep on the floor, his head cradled on a stuffed toy. The heavy silence was only broken by the screaming of gulls in the harbour. They would be fighting over fish heads thrown from the boats. My mouth was too dry to utter a word. I felt if I moved from the ramrod-straight position in which I was holding myself, I would disintegrate and shatter into little pieces.

Edward Rule took a deep breath and looked intently at me. 'When his mother looked at me in consternation with guilt written all over her face, what was I to think? I'm hoping you can tell me the answer, ma'am.'

I bowed my head and studied the hands in my lap as if I'd never seen them before. To my overstretched nerves, the wailing of the seagulls sounded like the cries of lost souls. I saw again the poor drowned bodies washed up in the sea-cave that terrible night when it had all begun. It was too much.

My self-control finally snapped and I sank back into the chair, my shoulders heaving with agonized sobs. Rivers of tears began to pour down my face, cleansing me of the last vestiges of the guilt I'd carried for so long. Scourging my very soul. And leaving me drained and as weak as a new-born baby myself.

Edward Rule had risen and was looking out of the window with his back to me, tactfully remaining silent until I'd cried myself out. Then he turned into the room and said quietly, 'I think you'd better tell me the whole story, right from the beginning, don't you?'

I nodded my head, defeated. 'I can't pretend any more,' I sobbed through a curtain of tears. Everything was closing in on me. In a smothering, suffocating fog. I'd already lost Joel, my rock, the cornerstone of my existence. I'd suffered appallingly during Joe's birth. Now I was about to lose Davy as well. It was too much.

I dragged myself up, sniffed and wiped my eyes. Then I began haltingly to tell him of the mental trauma I'd been suffering three years ago. Of the agony of mind which had led me to keep Davy as my own.

'I thought he was an orphan, you see.' I tried to explain – to justify – to those blue accusing eyes that never left my face.

'I assumed his father had been on board the ship as well – why else would a young mother have been travelling on a cargo ship? And he was so new. Just like my . . . my own little one . . . I guessed he must have been born on the voyage. So I convinced myself that nobody would have known there was a baby on board at all.' I gulped and spread my shaking hands.

'You see, Germany where the ship came from, seemed so remote – if I'd known you lived in Falmouth – it might have been different.'

I buried my face in my hands. 'I love Davy *so much*,' I whispered. 'I couldn't bear it if you took him away from me.' I stuffed a fist in my mouth. 'Oh, what are we going to *do*?'

Edward Rule rose to his feet again and paced about the room with his hands behind his back, carefully avoiding the slumbering child. 'I spent a sleepless night thinking about exactly that. And of course I'm not going to snatch him brutally away from you by force.' He darted a glance at me from under furrowed brows.

'Not that I don't feel like doing so. . . .' He swallowed. 'But we have to think about what's best for Davy.'

I licked dry lips. 'Are you going to report me to the law?' My voice faltered. 'And have me arrested for – kidnapping or something?'

Edward Rule gave me a stony look. 'Of course not. I'm not a monster. Besides, that would upset Davy even more. And the fact remains that you *did* actually save his life.'

I glanced up at him with eyes made sore with weeping. 'Mr Rule,' I paused and hesitated. 'How can you be so reasonable, and so calm about all this? I thought you would fly at me and shout and threaten. . . .'

'With violence?' His shoulders lifted. 'Fighting never solved anything, but don't think it hasn't crossed my mind,' he snapped. 'I spent a sleepless night, as I said, pacing the floor and calling you all the names under the sun.' He glowered down at me and I cringed.

Then he turned on his heel and paced towards the window again, speaking as he went. 'No. I'm a practising Christian, Mrs Penrose, and I believe that God works in mysterious ways. Ways we have no means of understanding.' He looked back at me and paused.

'And I decided, it was better that Davy's life had been saved, even in this way, than he should have perished. And that by a miracle, some form of divine intervention has restored him to me.'

I raised shaking hands to my cheeks. My eyes followed his movements as he seated himself again.

'The way we've been brought together now, you see – some would call it coincidence – but maybe . . . it was meant to be. . . .' He broke off and the poignancy in his voice penetrated my very soul.

I could have sunk through the floor. Against my will, I felt a flicker of admiration for this calm acceptance of his monumental shock. And it tore me to shreds to think what I'd done to this decent, kindly man.

'You can't call me anything that I haven't called myself a thousand times!' I shrank back in the chair and crossed my arms. I felt I might fall apart without support. 'But the longer it went on, the harder it was, you see?'

Edward had clasped his hands on his knees and was studying the floor, deep in thought. A blanket of silence fell. I found I was unwittingly rocking back and forth for comfort. At last he raised his head.

'Now, of course we must do what's best for the child. He's the one who matters. I want him upset as little as possible – as I'm sure you do, too.'

The ticking of the mantel clock suddenly seemed overwhelmingly loud as I waited for him to continue. Joe had woken up and was clutching at my knee, so I lifted him up and laid my cheek against his warm hair.

'And Davy adores his baby brother,' he continued as his gaze rested on the child. He took a deep breath. 'What I suggest is this. I shall be content for a while if you let me come here and visit as often as I can.' I nodded dumbly.

'I'll play with Davy, and gradually let him get to know me. He can look on me as a new uncle to begin with. Perhaps I could stand in for Joel and do some of the things they used to do together.'

He regarded me steadily. 'For as long as necessary. And you must bring him over to Falmouth from time to time to get him used to my home and surroundings. It will take a while, Loveday – I may call you that under the circumstances, may I not?'

I nodded again and relaxed ever so slightly, letting out the breath I hadn't realized I'd been holding. 'Of course. That's an excellent idea,

Mr – um – Edward. And I'm grateful for your understanding and consideration – under the circumstances.'

A ghost of a smile flickered between us and again I felt a hint of admiration for this man. For his quiet fortitude, astute mind and air of solid competence. Under different conditions I could even have liked him.

But, I told myself sternly, I must think of him only as an opponent. One who was eventually going to break up my close-knit little family and tear my beloved eldest boy away from me. However politely and considerately he might go about it.

'You'd better stay to lunch,' I blurted. 'As you're here, we may as well start as we mean to go on. The sooner Davy gets used to you, the easier the . . . break . . . will be for him.'

My voice wavered and I almost broke down again as I imagined life without my little boy. Pride however, strengthened my resolve. It helped me to hold my head high and swallow down the lump in my throat. For this stranger was not going to witness any more of my personal heartbreak. I'd made enough of a fool of myself already.

'Thank you. That would be very acceptable. I appreciate your kindness.'

I bit back the sharp retort that I wasn't doing it for his sake. That kindness was the least of my motives. But there was nothing to be gained from antagonizing the man. He held the upper hand and could still, if he wished, take me to court and charge me with kidnapping.

Then he, and the law, could take Davy away and forbid me ever to see him again. But I'd received the impression that Edward was an honourable man. And felt fairly sure he wouldn't go back on his word.

I wanted to know more about him. So, over the traditional Sunday roast, I asked a few questions as I passed plates and served the meal.

'Do you live alone, Edward, you and Daniel? I get the impression that you never – er – married again. So how do you manage?'

He paused with a loaded fork in his hand. His eyes were bleak. 'We rattle around, my son and I, in a large and splendid house far too big for our needs, but one so filled with memories that I cannot bear to leave it. For several years it had a couple of rooms furnished as a nursery, before I forced myself to clear it out.'

I kept my head down and looked at my plate. I might have been eating sawdust for all I could taste of the meal.

'As for managing,' Edward paused between mouthfuls, 'I employ a live-in housekeeper, Mrs Hocking. Also, my widowed sister Elizabeth lives in the house next door, and helps to look after Daniel. She's been very good to me – I couldn't possibly have coped without her.'

'Please Mr Rule, are you a fisherman?' Davy piped up. 'My papa was a fisherman. But he's in heaven now.' He stuffed a crisp potato into his mouth and munched on it.

Edward smiled. 'No, Davy, I'm not clever enough to catch fish. I work in a boring office, writing letters all day.'

'I'm going to be a fisherman when I grow up,' the little boy confided. 'I could teach you if you like, and you could come out in my boat with me.' He raised bright eyes and stared across the table.

Edward regarded him gravely. 'That would be very nice, thank you. I'll look forward to it.'

'Where *do* you work, Edward?' I turned to Joe in the high chair at my side and helped him scrape together the last of his dinner.

'In a shipping office. Fox's of Falmouth. That's how I first met Johanna. She came into the office a few times with her father, Captain Ritters. He took her to sea with him quite often before we were married.' He laid down his knife and fork and carefully wiped his mouth.

'I think she was his favourite daughter – the most adventurous of the three, you know. I'm sure he'd have preferred her to be a boy – he never had a son.' Edward tapped the fingers of one hand on the tablecloth and his gaze was a long way off.

'Three girls?' I echoed. 'So Davy has – aunts. In Germany?'

Edward nodded. 'And three cousins. Also a grandmother. My own parents are dead and I'm their only offspring.' He paused. 'Johanna had been visiting them – before her last voyage.'

I pushed back my own, far from empty plate. 'He'll have to get to know them too, in time.' I realized I'd denied Davy so much by making him my own; a shadow of my former guilt was creeping back.

But I raised my head and looked him in the face. 'He has "aunts" and "cousins" here too, whom he adores. And my parents as well.'

'I'm sure. And he must continue to see them of course.' A silence fell, broken only by little Joe's babbling and Davy's laugh.

My head reeled as I tried to imagine what this revelation was going to mean: I would have to tell my parents and tell Meg. The whole village would know. All eyes would be upon us when we went out. There would be wagging tongues . . . and people staring. . . . The story of my shame would be food for gossip for years to come. I would have to move out of Porthleven. I just could not bear to face living here any more. I was still dazed with the import of it all when Edward took his leave. I was left dreading his next visit.

I had to talk to someone or I felt my head would explode. After he'd gone, I bundled Joe into the perambulator, grabbed Davy by the hand and set off up the hill to see Kate. Yes, she was busy with the refuge, but I needed her too. And this was imperative.

With difficulty I wheeled the baby carriage up the gravel drive. I peeped through the window of the annexe where her own quarters were, crossing my fingers she would be there. I could hardly talk about this in front of strangers. I let out a sigh of relief when I saw her, alone, in the sitting-room.

I rapped on the window and she jumped up, startled. It was a mild day, so I parked the baby carriage outside. I told Davy to play in the garden for a few minutes and to keep an eye on Joe as well. Then I burst in before Kate could get to the door.

'Loveday! What on earth's the matter? You're white as a sheet! Come in, come in.' She seized my hand and dragged me inside. 'Are you ill?' She peered closely into my face.

I shook my head. 'No, I'm all right. Give me a minute to get my breath back.' I was gasping after the steep climb. Kate pressed me into a chair, slipped from the room and returned with a glass of water.

'Oh, I've so much to tell you!' I gulped the water greedily. Refreshed, I launched into my tale.

Kate's eyes grew more and more round as the story unfolded, until at last my voice faltered and came to a halt. 'So he's coming again next Sunday.'

'I can't believe it! Davy's *father*. And he was here in Cornwall all the time? Just a few miles away?' I nodded dumbly.

'Oh, Loveday, what are you going to *do*?' Kate's eyebrows rose and she raised both hands to her face.

'I just don't know.' I spread my hands despairingly. I suppose some of my desolation must have been reflected on my face. For Kate came to kneel on the floor beside me and put both arms around my waist. 'It all depends on Edward now.'

'And you say he's a decent sort of person?' Kate frowned and gave me a long look.

'He seems to be. At least he isn't going to take Davy away yet.' I swallowed hard.

Kate was nibbling her lip. 'So now you just have to wait.' She fell silent and for a second I had the impression her thoughts were somewhere else.

She gave my hand a squeeze and rose to her feet. 'Yes,' I said, 'nothing else I can do, besides worry. Oh, Kate, *waiting* is the hardest part of it all.'

She nodded. She *was* preoccupied. Yes, she been more than sympathetic and concerned over my plight, but knowing her so well, I could tell she had something on her mind. Understandably, with this place just established, she would naturally have all sorts of problems.

'Well, how are things going with the refuge?' I straightened up and changed the subject.

Then a huge smile lit up her face. 'Oh, better than I ever thought possible. We had a few small snags of course, but nothing major. Now we're in full swing and already we've taken in three desperate women.'

She clasped her hands together and took a few steps around the room as she went on. 'I've got some wonderful staff. James is a gem. He's quiet, but you only have to mention something to him and it gets done and Alice is an excellent cook.'

She reached the window and turned back, counting her fingers. 'We have two reliable girls whom Anne is training up, two maids, a groom and a groundsman. Oh, Loveday, I can't believe how much we've accomplished in such a relatively short time!'

'I'm *so* glad. I know what this means to you.' I looked steadily at her. 'I thought you might be having problems. You seemed a bit far away just now.'

She resumed her seat. I glanced around the little room as I waited for her to speak. It was comfortably furnished with the minimum of clutter. A writing desk with drawers and pigeon holes full of neatly filed papers stood along one wall. Another was taken up by the french doors leading to the garden, with long red curtains hanging at each side.

We were sitting on a comfortable sofa, upholstered in stripes of cream and red brocade. A small table at one end held a few books and magazines. It was a charming and practical room, reflecting Kate's own taste so well. It couldn't have been more different from the home she had shared with Arthur.

Taken unawares, Kate had bowed her head and was fiddling with the hands in her lap. 'Um, yes,' she said at last. 'There is something. But I didn't think it was so obvious.' She raised her head and our eyes met. 'Loveday, I've told you how much I've relied on Jonathan these last few months, and how good he's been to me, haven't I?'

I nodded, and wondered as I waited for her to go on. 'Well, he's . . . he's. . . . Oh, Loveday,' she blurted, 'he's asked me to marry him!'

'Oh, Kate!' I clutched both her hands in mine. 'That's *wonderful* news! Isn't it?' My smile slipped as she turned troubled eyes to me.

'Loveday, I just don't know! I've been turning it over and over in my head until I can't think straight any more. After Arthur . . . you know?'

I laid a hand on her arm. 'Arthur was a monster. We both know that. From what I've seen of Jonathan I'd swear he's a decent man, he's gentle, thoughtful and he does think the world of you. I've noticed it in little ways. A glance, a smile. . . .' I gazed into her face, willing her to believe me.

'Do you really think so?' She nibbled a thumbnail as our eyes met.

'Of course I do, but I didn't realize until now that he loved you so.' I spread my hands trying to convince her. 'You'd be a fool to turn him down, Kate. I know it's the . . . um . . . physical side of it that's worrying you, isn't it?' She lowered her head and nodded.

'But I'm *sure* Jonathan would never, um, force himself upon you. I just can't imagine his being like that. So, try and talk it over with him.'

'We did, briefly.' She twisted her hands. 'And actually, that's pretty much what he said.'

'Well, there you are then. For goodness sake, he's a *doctor*. You can't compare him with a warped individual like Arthur.' I urged her to see sense. 'It's the best thing that could happen, for both of you.' Her eyes widened as she looked up at me again. 'Kate, you do love him, don't you?' I persisted.

But as she drew in a breath to reply, a shout from outside made us both jump. 'What have you done with the children, Loveday?' She leapt to her feet. 'I did see them just now, didn't I?'

I gasped and straightened. 'Oh, Kate, I'd forgotten all about them! They're outside in the garden. I only meant to leave them for a minute.'

I was scrambling to my feet, but she pressed me back into the chair. 'You stay there. I'm up. I'll go and bring them in.'

Once the boys were with us the room became full of their chatter and we had no chance of further private conversation. Our talk turned to the refuge and developments there.

'I must go,' I said at last. 'I know you've such a lot to do.'

Kate took my hands in hers and pressed them. 'I'm so *glad* you came, Loveday. And I'll think over what you said about Jonathan, truly I will.'

'Of course you must. And don't turn him down, Kate,' I willed her to listen to me, 'or you'll regret it for the rest of your life.'

I turned away. 'Oh, I feel so much better for talking to you.' I heaved a sigh of relief. 'I had to tell somebody right away or my head would burst. And of course, you're the only other person who knows the truth about Davy. Apart from Edward now.'

She nodded. 'Let me know what he says next time he calls, won't you, Loveday?' She gazed earnestly into my face. 'I'm never too busy to spare time for you.'

I gave her a grateful smile and gathered up the children. 'I can't do anything until Edward makes the next move. But I feel better able to wait now I've shared it all with you.'

I lowered Joe into the baby carriage and turned away. 'And your news will give me something else to think about.' I looked over my shoulder. 'Don't keep Jonathan hanging on too long for an answer Kate, will you?'

So, building on the shaky start to our acquaintance, Edward Rule came to Porthleven a few times after that, bringing Daniel with him in the pony-trap. I gradually became used to his visits and the children positively looked forward to them.

I knew the village thought I had a new suitor. When we were on our way to the beach, and passing a knot of my neighbours standing by the harbour wall I could almost see their antennae working, in the way of those who live in small villages.

So I told Susan next door that Edward was a distant relation, a widower. That we'd lost touch as he'd been abroad until recently. Which was as good as telling the whole village. So, it was a lie, but I decided it was worth it in order to still the wagging tongues.

Then the day came when we naturally had to make a return visit to Falmouth. We walked along the quayside, looking just like any other family, I thought sadly. Then we stopped on Custom House quay and leaned on the railings to look out over the water.

Edward was showing Davy the harbour, which must have seemed gigantic to him after the one at Porthleven. The little boy was entranced by all the shipping, listening wide-eyed as Edward pointed out the different vessels and told him their names.

'That's a schooner over there, isn't it, Papa?' Daniel chipped in, not to be outdone. 'The one with the red stripe along her side?'

Holding them by the hand, one on each side of him, Edward listened to their chatter and carefully answered each of their questions in turn. 'Yes, she's come from Panama with a cargo of jute.'

Davy was jumping up and down with excitement. 'Where's Panama, Uncle Edward? What's jute?' he demanded.

What endless patience Edward has, I thought, and . . . how exactly *right* he looks with both the boys. I clenched my teeth on my bottom lip as my eyes began to sting.

It was on one occasion when Edward had spent the day in Porthleven, that he dropped his bombshell. He had come alone, as Daniel had a feverish cold and was being looked after by his aunt which caused Davy a good deal of disappointment. As he and Daniel had by now become firm friends.

Edward had lingered on long after he usually did. Davy and little Joe were tucked up in bed and I'd felt obliged to ask him to stay to supper.

I was slightly annoyed, as I had a hard day at the farm to look forward to tomorrow and had promised myself an early night.

In addition to my exhaustion was the ever-present worry of Edward and when he would decide the time had come to take Davy away from me.

I was sitting lost in thought, my elbow propped on the table and my chin resting on my hand. I could feel my eyes drooping with fatigue. I must have yawned, or sighed perhaps, for I glanced up to see Edward regarding me with a look of concern.

'Loveday, you're exhausted, aren't you? You work too hard, you know.'

I jumped and straightened up. 'Oh, I'm all right.' I tossed my head and rose to clear away the dishes.

'No,' Edward laid a hand on my arm as I passed. 'Sit down for a minute and listen to me. There's something important we have to discuss.'

My stomach clenched on a knot of fear. It had come then. This was it. The day I'd been dreading so much had come sooner than I'd thought. He was going to take Davy away and pretend I would have less work to do with only one child to look after.

I whirled around and clasped the back of the chair to steady myself. 'But it's too soon!' I blurted. My heart began thumping madly. 'He hardly knows you!' I gripped the chair harder and saw my knuckles whiten.

'Who's going to look after him like I do? I'm the only mother he's ever known!' A strangling sob rose in my throat. I gave a low, anguished moan.

'Loveday, *listen to me*!' Edward was on his feet too, clutching my arm and pressing me back into the chair. 'That's not what I was going to say at all.'

I gulped and wiped the back of my hand across my eyes. He shook his head and gripped both of my hands as he stared intently into my face.

'No. Now, calm down. I was going to make a suggestion for our future arrangements. I've thought of something that could be an ideal answer to the problem, for both of us.' He let go of me and took a few steps across the room, his own hands clasped behind his back.

'For both of us?' I echoed, dazed.

Edward nodded. 'I don't know why I didn't think of it before now, it's so simple. You see, Mrs Hocking my housekeeper is getting on in years and has been wanting for some time to retire and go to live with her daughter. She's only been staying on out of loyalty until I can find someone to replace her.'

He turned and faced me. 'And you're being run off your feet trying to work at the farm as well as keep house. Well, if you came to work for me, you and the children could live in.' He took a few steps then turned on a heel.

'Goodness knows the house is big enough for you to have your privacy. You could have Mrs Hocking's room for yourself, and what was going to be the nursery, for the children. Then I could be under the same roof as Davy and you wouldn't have to part with him after all.' Edward's voice died away into the evening stillness.

After a long pause he said anxiously, 'What do you think, Loveday? Would you be willing to leave Porthleven and give up your home?'

My head had been bowed, still waiting for some kind of blow to fall. But now I couldn't believe what I'd heard. I slowly straightened and knew my face was shining with joy.

'Edward, that would be absolutely *marvellous*! I can't believe it – I never thought for a moment there would ever be a way.' I rose and held both hands out to him. 'Oh, thank you, thank you,' I whispered. 'If I had to part with Davy now I truly think my heart would break.'

CHAPTER SEVENTEEN

KATE

I spent a long time after she left, thinking about Loveday's amazing story and what it was going to mean for her. Her life would obviously never be the same again. I worried though, about this Edward, however nice he might appear. Loveday had had more than her full share of heartbreak already. She would not be able to cope with any more suffering.

I'd been telling Jonathan all this, one evening when he'd called in during his rounds and stayed for a meal. We'd eaten and cleared away, and were in my little sitting-room with the coffee pot beside us.

After we'd finished the conversation, a brief silence fell. I was looking into the heart of the glowing fire and gave an involuntary sigh of contentment. I felt enclosed in an atmosphere of complete and utter comfort. And companionship.

The silence lengthened. I assumed Jonathan was also reflecting on what I'd just told him. Perhaps feeling as replete and relaxed as I was, but when I glanced at him with a smile and some trite remark, I realized he'd actually been deep in serious thought. Then he turned towards me, took one of my hands firmly in his, and looked intently into my face.

'Kate dear.' His voice was low and husky. 'You'll remember some time ago I asked you to think about whether we might become man and wife one day.'

I started. I hadn't been expecting this so soon. After telling

Loveday, I'd mentally shelved it for the time being. I'd been so busy with practical things lately. I realized with a stab of guilt, I'd been taking Jonathan very much for granted.

'Ah. No. I hadn't forgotten.' I shook my head as our eyes met.

All the thinking I'd done previously came flooding back to me. Jonathan was my rock, my anchor, the steadying presence I always turned to for sensible advice. But did I love him?

Well, I felt a warm tingle run through my body whenever he touched me. Yes, my heart beat faster when he kissed me. Yes, I looked forward with pleasure to being with him. But was this love?

I bit my lip. It was love of a sort. It must be. I wondered would it be enough to sustain a marriage? To last for the rest of my life? Granted I'd thrown away the first flush of my young love on the wrong man, for all the wrong reasons. It had only been infatuation I'd felt for Arthur of course, coupled with an eye for the main chance. With hindsight I could see how shallow I'd been then. So, granted I'd never known the heady passion and 'true love' so fêted in poetry and song. But how lucky I was to have been offered a second chance! And by such a good man.

Jonathan also knew me so well. Better than any other person could ever do. *He* had been with me at my darkest hour. He had witnessed my agony and had not turned away in disgust.

On the other hand, I'd scarcely had time to get used to my freedom. Or to recover from the trauma of my first marriage. How would it feel to be tied to another man? My independence had been hard-won. I was settled in a home of my own. I'd achieved my ambition. I had a responsible role running the refuge which I'd created. Life was good.

I reflected on all this as I tore myself away from that steady gaze. I stared at the carpet as if I'd never seen it before, my mind racing. Yes, I *had* done all that, but Phoenix Refuge was established now. And with brutal honesty, I faced the truth. It would continue to run quite capably whether I spent every day there or not.

There were times I admitted to myself, when I found living on my own could be lonely. I *did* miss having someone to talk to when I came back here at the end of a day, someone to share a joke, or to discuss a problem with. The evenings could be very quiet.

I was still a reasonably young woman – not yet thirty. I could even have children. In the years I had spent with Arthur, I'd longed above anything for a child of my own. I'd watched Loveday with her little boys and seen the delight and fulfilment they brought her. Then had cried into my pillow with frustration.

But Jonathan was waiting. And this time he deserved a definite answer. He'd waited patiently for a long time without pressing me. He wouldn't wait for ever. I looked into the familiar face that had become very dear to me. I tried to imagine life without him. And that, I admitted, I could not bear. 'Yes, I hadn't forgotten,' I repeated.

'It occurred to me that maybe the thinking time has come to an end,' he said. Jonathan played with the fingers he was holding. Then he gripped both my hands and squeezed them firmly as I lifted my head. 'Kate, will you marry me, yes or no?'

I looked into the warm brown eyes, the narrow, sensitive face and came to my decision. Snatching my hands from his grasp, I flung both arms around his neck. With a sigh, I laid my head on the shoulder of his soft tweed coat.

'Yes,' I whispered. 'Yes, Jonathan, I will. Gladly.'

Then he gathered me into his arms and our lips met in a lingering and passionate kiss.

'Oh Kate, my own, I've waited such a long time to hear you say that.' He was whispering into my ear and his warm breath was soft on my cheek. 'And I've been wanting to do that for even longer.' He drew away, and with a gentle finger tipped up my chin. 'Now all that remains is to set a date for the wedding. Shall it be soon?'

All my doubts and fears had blown away on the wind as if they had never existed. I looked into his steady gaze, felt the solid warmth of him beneath my touch and breathed in his unmistakable scent. Then I gave a blissful sigh.

'As soon as possible,' I murmured.

It seemed there was to be no end to life-changing events for both Loveday and myself. No sooner had I accepted Jonathan's proposal, than she was on my doorstep again, with more shattering news. This time without the children.

'*Moving*?' I felt my jaw drop. 'You mean – you're leaving Porthleven? For good?' I felt as if I'd received a heavy blow. Somehow

I'd never thought of this happening, but of course, it was perfectly reasonable. Edward wanted his son and he had a house large enough for them all. It was only common sense. And a wonderful solution to their problems.

Loveday nodded and when she bowed her head I thought she was upset. But when she looked up at me again I saw her face was calm and serene. 'It's all worked out amazingly well, Kate. I am so lucky Edward turned out to be such a good man.'

She touched my hand. 'We're *both* so lucky. That you and Jonathan have found each other too. . . .' She broke off in mid-sentence and gazed steadily at me. 'Have you . . . um . . . decided yet?'

I felt a smile of pure happiness spread across my face. Loveday must have realized what it meant, for her eyes lit up and she drew in a quick breath. 'You've accepted him, haven't you?'

I nodded, too choked for a moment to reply. She flung her arms round my neck and hugged me to her. 'Oh, Kate, I'm so *delighted*! I'm sure it's the right thing to do – for both of you. Jonathan has always struck me as being such a lonely man.'

'I know. And talking of luck . . . when you look back to the way we both were. . . .'

'. . . it sounds like a fairytale,' Loveday finished. I nodded in complete understanding and we gazed into each other's eyes in wonderment.

'We've been battered by so many blows, haven't we? Both our lives have been pulled apart and put together again. But we *have* come through.' I drew in a breath. 'And please God, we've reached a safe haven at last.'

'Oh, yes. Amen to that.' Loveday raised her clasped hands. Then a silence fell as we lost ourselves in our separate thoughts.

Loveday was the first to speak. 'Kate, I can hardly believe it.' She shook her head and her eyes were full of awe. 'For weeks I've been waiting for the next blow to fall. Dreading I would have to part with Davy, sooner or later.' Her mouth drooped and her voice faltered. 'I'd even started having nightmares again.'

'I'm so *thrilled* at the way it's all turned out.' I reached for her hand. 'But Loveday, how I'm going to *miss* you!'

'Oh, I know. I'll miss you too.' She dropped a kiss on my cheek. 'But

Edward says I can borrow the pony trap whenever I want. I'll be bringing the children back often to see Ma and Pa, and Meg too. I can visit you as well.'

'I'd like to come and see you, too.' I smiled. 'Arthur left the victoria behind when he cleared off and Roly is still at the livery stables. He'll enjoy the exercise. I must get him back soon. There's plenty of room for him over there still.' I pointed towards the french windows. 'We only turned a part of the stable block into living quarters for the Kingstons.'

Then I frowned as a thought suddenly struck me. 'What about Edward, though? Would he mind if I called sometimes?'

'Of course not.' Loveday shook her head vigorously. 'And I shall be so glad to see you, Kate. I'm going to feel very strange in my new life.' She nibbled her lip.

'I've lived in Porthleven for so long I can't imagine being anywhere else. And anyway, as Edward's housekeeper I get one day off a week. So please, yes, come as often as you like. I can't wait to show you around.'

'Loveday,' I paused as a thought occurred to me. 'I suppose you and Edward must have talked about this, but I was wondering. Are you going to tell everyone the truth about Davy?'

Loveday bowed her head and fingered her gloves. She rose restlessly to her feet and took a pace around the room. When she turned back she gazed steadily at me and sighed. 'Kate, we've discussed it over and over until we found ourselves going round in circles. And we decided, in the end, that, no, we're not.' She slowly shook her head.

'Think about it. What good would it do?' Her shoulders lifted. 'I can't think of one single good reason for doing so. Can you? And it would cause so much *harm* and heartache – for so many people.'

She turned on a heel. 'Can you imagine the ramifications of it all?' She held out her hands. 'They would be endless. Think of the effect it would have on our parents, on Joel's family and on the children as well.' Her eyes widened.

'I know. It doesn't bear thinking about.' I grasped her hands tightly in mine. 'Loveday I'm so *glad* to hear you say that.'

'You're the only other person beside Edward who'll ever know.' She paused. 'And I know the secret's safe with you. For ever.'

'I should think so. If I haven't given the game away after all this time, I'm not likely to now!' We laughed together and the atmosphere lightened.

Then I felt the smile slide from my face. 'I haven't even told Jonathan.' I shook my head. 'And I really don't like keeping secrets from him.'

Loveday pressed my hand. 'Thank you, Kate,' was all she said, but her heart was in her eyes.

I turned away and changed the subject. 'I'll come and help you pack up the house if you like, once you've decided when you're moving out.'

'Would you?' Loveday's face brightened. 'That would be marvellous. I'm sure I shan't know where to start. I'm not looking forward to it at all. In fact I'm dreading the thought of it.' Her face clouded.

'I can imagine so.' Our eyes met in mutual understanding. 'Because it's so full of memories. Is that what you mean?'

She nodded and turned away to gaze out of the window. 'So many years of my life are tied up in that house, Kate. All the major events that ever happened to me took place inside those four walls.' She gave a shuddering sigh.

I placed a hand on her shoulder and gave it a gentle squeeze. 'I know. Have you any idea at all when you'll be moving?'

'Well, Edward would like it to be in time for Christmas. So the children can spend it together. I thought that sounded quite a good idea.'

'It is,' I said. 'And with the new year coming, it's just the right time for making a fresh start. The excitement of Christmas too, will make it easier for Davy. It'll soften the break for him. And for you as well.'

'Right, before Christmas it is, then. And yes please, we'll do it together.' Loveday turned back into the room with a smile.

'What a lot of changes there are just around the corner. For us both.' She paused and looked towards me, resting a hand on the chair back. 'Have you and Jonathan set a date for the wedding yet?'

'We thought in the early spring.' I smiled. 'I know it sounds like a cliché, a spring wedding, but neither of us wants a long wait. We're now both sure in our own minds, you see.' I spread my hands and turned on a heel. 'And it's not as if we were giddy young things who have to get to know each other first.'

'Exactly. Oh, I'm so looking forward to it, Kate.' Loveday clasped her palms together. 'You certainly deserve to be happy at last, and Jonathan's such a lovely man. I couldn't be more pleased for you.'

'There's something else I haven't told you, too. We're not sure yet whether this is going to happen, you see. But Jonathan's hoping to leave the Infirmary. He's going to apply for a general practice in Penzance. He's heard on the grapevine that an elderly doctor in the area is due to retire soon and thinks he may be in with a chance.'

'Oh, how lovely! That would save him all that travelling to and fro.' Her brows knitted for a moment. 'Where are you thinking of living after you're married? You wouldn't stay here, surely?'

'Oh no, it's far too small. We've been talking a lot about that, and of course it depends on whether Jonathan gets this post. If he does, we shall get a house of our own somewhere between here and Penzance. Then I can come and go to the refuge, and he can easily get into his surgery.'

'Oh, yes, I see. That's the ideal solution.' Loveday nodded. 'Isn't it exciting! Now we just have to keep our fingers crossed that it all works out.'

CHAPTER EIGHTEEN

LOVEDAY

The time seemed to fly by after that. Soon I was packing up and preparing to leave for my new life.

I found it difficult to decide what to take and what to get rid of, for obviously a great deal of scaling down had to be done. I would sell the big furniture, of course, but I wanted to keep certain personal things I'd shared with Joel, for sentimental reasons. Pieces of china he had brought back from his travels, and a few pictures, which could hang in the children's rooms or my own.

I glanced with a lump in my throat at the carved wooden cradle Joel had lovingly fashioned for Davy. Both he and Joe had used it as babies. That was going with us of course, even if it was only destined to gather dust, and clutter up a corner somewhere.

Our clothes and the children's toys were already folded, sorted and packed into two big trunks Edward had lent me. Kate had spent half a day with me doing that, and helping to spring-clean the cottage ready for the new occupants.

Now, unable to settle, I wandered around the half-empty house. It echoed hollowly beneath my tread. I swallowed against the lump in my throat. But, look forward, not back, I told myself sternly.

I pulled open the kitchen door and went out into the back yard. Davy was sailing a wooden boat in a large puddle which had formed on the path. Joe, whom I'd tied to the fence by his leather reins for safety, clapped his hands and shouted encouragement. Both children were filthy, but it had been worth it to keep them out from under my feet while I had so much to do.

I watched them together for a moment and wondered, not for the first time, whether they would continue to get on so well when there were three of them.

Three boys to look after – and Edward. I was certainly going to have my hands full. Good, I was glad of it. For it would ease my transition from the old life to the new. And would stop me thinking too much about the past as well.

'Handsome, aren't they – them little boys of yours.' The voice startled me out of my thoughts. I turned to see Susan Trembath leaning over the low wall dividing our two cottages. 'How little Joe's *growing*, the dear of him.'

I smiled. 'Oh hello, Susan. Yes, they both are. You know how it is. As you said to me, ages ago now, they don't stay babies for very long.' I wiped my dusty hands in my apron. 'I've just been turning out all the clothes they've grown out of. Seems like only yesterday I was sewing them.'

I'd thought long and carefully how I would explain my departure to the neighbours. Eventually I decided that the plain truth was as good as anything. I needed employment and had been offered a job in Falmouth, as housekeeper to a widower with a small son of his own. End of story. To my relief it had been accepted at face value and no one had asked.

'I'm going to miss you some lot when you're gone, and they dear children too.' Susan sighed and wiped away a tear with the corner of her apron. 'But I'll be having new neighbours soon, I suppose.' Her face brightened.

I knew how Susan would relish finding out all about them and sharing her knowledge with the village. But she'd been a good friend when I needed her. The woman couldn't help being the biggest gossip in the street, it was second nature to her.

'I'll come in and say goodbye before we leave, of course. And now I must get those two cleaned up and ready for bed.' I smiled at my neighbour then turned away and walked down the path to fetch my children.

A few weeks later, I was leaning out of the window of my new room in Edward's house, my elbows on the sill and my face between my hands. It was so tranquil, such a contrast to the more exposed conditions I'd been used to all my life.

Here, sloping and heavily wooded spurs enclosed the gently rippling sea. There were mysterious creeks where trees grew right down to the edge and dipped their leafy fronds in the water. The dried wrack thrown up by winter winds sometimes clung to their branches for weeks after strong winds, a strange kind of foliage.

I gazed out to where the winter sun was slowly sinking and painting the sky of faded blue with streaks of lemon and powder pink. The silver-tipped ripples on the sea reminded me of fish scales. A couple of small sailing boats too, were silhouetted against the darkening horizon as they rounded the point.

Below me in the garden, Edward was playing with the three boys. He was always scrupulously fair in dividing his time equally between them and never favoured his own two over Joe in any way. I watched fondly as they romped together and he played at mock wrestling on the lawn with the older ones. Davy loved the space of this new garden, which had plenty of room to run about and mature trees just made for climbing. To have such a large house and grounds, Edward must be quite a wealthy man, but it was not my place to enquire after his means. Certainly the salary he paid me was generous enough and I wanted for nothing; I had only to ask and it was provided for me.

I'd been so lucky that Davy's father had turned out to be this decent, kindly man. Edward had already secured a place in my heart simply for his goodness, and his consideration for my feelings. It could so easily have been different. If he'd been a man who harboured a grudge, he could have taken Davy away from me for ever, as was his right.

Edward glanced up then, as if he had read my mind, and raised his hand in a wave. As our eyes met, a boyish grin spread across his face, easing out the worry lines across his brow and making him look half his age. Oh yes, I thought as I returned the greeting, I'd been lucky all right. To have so much that was good come out of my original deceit was almost unbelievable. So maybe I'd finally paid my debts and this present contentment was my reward. And the future? The future remained as always, to be seen.

I came back to the present, withdrew from the window and ran lightly downstairs to prepare supper for my family.

Kate and Jonathan were married on a warm day in late April. Kate's gown was a floating creation of palest pearl-grey chiffon, with a spectacular hat of dusky pink smothered in silk roses. She carried a bouquet of real roses, white and pink, whose scent wafted behind and around her as she walked up the aisle.

We were in the little whitewashed Methodist chapel, for of course a divorced woman was not allowed to re-marry in the Anglican church. Kate had asked me to be her matron of honour, but while appreciating her offer, I'd talked her out of the idea. This was her day, hers and Jonathan's. I told her that with the simple ceremony, which was what they both wanted, there should be nothing to detract attention from the happy couple.

I was sitting in a front pew with Mama, a well scrubbed and an over-awed little Joe on my lap. Davy in his first grown-up suit sat beside me. Edward had had no objections to my taking him with me on this special occasion. If he had, I would have found it very difficult to explain his absence to all our relations. So I sent up my own private thanks in a prayer for my new employer's gentle kindness and understanding.

I felt my eyes misting as my sister passed on Pa's arm, and a lump came to my throat as I thought back over the last few years. Both of us had had more than our share of anguish and torment, pain and suffering, and had come through. Today, all that misery seemed to have been finally washed away by this wonderful occasion and by the almost palpable happiness surrounding the couple.

The wedding breakfast was to be held in the Sunday-school building not far from the chapel. As the newly-wed couple emerged, they were greeted by shouts of goodwill from the village people gathered outside, and a shower of confetti and rice rained down on them. As we all walked in the warm sunshine from one building to the other, the company all dressed in their best finery, looked to me like a cloud of colourful butterflies. I smiled as I held up my face to the sun, hugged my precious children to me, and sent up a heartfelt prayer of thanks for the way things had turned out.

As the wedding breakfast was under way I looked down the long room from my seat at the top table at all our family and friends. Of Kate's staff from the refuge, James Kingston whom I'd met, was here with his daughter, and also Anne Barrington, together with several people I didn't know.

After the speeches, the toasts and the chatter were at last over and the guests had begun to leave, I noticed Kate trying to attract my attention, and I moved towards her.

'Loveday,' she said quietly, 'I really feel like a stroll along the beach before we leave. Do you want a breath of fresh air?'

She and Jonathan were having a short honeymoon in Torquay. As neither of them could be spared for very long from their responsibilities, they had decided not to venture any further away.

I realized then my head was feeling dizzy with the effects of champagne and rich food, so I nodded. 'Actually I do. Ma's taken the children for a while to show them off to everybody, so that's fine.'

'I'd better just ask "my husband" first if he minds.' Kate smiled and moved away. She was back in a moment, smiling broadly. '"My husband" is deep in conversation with Pa and doesn't mind a bit. I gather that the burning topic of the hour is whether the cause of women's suffrage will be helped or hindered, now that Mr Asquith has become PM.'

I shrugged and laughed. 'Personally I can't get worked up about it – it all seems so far away at the moment.'

Kate nodded. 'Just a minute.' She reached up to remove the pins from her elaborate hat, setting it carefully down on a table. 'Hardly the thing for a walk by the sea, I think.' She laughed and shook her hair free, sending it tumbling down her back in a shimmering blonde curtain.

I did the same, then arm in arm we made our way first around the harbour and then up the slope towards the cliffs overlooking Megiliggar rocks. With my thoughts wholly in the past now, I felt a shiver flutter down my back as I glanced over the edge. For this was where it had all begun, on that shelf of black, treacherous stone.

For an instant the sun went in. Then my vision was eclipsed by the driving rain, howling gale and raging storm that had brought baby

Davy to me on the wings of the wind. The image was so clear it could have happened yesterday. I took in a deep breath and my head reeled. The vision faded as quickly as it came and was replaced once more by balmy spring sunshine. And Kate, who must have guessed what was going through my mind, met my glance with understanding in her eyes.

'We've all been through a lot since then.'

I nodded, thinking just how much, as we strolled on.

'Loveday, are you happy?' Her eyes were on the sparkling sea. Caught unawares, I paused for a moment. 'I think so. I'm content, at any rate. Edward and I get on so well, you know, and it could have all been so very different.' I bent my head. 'Sometimes I even catch him looking at me in a certain way, and I wonder whether . . . in time . . . I – we – could. . . .' I left the sentence unfinished, but Kate pressed my hand in mute understanding.

'Of course, there's no need to ask you that question.' I glanced up at her. 'It just shines out of you, Kate.'

She nodded. 'I took a while to make up my mind, you know.' She fingered the new wedding ring on her left hand.

'Understandably so, after the first time.'

Kate's eyes flashed. 'That was a nightmare.' Her expression had become serious. 'It took a long time, but now I feel I'm finally free of the past.'

'That's exactly how I feel myself,' I whispered, pressing her hand. I took in a breath. 'So in a little while we shall part to go our separate ways. A new life for each of us.'

We'd paused before climbing back up the slope to the top. Before us lay the shimmering sea, gently rippling in a breeze which hardly disturbed its peaceful surface. The breeze lifted the hair at the back of my neck and set Kate's gold mane dancing. Above us the paler blue bowl of sky stretched to infinity, studded with lazy little puffball clouds.

Then, making a fist of my hand, I smiled at my sister and raised an imaginary glass. 'To us both and to our futures. May we remember this perfect day and always be as happy as we are now.'

Kate turned to me and smiled as she joined in the little ceremony. 'To us,' she echoed, 'and to the future.'